THE FIRE KILLER

A DI BARTON INVESTIGATION

ROSS GREENWOOD

Boldwood

First published in Great Britain in 2022 by Boldwood Books Ltd.

Copyright © Ross Greenwood, 2022

Cover Design by Nick Castle Design

Cover Photography: Shutterstock

A CIP catalogue record for this book is available from the British Library.

Paperback ISBN 978-1-80048-662-1

Large Print ISBN 978-1-80048-663-8

Hardback ISBN 978-1-80426-233-7

Ebook ISBN 978-1-80048-664-5

Kindle ISBN 978-1-80048-665-2

Audio CD ISBN 978-1-80048-657-7

MP3 CD ISBN 978-1-80048-658-4

Digital audio download ISBN 978-1-80048-660-7

Boldwood Books Ltd
23 Bowerdean Street
London SW6 3TN
www.boldwoodbooks.com

In memory of Paul Bradshaw
One of the good guys
1970 – 2021

Light a fire they can't put out.

— AVICII

1

DI BARTON

Present Day – August 2020

DI John Barton watched all four passengers in the Range Rover they were overtaking do a double take as DS Shawn Zander accelerated past them. He supposed it wasn't every day you saw two large men, both well over six feet, one black and one white, zip past you on the four-lane A1 motorway in an MR2 sports car with the top down, doing well over a hundred miles an hour. At least the vehicle was light blue. If it had been red and yellow, there would have been Noddy jokes every time Zander gave him a lift.

Despite the speed, the air that raced over both their bald heads was bearable. In fact, Barton found it pleasantly bracing. The extreme weather had begun to exert its toll over the last month and it seemed as though there'd never be an end to the heatwave. It was only in the last few days Barton had worn a tie again, without it feeling like a noose.

He was returning from a meeting in Huntingdon in Zander's

pride and joy, which had developed a roof fault when they arrived, whereby it stubbornly refused to lift back into place. At this speed, the wind howled around the windscreen into their faces now they were returning to Peterborough. The air smelled different. By that measure alone, a storm was coming. The men looked at each other, but it wasn't the time for smiles. After working together for over twenty years, no words were necessary.

Barton observed the weather front massing on the horizon, but they didn't have far to go now. The dark clouds gathering above cast moody shadows, although there were still breaks where sunlight flooded through.

Barton shifted down in his seat so he could answer his ringing phone. It was DS Kelly Strange. She and DC Nicola Pignatiello, who went by the nickname Pigs, had left south Peterborough ten minutes ago and were meeting them at the place where this nightmare had begun.

'Barton speaking.'

'John, we've reached the address. There's a very big problem with the house.'

'Now what?'

'It's on fire.'

2

DI BARTON

Barton's phone whistled with the air turbulence, and whatever Strange said next was stolen by the wind.

'Say that again. What do you mean by on fire?'

Again, the reply was lost.

'Slow down,' shouted Barton to Zander.

They were pulling off the motorway for Peterborough anyway.

'Please repeat, Kelly.'

This time, her voice was loud and clear.

'We can see flames licking at the back wall of the upstairs bedroom, lots of them. The blaze is building in there, but the rest of the house seems untouched.'

'Ring the brigade.'

'Pigs is on the phone to them now.'

'What about the residents?'

'That's why I'm ringing. The Fire Killer is sitting in a car outside the house, watching.'

'Pardon?'

'Yes. Hang on! There's someone at the upstairs window.'

'Don't enter the building!' he bellowed down the phone. 'Wait for the fire crew.'

'The person at the window has their hands pressed against the glass. Hang on.'

Barton listened as Kelly asked Pigs how long until the first engine arrived. Strange came back on the line.

'John, ETA for the closest appliance is at least six minutes.'

'Stand down until they get there. Arrest The Fire Killer. We'll be there in five.'

There was a gap with only static. Barton felt like crushing the phone in his huge hand. The line buzzed, then cleared.

'John, we have to try. Otherwise, anyone in there will burn to death. It doesn't look too bad right now, so we're going to check it out.'

Barton thumped the dashboard in frustration. After a small pause, where Barton listened to footsteps hitting the pavement, Strange spoke again.

'Are you with Zander?'

'Yes.'

'Tell him, tell him...'

Strange stopped talking. There were a few quiet seconds, then Barton heard a creaking sound.

'The front door is unlocked,' said Strange. 'We're going in.'

3

DI BARTON

Barton shouted Kelly's name into his phone. But the line was dead.

'Drive, Zander. As fast as you can.'

Zander didn't need asking twice. He'd made out enough of the conversation, and he knew where Strange had gone. Barton looked across at his friend and colleague. He still hadn't put the weight back on since his son had become ill, even though it had been years now.

Zander had enjoyed a few dates with Pigs, but there were words that remained unsaid between him and Strange. Unsurprisingly, Zander's face was stone, eyes narrowed. His knuckles white on the steering wheel.

Barton was pressed into his seat as Zander tore through the next roundabout, stamping the brakes to career through the bend. Zander accelerated hard again, and they roared up the slip road and down the parkway, pulling off three minutes later onto Fulbridge Road. Barton moistened his lips. He removed his tie. They were almost there.

They flew past lads playing football on the field to their right, where the van fire had been, and children screaming with delight in the play area on his left. All blissfully unaware of what had occurred or what might be about to.

They were less than a minute away now. The first heavy drops of rain fell onto them, but any concerns about getting soaked were irrelevant. They rapidly approached a badly parked white Transit van, which blocked their view of the way ahead. To the sound of screeching tyres, Barton was jerked back by his seat belt. A little girl wandered into the middle of the road and stood staring at them as Zander's car juddered to a halt, mere metres away from her. Before Barton could get out, a woman sprinted into the street, scooped the child up and ran to the pavement, and Zander was on his way again within a second.

They soon turned right onto Fig Tree Lane. A fire engine's siren wailed in the distance. Barton swallowed as he spotted a string of black fumes rising above the houses. The clouds beyond had darkened considerably and seemed to boil as the storm approached. Destruction was in the air as the wind picked up the smell of smoke and blew it towards them. Zander slammed on the brakes outside the property and Barton clocked The Fire Killer sitting in a car next to the kerb, but he had more pressing concerns.

He and Zander jumped out of the MR2 and frantically assessed the scene. Barton stared up at the bedroom window where he saw someone, looking to their left. Grey smoke swirled and amassed behind the glass, temporarily concealing the occupants. Barton noticed a hazy arm and hand appear. The window opened, but only a few inches. Two seconds later, to the accompaniment of a crack of thunder, what looked like a small bedside table bounced off the inside of the glass.

Barton knew modern glazing would withstand a brick, or even an iron bar. The smoke cleared a little. Through the teeming rain, he watched someone in a white blouse approach the bedroom window. They put a hand to their mouth and bent double. Then

Barton saw a stool or a chair hit the glass. A crack appeared this time, but nothing more. With the increasing smoke, Barton couldn't tell if it was Strange or Pigs who was trying to break the glass.

He felt a blast of sound and air, combined with a throaty growl as the fire engine braked behind them but Barton kept his eyes on the house. Darkness seemed to descend as the black clouds raced overhead. The front door was ajar. The creeping smoke was now pouring around the sides of it. Barton stepped a few paces forward as another deep rumble of thunder echoed above them. He fought the urge to race in, but sensed Zander edging past him towards the door, which suddenly spewed black smoke out like a desperate, dying gasp. Barton managed to catch Zander's sleeve, and with all his strength, hauled him back.

'No, no!' screamed Zander.

Barton didn't reply. He tried to put his arms around Zander's waist to stop him moving, straining every sinew to hold him still. Sheet lightning lit the house up for a second. Zander's suit jacket ripped as he struggled out of it.

Then an ear-splitting, booming bang filled the air and Zander froze. They both looked up. The window vibrated, and then another louder explosion shattered the glass outwards, blasting shards like bullets in every direction. Barton covered his face with his hands and bent double. After a few seconds, he straightened up and frantically waved his hands to clear the smoke in front of him. When he could finally make out the window again, all that was visible were large roaring flames, which reached out of the blackened hole like the fiery claws of an escaping demon.

4

THE FIRE KILLER

Many years ago

My mother pulls the blanket up around our chins as we snuggle on the sofa. We were toasty as hell after tea, but the fire has been off for well over an hour now, and the room is chilling fast. He'll be home soon, and the heating is the first thing he checks. It's the same routine every Friday. He gets paid, he visits the pub after work, we wait. The time he returns matters.

Tonight, it's already eleven p.m.; I'm fourteen years old, and it's way past my bedtime. My mother and I hold hands. Our grips tighten with each ticking second; we know what's coming. The small TV is on, but we can't concentrate on the film.

Our house is unloved and poorly insulated. Double glazing is a modern miracle, in which my father or the council has yet to invest. That could also apply to his relationship with me.

We can always hear him crunching up the gravel drive. We

listen as he bangs open the gate. How he comes home is the second sign.

Tonight, the approaching footsteps are slow and thudding. I imagine the breath steaming from his mouth as though from an exhausted beast, deadened by whisky, not hard labour. He fiddles with the latch, momentarily beaten by his drunken fingers. He scrapes along the brick wall for a few seconds, then silence, before another scrape. It's the worst sign of all. He will be angry, he always is, but he'll be capable.

'Quick, upstairs.'

My mother drags me out from the warmth of the blanket and shepherds me up the stairs. I race up, giving her one final glance back at the top.

'Be quiet,' she implores with wide eyes.

I used to think my presence would help if I stayed with her even though I'm small for my age and delicate. But it never did, especially at this time of night. Not having put me to bed is just another thing that riles him, although he never needs much of an excuse to remove his belt.

'Be careful, Momma. Get him a drink.'

'There's none left,' she whispers.

Then she scoots out of sight. I scamper into my bedroom and slip under the blankets fully clothed, knowing that, despite all the layers, the cold will have filled my bones when I rise in the morning. My heart drums in my chest. I can imagine his key being dragged and stabbed around the entrance to the keyhole. He curses loudly at the door as though it is personally trying to prevent his entrance. The words slur together into one long sentence.

I put my hands over my ears, but it's pointless. Now he's inside, his voice is loud. The angry tone rises in volume, separated by my mum's quiet pleading. Then a thud. Shouts. Whacks.

My father isn't a bad man most of the time. His job is boring, and he despises it, but he goes every day to provide for our family. He tells me this often. I'm ordered to study hard or I'll end up the same way. It's difficult to imagine anyone accepting a life like this. When I first realised what was occurring, I assumed it was a stage that would finish, but now I can't remember anything else.

As always, it doesn't last long before he drags her upstairs. Occasionally, he will stop at my doorway, when I know to lie deadly still. In their room, he makes strange noises for a few minutes, as though he's struggling to get his clothes off. This part is over fast. Then his snores echo through the walls. This is the bit I can barely tolerate. It's as though he's lying next to me. I can smell him.

Even though my mum's ordeal is over, it's only now that she sobs.

I slip out of bed, pull on my thin, mildewy dressing gown, and tiptoe down the stairs. My breath is visible in front of me. I open the lounge door and see Dad has left his cigarettes and matches on the sofa. Weirdly, I find the smoky aroma from them comforting. Perhaps, long ago, things were different.

I've played with matches before. There's an attraction to warmth when you're often cold. I light one of his fags, as he calls them, and take a tentative puff, coughing slightly. I've had a few in the past and, despite the light-headed feeling, still can't fully understand the appeal.

After a few minutes, I stub the cigarette on the side of the ashtray, but it continues to smoulder. The ashtray is overflowing with the remains of both my parents' smoking, and I worry he'll know if there's a half-finished one, so I empty the ashtray into the lounge bin. There's a heavy thump upstairs. I freeze. It's not unusual for him to wake up on his bedroom floor, but if he comes downstairs, I'll be in trouble.

I open the door to the staircase and listen. Blood pounds in my head. Treading on the sides of the stairs, I sneak up. A growl makes me jump, but it's just part of his snoring routine. I slip back into bed, praying that I don't get a late-night visitor.

5

THE FIRE KILLER

It's a familiar acrid stench that wakes me up. My dad tends to burn things in our back garden. I always think it seems a lot of bother compared to filling the boot of his old car with the rubbish and driving it to the household waste place, so maybe he just enjoys it. Once he threw on a heavy curtain, which I thought would put the fire out, but it merely held the flames back until there was a whooshing sound as the fabric lit. I can still recall the strange gleeful expression on my father's face, distorted by the hungry flames as they reached for the sky.

The thick, bitter aroma I remember from back then is in my bedroom now and it's an effort to make myself move. I force myself to throw my sheets back and get out of bed. When I pad onto the landing, I immediately feel the warmth in the carpet, which must be coming from below. I slide my feet into my slippers, which I left at the top of the stairs, and creep halfway down. The smell is stronger here and it's smoky, which makes me cough. The smoke filters through the air as if from a giant cigarette. I can hear a strange sort of snapping, popping sound and I notice that it's not as chilly as when I went to bed.

I edge down the stairs, putting a hand to my mouth at the door to the lounge. I press the handle and push it open. The fire is still off, but the mirror above it is full of flames.

I take a stride inside the room and peer to my right. The blackening sofa against the wall steams while flickering tongues of fire taste the air. My mum's crossword-puzzle book is on fire. The picture frame above it smokes.

The heat is a force that increases during the few seconds I stand there gawping until I slam the door, race back upstairs to my parents' room, scuttle to my mother's side, and shake her shoulder.

'Mum, quick! The sofa's on fire.'

I grab her hand and try to pull her from the bed. She stirs, then jolts upright. Even in the twilight of their room, I recognize the look of pure terror on her face a second later. She turns to wake my dad.

'Leave him,' I urge.

She jerks back to look at me. Her natural instinct to protect rapidly dwindles as she knows what he's become. The internal war only wages for a few seconds before he loses. She slides out of bed and I pull her towards the door. We stumble over shoes and fall onto the landing.

We pick ourselves up and race down the stairs. I burst into the lounge first and stare at the flames that are crawling across the lounge carpet, having already set fire to the door to the kitchen. The sofa has become a ball of furious, spitting sprites.

We don't use the front door; my dad having lost the keys a long time ago. The only way out now is through the kitchen diner, where there is a door to a cheap wooden conservatory that leads to the garden, but most of the floor is black and smouldering in front of us. Dark grey smoke rises from it. More flames pop up. My mum has bare feet.

I point twice to the kitchen, and my mum nods. As I sprint across the floor, hurdling the odd leaping flame, I realise the ringing in my ears is sirens, hopefully from emergency vehicles as opposed to the police who visit our estate regularly to sort out the mischievous local lads. I pray that the fire brigade are coming.

By the time I reach the dining room, my thin soles are painfully warm and the skin on my ankles is hot. My clothes feel the same as they do when I put them on straight after being on the rail in front of the fire. I glance back through the doorway, which now resembles a burning picture frame. My mother crouches, shrouded in smoke, still against the stair door. Her teeth are bared. Her eyes desperate. She shakes her head. I want to return and grab her, but I'm frightened of us both getting hurt.

Maybe I can get help from outside. My eyes sting, and even the few metres I could see clearly a few seconds ago begins to blur as billowing smoke envelops me. I close my eyes, reaching out like a blind person checking their way to locate the door to the conservatory. The surface jars my fingers, but I manage to make out where the lock and key should be. There is no key. I tug on the handle. The door is locked.

I can't hear the sirens any more, only the crackling and roaring of the encroaching fire. A huge bang comes from outside. There's a panicked scream, more animal than human, from behind me. I crouch and turn and, through slitted eyes, try to locate my mother in the lounge, but she's disappeared from view as the doorway becomes a solid block of flames.

The swirling black smoke is so pungent that I can't swallow. Dropping to my knees, I realise there is nowhere to run. Dizziness rushes over me. Sickness roils in my stomach. Intense heat washes over me and my head burns. My back arches as I cough, but then there's another crash and the sound of wood splintering. The air clears slightly, and a cold breeze kisses the right side of my face so I turn in that direction.

The kitchen door flies off its hinges and an immense black and yellow shape barrels through and towards me. An enormous gloved hand grabs me under the armpit and lifts me as though I've already burned away. There's a creaking sound above me and more cracks. I hear his fast, heavy, long strides as he thuds through the greyer smoke in the conservatory.

Then we're outside. It should be cold, but it's as though I'm running into the sun. A blast of freezing water covers me. I open my mouth and nothing has ever felt so good. I'm carried towards more people in black and yellow and a woman with a concerned face delicately takes me from my rescuer, who I now see has a big transparent mask on. The giant towers over me for a moment, turns around, and vanishes.

A strange silverish blanket is pulled over my shoulders while I cough repeatedly. More water is poured over my head, which splatters on my scalp.

There are loud noises everywhere. Sounds like clanging bells and whirring, grinding machinery. There are shouts and screams, more sirens and pounding feet. I blink my sore eyes at the bright lights and flashing images.

Looking around, I manage to focus and see all our neighbours have come out of their houses. They are standing with open mouths and slack jaws while spitting flames pour from the windows on the bottom floor of our house. But the top seems dark and silent. There's an explosion in the house. A big shape appears and strides up our path, holding something heavy, and I realise it's my mother in the arms of a firefighter. As they approach, I notice her hair has gone. She wriggles frantically from the man's grasp, eyes seemingly on fire, and limps over to me. Her face is filthy, black, and dark red, but her smiling teeth are white.

She pulls me into a hug. Glancing over her shoulder, I watch the firefighter yank off his mask. He shakes his head at another older woman in uniform. There's a loud smash as the lounge window disintegrates under the force of three jets of water. The flames are beaten back, but they aren't so easily vanquished. They fight again, billowing out once more. The two windows upstairs light up in orange like a waking dragon. Another firefighter returns from the side of the house, pulling off his mask, too. He's empty-handed and grim-faced.

6

THE FIRE KILLER

Time seems to stand still as I cling to my mother, but she's gently coaxed from my grasp. She mouths something, but no sound comes out. An ambulance quickly takes her away. I feel strangely calm now, sitting in the back of another ambulance. I'm not cold, even though they covered me in something to cool my skin and my burns.

It was quite a surprise touching the damaged hair on my head, but my hair was short, anyway.

'We'll have you at the hospital soon,' says the paramedic. 'The commander would like to ask you a few questions first.'

'Can you tell me who else was in there?' the older woman from earlier says.

'Just my father. He was upstairs in bed.' I look into her eyes. 'Did you save him?'

Her right cheek twitches. She must be used to giving bad news and knows that there's no point in any sugar coating.

'No, I'm afraid we only managed to get you and your mum out.'

I digest that fact for a moment.

'Will she be okay?'

'Yes, she has some burns on her face and feet, but they seem reasonably superficial. We're a bit worried about the smoke that got to her lungs, which is why we've been cautious and rushed her off to hospital.'

I glance in the direction of the house.

'Is he dead, then?'

The woman tries to give me a comforting smile. But what can you say in such circumstances?

'We're damping down at the minute. When it's safe, we'll go back inside and find him, if he didn't make it out. Do you have any idea how it started, or if there's anything dangerous in there?'

'My father drinks and smokes. And no, I don't think so.'

All of a sudden, my shoulders drop as though they've turned into lead. It's quiet now. Just the sounds of whispered voices and splashing water. The lights from the emergency vehicles light up the fire lady's face. She looks kind.

'Thank you for saving us,' I say.

'You've been very brave,' she says, giving me a real smile. 'A true hero. Now get going. You'll be fine.'

The paramedic slams the door shut, and we're soon travelling at speed. The sirens aren't on, which I guess is a good sign. I close my eyes and try to organise my thoughts.

'Keep awake for the moment,' says the paramedic, who is an oldish man with a crinkly face and grey hair. 'You'll have plenty of rest once we've got you checked out.'

As the vehicle swings around corners and roundabouts, it dawns on me what I've done. I've killed my father. Could we have saved him? Should we have? Tears stream from my eyes, but I'm not sure why. I already know without a shadow of doubt, given a second chance, I'd do the same again.

7

DI BARTON

Thursday 2nd July 2020

Things had been quiet since the end of The Cold Killer case. There were the usual unpleasant serious domestics and general violence in the city, but no major drug inquiries or suspicious deaths. Peterborough was becoming a large city with over two-hundred thousand residents, but the crimes were relatively low scale compared to big established towns. The burgeoning population was bringing her visitors though, who could smell the opportunity that a fluid working population provided.

Barton was enjoying the relaxed pace for the moment, even though he could sense the team was raring for something challenging.

The only slight niggle he had was the relationship, or lack thereof, between his two sergeants – Zander and Strange. They'd had an entanglement, for want of a better word, but then not talked about it. They remained professional at work, but DS Zander had been out for a few drinks with the new DC, Nicola 'Pigs' Pignatiello. Barton could see the attraction. She was olive-skinned, tall, warm-natured, and had already proven to be a natural detective. Barton knew her nickname in uniform was Pigs, but had concerns about the team using it in her new role, despite her confidently declaring when she joined them that they were all to call her exactly that.

DS Kelly Strange, on the other hand, was ten years older, not much over five feet tall and blonde. She was a much cooler character and Barton considered her unflappable nature a real asset.

Even Barton heard the gossip going around the department about Zander and Pigs, so Strange must have too. She was sitting opposite Barton now, tapping away at her keyboard. He wasn't sure if it was just his perception or not, but she seemed to have started dressing smarter of late. He looked up as Zander and Pigs came into the office at the same time. Zander had been training her since she joined them and Barton watched them comfortably laughing together, before he realised he wasn't the only one observing the pair. Strange abruptly averted her gaze and instead caught Barton's eye as she returned her focus to her screen. He noted her forced smile in reply to his.

Pigs said something to one of the civilians who was walking through the room. They both laughed afterwards. She moved around the room with a grace and confidence that was extremely rare for a new detective.

Even though their shifts were almost over, Barton decided he'd talk to Zander now, and rang his mobile. He smiled as Zander took his phone out of his pocket, looked at the display, then laughed in Barton's direction.

'Come on, Zander. I'm going for a walk to see the bluebells.'

'Tempting offer, John, but I already have a date tonight.'

'It's an order, not a proposition.'

The two men walked outside together and turned left. Thorpe

Wood was next to the station; hence it being called Thorpe Wood police station. Most locals called the wood Bluebell Wood because it had one of the best displays in Cambridgeshire. Even though the bluebells were gone for another year, it was still a tranquil place in mid-summer.

A series of storms had been passing over the city for the last few days and it was blowing a gale outside, causing both men to do up their coats and lean into the wind, but it was sheltered within the trees once they got inside the wood.

Barton followed the path and took his coat off. With cover from the elements, it was mild and a portent of what was due to arrive soon. The newspapers had been going on about the upcoming heatwave for a fortnight.

Barton's mother had died at the end of the previous year, which had been an unsettling experience for him. She had a plaque in the grounds of her local church, but Barton never sensed her there as he could amongst these trees. She loved walking around here after spring had sprung, and she adored bluebells. Here, Barton could remember her clearly and fondly. Zander knew this and had walked in relaxed silence along the peaceful path with Barton on numerous occasions after she'd gone.

The enchanting sea of bluebells this year had been the best Barton had ever seen, but nature moved on. Barton was doing the same. He loved the smell of a wood in mid-summer and took a deep sniff of the intoxicating fragrances. Then he turned to Zander.

'I'm going to take Pigs off you.'

'Eh?' replied Zander.

'If you're getting close, it doesn't make sense on any level to have you mentoring her.'

Zander paused, looking up into the canopies as he considered his answer.

'Fair enough.'

'Does that mean you're an item now?'

'Not officially, I suppose, but we've been out three times and things might progress. I was going to talk to you about it. Who will you get to train her?'

'I only have one other sergeant.'

Zander looked back at Barton.

'Is that wise?'

'I'll keep an eye on it, but they're both professionals, so I think she'll be fine. Kelly's our best interviewer. Pigs will do well by learning off her.'

Barton wondered whether he should mind his own business, but he thought it worth a final query.

'Did you ever talk to Kelly about your night of passion after The Ice Killer court hearing?'

Zander chuckled because neither he nor Strange could recall much about it.

'I guess we talked around what happened. It was weird. We were like teenagers. I'm not going to pretend I don't have strong feelings for her, but it seems so natural with Pigs. The reason I've been taking it slowly with her is because I feel torn between the pair of them. Perhaps I shouldn't date either.'

Barton laughed out loud.

'That's like struggling to choose between a Grand Big Mac or a Double Quarter Pounder with cheese, and deciding to have neither.'

'So your advice would be to have both?'

Both men giggled like schoolboys as they turned around and began to walk out of the wood.

'Good point,' said Barton. 'I've never been in your position, sadly. Maybe you should talk to Holly about it.'

Zander pulled a face. 'Not tempting,' he said. 'Your old lady can be scary. I also know how much she loves Kelly. I might say the wrong thing and she'd remove my testicles.'

'Perhaps it's a risk you should take.'

'Will they grow back?'

'I doubt it. Mine haven't.'

They stepped from the wood, grinning wildly, and put their coats back on as a squall hit. They were doing their coat zips up as a car driving past stopped, and the window wound down. It was DS Strange.

'I always suspected as much,' she said with a knowing grin.

8

THE FIRE KILLER

Later that night

Staring out of the bedroom window, I think of the convenience store a few roads away. They'll be closing shortly at ten p.m. They have a large skip outside their shop, which is full of paper and cardboard. It's been a red rag to me ever since they filled it up a few days ago.

A Syrian family runs the place. The older parents are lovely, but one of their new workers always looks at me like I'm trying to steal things. I've been daydreamy these last six months, what with all the changes, so I once walked out of their shop with a copy of the *Peterborough Telegraph* without paying for it. He chased me down the street past a huge queue of people waiting for the bus, while shouting 'thief' at the top of his voice. I haven't dared look my neighbours in the eye since. Not that I used to do that much anyway.

I'd love to see his face when he looks out of his window and sees the world on fire. I want to watch it burn, too. Normally I wouldn't set light to something that large, but it's well away from all the cars. I could watch next to the wall, where I'd be almost out of sight too. It'd be like having a ringside seat for the big fight. My skin tingles at the thought of what might happen. A much bigger blaze is an added risk though, but they'll think it's young kids like they usually do.

At eleven, I pull on a large ski jacket and steady myself at the door. As always at this point, my fingers lack dexterity and my toes are numb. My feet feel like I have heavy wooden clogs on them as I step out from the house and trudge down the road. It's a cruel, wild wind that hurries me towards my target. The air has a hint of rain in it again, but it never seems to get going. Heavy clouds bulge and rumble, but rush away as if protecting their load. Strange weather, for strange times.

There's nobody else about, which isn't surprising. The local paper has regular reports of muggings. I walk past on my first sweep to make sure no one's coming around the corner. When I approach the bin on my return journey, I stand in close to the edge of the skip. I've decided to use a Zippo lighter because of the wind and I force myself to calm down as I struggle to light it. In the end, I open my coat to shelter the flame.

Once it stays lit, I take a last glance around and slide the flickering lighter into a cereal carton near the top of the skip on the other side from the shop. There's a small path that leads to our cul-de-sac along the back of some gardens. I hustle over there. The foliage of a tree in one of the gardens hangs heavy over the wall, and I'm almost invisible underneath it, so I decide to stop and wait here.

This stage – the anticipation and planning – can be enjoyable. I sense the need coming months before I act, and it's like springtime inside me. Afterwards, I pretend that I won't weaken again, but I always do. It's what I do. The fire engine arriving is the best bit. My knees weaken at the imminent arrival of the big machine and then the uniformed firefighters will jump out purposefully.

If there's a sizeable crowd when they turn up, I'll sometimes mingle, getting close to those strong men and women, but I'm pretty sure the police would look at the bystanders if they were investigating a serious blaze. I usually just wait and pretend that I'm walking past, or stand at a distance if I've lit up something big.

There was a warehouse blaze once, many years ago, not too far from my house. A warm feeling comes over me now when I remember parking up and observing. The heat was incredible, even through the windscreen. The sky glowed better than any sunset I've seen before. I almost left my car and ran towards it. It was stupid to go, even though I had nothing to do with it and the cause was found to be an electrical issue.

I'll stick to my little fires, but the urge to progress has always been there. As I ponder how I've managed to control these strengthening desires, I spot the first sign of life. There's a slight radiance to the far side of the container. It's a large skip, twelve feet at least. As the seconds pass, the glow grows. I try to steady my breathing as the flames rise, but my breaths are rapid and shallow. After a few more minutes, I sense movement at the dark shop. The door has opened and a man has appeared. He halts with obvious shock. It's the bloke who embarrassed me. I can see him reach for his pocket and take out his phone. He pauses, hustles back inside, then rushes out a minute later with a small red fire extinguisher.

I worry that he and the weather will beat the fire back, but the pathetic stream from the extinguisher is as effective as him shouting into the wind for it to stop. Each meaty gust picks up burning material and blows it into the air. The pieces swirl and race into people's gardens, onto their cars, and over fences, as though they are swallows from hell in flight. It's a beautiful sight, but I know paper burns hot and fast, and the fire might spread.

The flames leap twenty feet when the man throws the extinguisher into the fire and returns inside the shop. Most of the skip is ablaze. I hear a siren in the distance. I place my hand on the wall to support myself as the euphoria threatens to swamp me. Then a scream fills the night. I scan the area to see where the sound has come from but then I hear it again. I realise with horror that it's not a scream of fright, it's one of pain.

I stagger backwards when I see movement at the edge of the skip. A clawed hand rises out of the furnace, then sinks back out of sight.

9

DI BARTON

Barton stepped out of his front door the next morning and picked up the rubbish bags his wife had left outside for him to carry to the bins at the side of his house. A guy from the bottom of his cul-de-sac walked past with his timid terrier.

'Morning, John.'

'Morning.'

Barton searched his mind for the man's name. He could remember the dog was called Harry, but Kevin's name only materialised when they were both out of sight. Barton breathed in a breath of air. He liked living on the edge of Peterborough in Longueville Village. The house prices had been reasonable when they'd bought, but he'd struggle to buy now, so he really appreciated the peace and quiet.

It was only a 1950s semi, but it had an extension, which they used as a lounge, and a garage, which they'd converted into another bedroom. Holly often went down there to watch TV and to have a little peace. Smiling to himself, he noticed the side gate to the front garden was open. He wandered over and grimaced. It was as though the patio out there had witnessed a hurricane judging by the discarded toys, bikes, scooters and past-saving wicker furniture. A distant memory of promising to clear it surfaced from a year ago.

Luckily the hedge, which needed trimming, concealed most of the wreckage. He made a weak promise to do it at the weekend, shut the gate, got in his car and drove to work.

The police station, on the other hand, was an ugly warehouse-type building, which had been designed without any love. It was surrounded by more office blocks and a gym, but Barton had a soft spot for the area after so many years. He didn't mind if the station looked a bit foreboding. After all, theirs was a serious business.

Barton had only been at his desk for five minutes when he found Chief Inspector Brabbins standing beside him, looking immaculate in his uniform.

'Quick minute, please, John.'

Barton smiled as he followed Brabbins into an empty office, although he suspected some shit was about to be shovelled in his direction.

'I've spoken to DCI Cox, and she's happy for me to explain the case directly to you.'

Barton hid his grin. He bet she was.

'We'd like you to investigate a fire.'

'The one last night in Welland?'

'That's it.'

'I just read the report. I thought there wasn't any significant damage or injuries.'

'That's what we believed, but daylight revealed extensive burns to a telegraph pole and the guy who'd ordered the skip says his car is covered in scorch marks. He reckons it was done deliberately, possibly because of race.'

'Okay, but I'm still not sure why Major Crimes would get involved.'

'That's the final element. It was an old skip without a drain, so it filled with water when they doused the flames last night. They aren't waterproof, so it's gradually emptied itself overnight. We left a constable to guard the scene, and he noticed something unexpected at the bottom in the morning.'

Barton raised an eyebrow.

'Yes,' said Brabbins. 'It appears to be a charred human body.'

10

DI BARTON

Barton's brain chugged into action.

'Any chance it's a mannequin?'

'Not judging by its teeth, no.'

'Our case, then?' Barton said after a pause.

'Yes. Do you have the manpower? We're flat out at the moment. Not that there's an enormous amount of offending going on, but we've got loads of staff off with Covid or self-isolating.'

'Yeah, we're quiet, too. The shops are closed for theft, folk are in their houses all the time so burglaries are down, and a lot of pubs are shut, so drunken violence generally has decreased. The opportunity to sell drugs has been curtailed too. I suspect domestic abuse cases will accelerate the longer the restrictions continue. Holly's already threatened to kill me on more than one occasion.'

Brabbins laughed.

'My wife's home-schooling the kids,' he replied. 'You'd need a samurai sword to cut the tension.'

Barton chuckled, but he knew that on average the lockdown would hit women harder than the men. They would be the ones trying to juggle their jobs with home-schooling. He made a mental note to help out more at home and to chat with the children, so they also stepped up. To be fair, the older kids had just got on with it, but Luke was still at junior school and needed almost constant supervision.

'Right,' he said. 'Where are we with the fire?'

'CSI have been called. The fire investigator has been appointed this morning and should be there at ten. The manager of the skip-hire company is on his way too. Of course, the scene is secure, and there have been no people reported missing over the last couple of days that haven't been located. Nothing else so far.'

'Okay, thanks. I'm going to head down there and talk to everyone face to face, get a feel for the area and the people. I seem to remember there being a spate of arsons around there. Mostly in a variety of rubbish bins.'

'Yes, it's been an ongoing annoyance. We managed to catch a kid on CCTV for one of them, and he confessed to two more, but there have been a lot over the years. We also caught a girl who said she'd got the idea after seeing a blaze that someone else had started.'

'Great. Learned behaviour. And you never caught anyone for the others?'

'Nope. You know what arson is like. Fire doesn't leave many clues behind. We've received no intel so far for this one. It's on the Peterborough Matters website, but they aren't aware of its gravity yet. Cox has said she'll handle the media aspect, just give her an update when you're ready and we'll get it on the evening news.'

After Brabbins had left, Barton spent a few minutes running through his options. Racially motivated crimes were more serious than ones that weren't, so it was important he kept that fact at the forefront of his mind. An aggrieved party might be more likely to want revenge.

That said, it was more than likely arson. A skip full of burnable rubbish was a tempting proposition for young boys. Barton could remember playing with matches when he was a teenager, and there were going to be a lot of bored children around right now. Young people didn't care about the virus. A sense of invincibility was a recurring theme for each new generation until life taught them otherwise.

As for the body, it was a bracing breeze last night. It was possible that someone could have climbed in for a nap to get out of the wind. That sort of thing happened regularly, but generally when the pubs and clubs were open.

It was tough to think about a person being burned alive, but the ends of skips weren't that high. You'd have thought that whoever it was would have been able to scramble out once they realised what was going on. Which meant there was the possibility that the victim was put in there when they were already dead. The fire might well have been started deliberately, perhaps to burn the remains. Or maybe a passer-by threw a cigarette butt in as they walked past.

Barton picked up the phone and rang the morgue. Mortis, the curmudgeonly pathologist, answered on the second ring.

'Morning, John. Are you booking yourself in? I thought you looked a bit peaky last time I saw you.'

'It depends,' replied Barton. 'Are you offering liposuction yet?'

Mortis and Barton had worked together for many years. Mortis was Scottish and close to retirement.

'I'd need to hire two new members of staff to do that for you.'

Barton laughed, then explained what had happened.

'That sounds most interesting. I'll meet you there within the hour.'

Barton returned to the office, where he found all of his team. He cleared his throat, causing all of them to look up.

'Okay, listen in. A body has been discovered.'

'Where?' asked DC Leicester and DC Malik in unison.

Barton smiled at them. Despite the difference in their skin colour, they really could be twins. He gave them a quick update.

'Probably a homeless person,' said Malik.

'It could be a domestic murder,' said Zelensky, a young detective who was similar to Strange in both looks and demeanour.

'It sounds suspicious,' said Leicester.

'The Barton belly would agree with all of you.'

11

DI BARTON

Barton directed Strange to take Pigs. Zander and Malik would drive together, and he took Leicester in his vehicle. When they were en route, Barton could see that Leicester was considering the case because he had a habit of running his hands through his short, thick ginger hair when he was deep in thought. With a tell like that, Barton made a mental note to restart poker night.

'Have you been involved in many similar cases?' asked Leicester as they raced along the parkway.

'I'm not sure what we're dealing with yet, but people have been covering their tracks with fire for years, or at least attempting to. Don't let the fire angle complicate things. If you believe someone was murdered, then you start at the victim and work outwards. Not many people are capable of murder, and, of those who are, few would then have the calm to dispose of the corpse in this manner.'

'Yes, that does seem hardcore. Organised crime?'

'It could be. If it's Joe Public that's died, relatives have usually missed them within twenty-four hours. If they see that a body has been found on the local news, they would be even more worried, so we might get a call later today when the facts are released. Whereas criminals, either home-grown or imported, are less likely to be missed and also more at risk of meeting a grisly end. Keep your mind open. This really could be anything.'

'It takes a cold heart to lob a dead body into a skip and torch it.'

'Yes, and a strong one. Dead bodies aren't easy to manoeuvre without the right equipment. From what Brabbins said, that skip was in the open. You'd expect someone to notice two people lugging a body-shaped roll of strangely heavy carpet up the road.'

'They could have driven up and lobbed it in off a truck.'

'Excellent thought,' said Barton. 'Let me know how you get on later with local CCTV for any recent trucks or hearses passing by.'

Leicester groaned good-naturedly. They arrived at the location, and Barton parked up in one of the parking bays for the row of shops. There was a dry cleaner, a newsagent, a Chinese takeaway, a chemist, and a couple of units that appeared vacant. Barton and Leicester stepped from the vehicle and looked around. Thanks to so many people working from home, apart from the figures gathered around the skip, there wasn't a single person or moving car in sight.

Barton checked for CCTV. He hadn't been joking earlier with Leicester. They solved so many crimes nowadays with technology that sometimes it took some of the challenge out of it. He grimaced as he wondered whether it was acceptable to think like that in this day and age, but he still hoped for cameras. There was nothing obvious. He spotted one on the corner of the last shop, but it was pointing down, not out.

The big plus of CCTV was that in court there was less risk. CCTV didn't turn up late or not at all, and it didn't change its mind under duress, or forget things. Barton strode over to the group next to the skip. There was Sirena, who was the crime scene manager, Mortis, a young, female uniformed PC called Adams, and the guy from the local fire investigation team, Leigh Beddows.

They all knew each other, no introductions were necessary, so while Barton waited for the other detectives to turn up, he put some shoe coverings on and walked under the tape and around the skip, peering inside as he did. The weather was beautiful. There was a cloudless sky, and the sun was rising, yet there was still a little nip in the air. The wind had blown itself out. It seemed like the forecasters were right and summer was going to be a period of blazing glory.

The skip had more in it than he imagined. He'd expected the contents to be burned up and melted inside, but there were many intact items in there, including a bicycle frame and what looked to be parts of a garden swing. There were also bits of soggy magazines, pictures of a bodybuilder still discernible, a blackened microwave, and a half-melted toaster. Visible at the side of the skip, protruding from wet ash, were the chargrilled head and neck of the victim. The lips had retreated to reveal a terrifying grin that wouldn't have looked out of place in any horror movie.

It felt surreal to be standing near human remains on such a lovely, quiet morning. Barton gathered everyone around when the other cars turned up.

'Okay, we'll all be able to read each other's reports, but let's see what we come up with collectively before we begin questioning the shop owners and going door to door in the neighbourhood. It's a fire, so let's start with you, Leigh.'

'We got a call last night not long after eleven. The caller gave full details, so we only sent one appliance. The commander was pitching in due to staff shortages, so he went out with the crew. He estimated the fire had only been burning for a few minutes before it was rung in, and the station is only around the corner. You can see how visible the skip is from quite a few houses, so perhaps that's not surprising. There was no danger to cars, the public, or personnel. We put it out in less than a minute. We stayed for a while but a joyrider had come off on the A1 and we were needed to free him.

The police said they'd set up the perimeter here and secure the site until this morning.'

'At the time, was nobody suspicious it might have been more than a fire?' asked Barton.

'No, there was nothing to indicate that. Nobody came forward to say they'd seen anything. One of the people who reported the fire remained at the scene. He just saw the flames and called us. It was over so quick that only a few people came out of their houses to watch. I'm guessing all the debris and burning residue would have concealed the body, then the fire crew's water would have. The only reason we wanted to follow it up first thing was that two of the fire-fighters reckoned they might have got a whiff of meat being cooked when they first arrived.'

'What type of meat?' asked Zander.

'I'm sure you know the smell. At first you think it's pork, but then there's that other scent, that's not quite bacon, from the burning blood and all the fat. It was windy last night, so the fire had blown scraps of paper and cardboard all over, and it would have dispersed the smell, but human flesh has a subtle scent of its own. You don't forget it.'

'Right,' said Barton, knowing that, sadly, most police could confirm that. He considered whether the fire crew should have reported their suspicions last night, but decided not to mention it. 'Will you get much from analysing the skip and its contents?'

'We might. If a strong accelerant was used, it would affect how everything it touched burned, but there's a lot left in there. Even the corpse is still human-looking. It seems there was plenty of paper and card inside, so a match might have done the trick. The high sides would shelter the flames until they were well established.'

'Do you investigate most fires like this?'

'No, resources are thinly stretched. We only investigate if certain factors are present. For something this size, we'd obviously come back to see what had been burned. My initial guess is that this is mostly a paper fire, so maybe between five hundred and six hundred degrees Celsius. A lot of things won't burn up in that kind of heat.'

Barton turned to Sirena. She still had a strong Greek accent, despite working in the UK for many years.

'Fires ruin evidence, but not all of it. We'll get fingerprints from the surrounds of the skip too, which might help let us know if the person climbed in, or was put in. DNA won't be a problem either if the body is only charred, but any fingerprints and footprints don't do well in these circumstances. I agree with Leigh. This looks like a standard fire from first inspection, so it won't tell us much. If we can identify the victim, that should get you started. We'll start taking photos now, and remove samples, then we'll move the body.'

'Who knows, there may be a driving licence in her pocket,' said Mortis.

'Her?' asked Barton.

'An educated guess.'

'Excellent,' said Barton. He turned to Mortis with half a smile. Mortis had a tendency to give lots of details very quickly, not all of which were pertinent. 'Go on, let's hear the reasons.'

'Interesting case. As you can imagine, I've seen many such remains. I'd agree with what's been said so far. The best way to tell if this person was already dead by the time the fire was started is by analysing the lungs. They'll be full of deposits and damage if the person was breathing while they burned. A few hours after receiving the body, I'll know their approximate age, sex and health. Teeth and bones aren't destroyed unless it's incredibly hot. I'd guess it was a female by the size of the shoulders and the bone structure of the head. It's not a young child because those teeth are too big.'

'Okay. Let's get to it,' said Barton.

He beckoned his team to the side and instructed them to go

house to house in pairs for all properties that had a visual on the skip, while he and Leicester would have a word with the shop manager who'd made the race accusation. Barton hoped they'd catch a quick break because this woman's family would be missing her. Whether it was an accident or deliberate, their lives would be forever changed, regardless.

He looked up at the shops and saw a man with his arms crossed in the doorway of the convenience store, staring hard in their direction. Barton was just about to take Leicester over for a chat when a skip lorry arrived with Craster's Skips written on the side of it in faded paint. The driver pulled up next to him and scowled down.

'Who's paying for the repairs to my skip?'

Barton realised it was going to be one of those days.

12

DI BARTON

Barton took a deep breath.

'Park up and then come over, please,' he said to the driver.

He watched as the man expertly manoeuvred the big lorry into a tight space between two cars. Barton had met a lot of skip drivers over the years and found they came in all types. He initially imagined them as burly, sullen types with dirty overalls, but the last one he'd encountered used to work as an engineer for Rolls-Royce and just wanted a slower pace of life.

Sure enough, the man who got out was a surprise. He was rake thin, completely bald and wore smart shoes, brown trousers and an ironed shirt. He did, however, have a mean face, and his lips were tight as he stomped towards them.

'Look at the state of it,' he shouted while he was still twenty metres away.

Barton stepped forward.

'I need to ask you what you know about the dead body in it.'

The skip owner slowed, deflating slightly.

'That had nothing to do with us. I'm just trying to earn a living here.'

He strode forward again.

'No compassion for the young woman who died, Mr Craster?'

Craster stopped in front of Barton, grimacing while avoiding eye contact.

'That's very sad,' he eventually said.

'That's good to hear. Now, I know you'd like to help me swiftly, answering all my questions so I can understand the skip business in less than five minutes. I have my suspicions. I'd hate to need all of your drivers to come to the station to make statements. Bring ID, that type of thing.'

Mr Craster almost smiled. Clearly, he wasn't daft. Barton knew that in his line of work, the ebb and flow of dropping the skips off and picking them up was the way to make money. His whole team losing a day would screw most of that up, not to mention there was the chance employee records might be incomplete or absent.

'Of course. There shouldn't be any call for that,' said Mr Craster.

'What's the process from the customer ringing up? Do they have to set up an account, pay by card, how long does it take, how much is it?'

'Right. The customer rings. Repeat customers would have an account and ten per cent off. New customers would pay by card. It's anything from two hundred pounds up. We deliver it on an agreed day, collect the same way. They get up to a week maximum for the fee. If they want more, it's extra.'

'What kind of skip is this? Can you put anything in it? Does it go straight to be buried somewhere?'

Mr Craster was certainly on the ball.

'Are you asking if someone could stick a dead body in here and we'd just take it to landfill?'

'More or less.'

'No, they couldn't. The cost of each skip depends on what it's for. If it's for concrete, stone or bricks, it's cheaper because we break up what we take away and sell it on elsewhere as aggregate. This is a mixed skip, so they can ram any old shite in it. Bikes, toys, books, baths, bogs, but we still sort it. It needs to be recycled. We'd find a body straight away.'

Barton considered his answer. Obviously the skip would have arrived empty, and the company wouldn't want any involvement in this kind of situation because it was so easily traceable. He'd put the skip crew to one side for now, although there was no accounting for what people might do if they wanted to dispose of a body.

'Okay, thanks for that. The skip will be examined here, then taken to a compound to be emptied. Leave your details with one of the CSI team. They'll be in touch.'

'Look, I need that skip. It's due over at Werrington tomorrow afternoon.'

Barton raised an eyebrow.

'Okay, here's my card,' said Craster. 'Anything at all, ring me.'

Barton was about to walk towards the shop when he had a thought.

'Why were you so tetchy first thing?'

Craster finally seemed to relax, and Barton suspected he was actually a decent guy.

'This is a tough game to be in. People order the wrong skip, fill it with the wrong stuff, then refuse to pay the extra. They put asbestos and full tubs of paint with loose lids inside. If they run out of space, they overfill them, and some assholes even set fire to them to reduce the contents, which is massively dangerous.'

Barton gave him an appreciative nod.

'Good to know,' he said, as he beckoned to Leicester to follow him. Barton walked with interest towards the still scowling shopkeeper.

13

DI BARTON

Barton and Leicester headed for the shop but just before they got there, the man disappeared inside. Barton groaned under his breath and followed him in. When they entered the shop, there were only two elderly, Middle Eastern people at the till. Barton had assumed the person in the door was Rafiq Majid, one of those who'd rung in the fire.

The couple waved at him and Leicester, giving them big grins.

'Morning, sirs. Please, he waits in the back,' said the woman, gesturing to a door further down at the side of the shop.

Barton ambled down the shop, looking around. He stopped at the door and, not wanting to appear rude, knocked. Barton had seen enough angry men to know what was in front of him when it opened.

'Mr Majid?' asked Leicester.

With a quick nod, Majid retreated to the back of the shop and stood behind a desk. Barton nodded. Normally, he'd offer a hand, but Covid had put an end to such barrier breakers. Majid paced up and down behind the desk.

'You rang about the fire last night,' said Leicester.

Majid wasn't just cross, he was fuming. If he'd been a big man, Barton might have had some concerns, but he couldn't have been much over five and a half feet and was slim. Up close, he was also much older than Barton had first guessed. Maybe pushing fifty like Barton. Majid stopped pacing, turned to them, placed his hands on the desk, and vented. But he did it in a harsh whisper, as though there was a baby sleeping upstairs.

'This is bullshit. I ring and ring about all the abuse, threats, thieving, burgling and graffiti, and no one's interested. The odd copper turns up, but I never hear anything again. Then I call up for a simple skip fire, and you turn up en masse, and talk to everyone else but me. I've had enough. I'll, I'll—'

'There is a complaints procedure, sir, but this isn't just about a burning skip. There are other factors in play.'

Barton briefly wondered if Leicester was being facetious, but that wasn't his style. Sometimes Barton would calm the complainant down, but in this kind of irate state, he liked to keep them talking and shouting without engaging their brains. Usually, the unvarnished truth came out, even if they didn't want it to.

'Why do you think this is to do with race, and is personally directed at you, Mr Majid?' asked Barton.

'This might as well not be a store. I should get rid of the tills, save them having to hide the stuff in their pockets. They can tell me what they've stolen. At least that way, I would know what had gone. I also wouldn't have to put up with threats of violence when I challenge them. I've had shit smeared on the door. Someone even threatened to burn the place down when I followed them in the shop because they were acting suspicious.'

'Really?' said Barton. 'Who was it?'

'He was just a kid. It was when I first took over. I haven't seen him since, although they come in with hoodies and scarves on, so they're hard to tell apart.'

'That doesn't mean they wouldn't do it.'

'I suppose. I'm more bothered by the druggies and goths hanging around outside scaring off the decent passing trade.'

Barton glanced around at what appeared to be a storeroom. It seemed badly organised, if indeed there was any order. Next to him were toilet rolls and Mars bars. He'd also noticed empty shelves as they walked through the shop.

'Is this your establishment?' asked Leicester.

'Does it matter?' replied Majid.

They were missing something here. Barton gestured to the seats around the desk.

'Shall we take a seat?'

Majid looked as if he was going to say no, but instead gave them a little nod. Majid pulled up a chair, then surprised them by resting his head on the table. After a few seconds, Barton reached over and gently placed his hand on the man's arm.

'Do you want to tell us about it? You look as though you're under a lot of pressure.'

When Majid looked up, Barton saw tears. Barton gave him a reassuring smile and gestured for Majid to talk to them. Majid took a moment to calm down.

'I'm sorry. Last night I felt like I was losing my mind. This isn't my store. It's my friend's upstairs. We've been mates for over forty years, ever since we went to playschool around the corner together. I work from home in IT, he ran this place. He was busy, and I have a family, two daughters, but we still looked out for each other. Us against the world, you know.'

'What happened?' asked Barton, softly.

'He had a stroke. Must be six months back now. Basically, it paralysed his left-hand side, from top to bottom.'

Majid leaned back in his seat and blew out a big breath, then wiped his eyes.

'And you've been helping out?'

'Yes, his parents who you just saw helped him run the shop, but they're old now, and merely pottered about before their son became ill. They want to keep it running until he's better, but I don't think he's ever going to recover enough to run this place. It's bloody tough. I can't be here all the time. The kids on the estate know the parents aren't up to it, and if I'm not here, they get up to all sorts. But it's not only them. Adults wander out with things too. People are rude. A woman in her thirties was sick over the sweets, never even said sorry.'

'That must be hard, having your own work, too.'

Majid looked in Barton's eyes, as if to check he was being genuine.

'Yes,' he said, in not much more than a whisper. 'It has been exhausting. Last night was the final straw. I could smell burning. I thought back to the kid who'd threatened to torch the place and went outside. That's when I noticed my skip was on fire.'

'Your skip?' asked Leicester.

'Well, it was supposed to be.' Majid let out a grunt that might have been the beginnings of a chuckle. 'I ordered it three days ago. I'd just taken the cover off it yesterday morning when Jerry upstairs had a fall, so I took him to the hospital. With all the recent precautions, we were there for ages. When I got home, the skip was full of stuff. Chairs, carpet, tons of newspaper, cardboard, thousands of leaflets, which I assume someone couldn't be bothered to deliver, loads of polystyrene, you name it. Almost spilling out, it was. None of it mine. Even had a framed photo of George Michael in it.'

And a body, thought Barton. He decided to ask the obvious.

'You didn't burn it to reduce the contents?'

'No, of course not. There's a huge sign on the side of it saying no fires. Besides, I have a BMW Z3. I love it more than my wife, and she's amazing, and it was parked close by. Burning paper blew over it and damaged the paintwork.'

Barton hesitated for a few moments, flashed a quick smile at Leicester, then turned back so he could study Majid's expression.

'I'm afraid to say that there was someone in the skip when it burned,' said Leicester.

Majid's reaction was instant and genuine.

'Oh my God, who?'

'We don't know yet. Perhaps a woman. Do you have any thoughts on who it could be? It might be a beggar or a homeless person. Are there any around here? Maybe even a streetwalker.'

Majid frowned.

'How awful. We do get all of those types here. A woman nicked a bottle of whisky yesterday while I was at the hospital but Jerry's parents didn't notice. They're just too innocent of what some people are like. I saw it on our CCTV last night, but the shoplifter had a mask on, sunglasses, and a hood up.'

Barton exchanged another look with Leicester.

'Why do you think it was a woman thief?' asked Leicester.

'She had woman's boots on, you know, with thin high heels. Looked a bit weird with the chunky coat, but what would I know? I'd already had enough of running the shop when I saw her stealing it, and that was before the fire. Jerry's parents will be heartbroken, but I'm going to shut tonight, and not reopen.'

'Okay, I'm sorry to hear that,' said Barton. 'I know this is a tough time for you, but we'll need you to come to the station and make a full statement.'

'No, I don't want to. I just want to close up and forget about it all.'

'I understand,' said Barton. 'But this could be murder. You need to help. If we don't catch them, it might be someone else's daughter in a skip next time.'

Majid's eyes widened. 'Can I come tonight after I close up?'

'First thing tomorrow will be fine if you need to get this place in order,' said Barton. 'But let's look at that CCTV now.'

An hour later, Barton and Leicester stepped from the shop.

Barton's mind was racing. He suspected his brain would look like a firework show on a brain scan. The girl who'd walked in and stolen the whisky had been staggering. She could easily have been a homeless alcoholic who climbed in the skip to sleep it off. Yet, even with the grainy CCTV, which showed nothing of her face, Barton could see that she had been dressed well. She was also carrying a small suitcase. That didn't add up to his idea of a homeless person, so what was she doing climbing into a skip?

In any case like this, the first step was victim identification. All roads would lead from there. Her death could have been a terrible accident, but something was definitely out of kilter.

Barton updated the rest of the team and left them to their house-to-house calls, and Mortis and Sirena continued their more gruesome tasks. Barton had a lot of paperwork to do, and an incident room needed setting up. He had a serious investigation on his hands.

14

THE FIRE KILLER

It's late morning when I wake up. Usually after setting a fire, I sleep most of the following day. A couple of times, I've slept for over twenty-four hours. When I finally get up, it's as though I can breathe again.

My mind wanders to the hand coming out of the skip. Perhaps it was a clothes dummy. I yank the duvet off, knowing I'm deluding myself.

I plod downstairs, dreading turning the TV on. Nothing good will come of this, but I should be safe. I don't know much about police procedures or fire investigations, but they'll struggle to connect anyone to a discarded Zippo lighter with no fingerprints on it, unless someone saw me. Would they see it as murder, or an accident?

I'm aware we don't get too many murders in this country, so the authorities probably throw loads of resources at them when they do come up. I live nearby so it's likely they'll knock on my door. Do I open it? Surely, the answer to any questions is to shrug and say you were watching TV. Act normally. I shake my head. I'm not even sure I was born normal. My father certainly wasn't.

I rarely watch the news. It's too depressing, but I click on the TV now. There's no mention on Sky News about the fire, and I've no idea when the local programmes come on. After a quick shower, which does nothing to ease my agitation, I try to force some breakfast down my neck. The toast sticks in my throat as I picture the toxic smoke closing the victim's airways. What the hell were they doing in there? Jesus Christ. Imagine if it was kids playing a game. What if there was more than one child in there? My cup of tea threatens to re-emerge.

I need to get out of the house and do something, even if it's only to go for a walk. Just as I'm ready to leave, I realise I've put the same ski jacket on that I was wearing last night. A short denim one will do instead. I don't want to jog anyone's memories.

Outside, I'm glad I didn't wear the long coat because it's noticeably hotter than yesterday. There's a real feeling of summer, or at least the promise of it. I'm not happy though, or at peace. That's how I usually am after the event, but I guess it isn't surprising that this time is different.

I didn't get to gasp when the ground shook as the big truck arrived, or hear the clamour of the equipment and sense the urgency of the crew. Even the smells were stolen from me due to some imbecile climbing in where they shouldn't.

I breathe out long and hard to attempt to relax. Besides, it's more my fault than theirs. They must have been asleep in the skip. Imagine the horror to wake up cooking. The disorientation and panic would have been all consuming, as they were consumed themselves. I never saw my father's remains after he was burned, but there were some. Even in that ferocious heat, the body endures.

I recall my father's funeral. For such an arsehole, he had a lot of friends. My father was a big, strong man. My mother and I knew that well, and I remember the strain and focus on the faces of the pall-bearers as they carried him into the crematorium. I had to go with Aunt Tabitha, who they had forced me to live with for a while. She stank of cigarette smoke, and that made me think back to what I'd done every time I was in her presence. My mother couldn't be there. It was two months before she left hospital. She would never be the same.

I decide to wander the long way out of our street, reaching the main road around a hundred metres from the shops. It was a good choice because there are emergency vehicles and people in crime-scene suits all over the place. I keep my head down, turn left and stroll past a block of flats. There is tension in every joint of my body.

I spot the line of bins against the side wall of the flats. It'll be collection day in a few days. They only collect them fortnightly now, so they're all overflowing by the time it comes around again. My eyes flick over them and, despite the warmth of the sun, a chill washes over me.

Last night wasn't enough, but I swore if I ever hurt anyone innocent, then that would be the end. Which would mean it would be my end. Because I would have nothing to live for if I stopped. Everyone hurts me eventually. All I have left are the fires.

Last night wasn't enough. I suppose it never is. I will have to do it again, and soon, but this time I really will make it my last.

15

DI BARTON

Barton had a busy morning, setting everything in motion back at the station. He didn't notice when DCI Cox appeared beside him until she cleared her throat.

'I've got meetings all afternoon, then I'm at a strategy day tomorrow in Huntingdon, but I'll be contactable. Anything I should know about the fire?'

'Could be anything at this point.'

'Okay. One quick point before I leave. Have you heard of the Bates gang in London?'

'Can't say that I have.'

'That's not surprising as they're an east London outfit. I've only heard of them in passing, but they're serious gangsters for want of a better phrase.'

'Are you saying that Peterborough's Greasy Chip Shop Gang operating out of Thorney aren't a force to be reckoned with?'

'Quite. The Bateses are into guns in a big way, but they have their fingers in prostitution, drug dealing and extortion.'

'They sound lovely,' he said.

'One of the brothers is under around-the-clock observation, but a different brother was seen getting into a car last week that ended up in our city.'

'And?'

'That's it. There was nothing more to it, but they let us know in case anything happened here. For all we know, he might have been coming to see the cathedral.'

Barton imagined a Reggie Kray type parking his Jaguar up at Asda, wandering past Poundland and Greggs in his moleskin suit, and slipping the beggars a few quid down a littered Bridge Street before admiring the famous imposing early English gothic west front. He also recalled the Salisbury poisonings, where the Russians said that they had been there to see the cathedral, which reminded him of Leicester's earlier comment about whether the fire was connected to organised crime, but this guy had been long gone by the time the body was put in the skip.

'I'll listen out for gunfire,' said Barton.

'That's the spirit.'

It was mid-afternoon when the team returned from canvassing and he gathered them all in the incident room.

'Okay, what did we find out?' he asked.

'If we're honest, not much,' said Zander.

'Anything at all?'

'No, not really,' said Strange. 'It's a bit rough around there, and people were cautious about talking to us. A few of the houses need condemning, but there's still a sense of community. The area appears to have a fluid situation with immigrants moving in and out, but many wanted to help. I could live there. My first gaff in London was way worse. I lived at the end of the line. We used to joke we were catching the last train to crime central.'

'I bet everyone was relieved when you left,' said Zander with a big grin.

Barton tensed, wondering whether Kelly would be in the mood

for her colleague's banter.

Strange gave him a filthy look, then laughed. 'Yeah, you're right. They all knew I was Old Bill. It's hard to flog hooky gear when there's a panda outside your house.'

Barton chuckled along with everyone else, while stopping himself from wiping his forehead.

'No eyewitness, then?' he said. 'No one with suspicions? What were people's views of the shop, and its owners?'

'No eyewitnesses. The shop was held in high regard. They sell cheap booze, and they were open during lockdown. It's like an essential service,' said Zelensky, earning herself another group laugh.

'A few of the people I spoke to mentioned groups of kids were regularly up to no good, but it had always been that way,' said Strange. 'A guy who moved in some time around the millennium said he'd often seen the odd bit of arson.'

Barton rubbed his hands together while he thought.

'Okay, get on with your paperwork. Let's get it done before we leave. This case might explode. Sirena and Mortis will report back this afternoon, as will the fire inspector. We need to be ready to roll. This woman could be anyone. Someone important, famous or connected, or someone lost and alone. She might be an abductee, or life could have knocked her over. We owe it to her and her family to find out what happened.'

Mortis had swiftly confirmed at the scene that the deceased was female, but Sirena was his best hope for concrete identification. Barton stared around the room at his team.

'I have admin gathering all the misper reports from the neighbouring counties to add to ours, but it's open season. Hopefully by the time we leave here tonight, we'll know who our victim is. Get to it.'

Barton's phone rang as the team noisily filtered from the room.

It was Leigh Beddows from the fire brigade.

'Afternoon,' said Barton. 'Give me a minute to get some peace and quiet.'

Barton closed the door after the detectives had left and took a seat.

'Shoot,' said Barton.

'Okay,' replied Beddows. 'As we suspected, our investigation was inconclusive. We have found one piece of strong evidence, but it might not help you.'

'Intriguing.'

'It's a scorched Zippo lighter.'

'The source of the fire,' stated Barton.

'Probable source, but not great for leading you anywhere, except to say that it's now more likely that the fire was not accidental.'

Barton pondered for a few moments. Zippos often had a personal connection. They could be irritating to keep filled with fuel, but people received them as presents and would be unlikely to casually throw one away, although they might if it was broken. It was a piece of the jigsaw. Time would tell if it was an important one.

'As the likely method of ignition, it's badly burned, so it's doubtful there'll be prints or DNA, but it looks to me like the fire was started deliberately.'

'Perhaps they were trying to burn the body and hide evidence?'

'I'm guessing not.'

'Oh,' said Barton. 'Why's that?'

'If you were going to destroy a body, and therefore the evidence, nearly everyone knows that you would require a big, powerful fire. It would also need to burn for a while. The longer it burns, the hotter it gets, particularly as the sides of the skip will continue to heat up and increase the temperature. I guess most people would use something like lighter fuel or petrol, but you could pour in oil or very strong spirits.'

Barton tried to think back to his last refresher course on fires.

'Those accelerants burn much hotter, and would therefore discolour and maybe even warp the skip or bend the metal things inside it,' he said.

'Correct, and there isn't a sign of that. I'd say someone deliberately set fire to the skip but didn't know the person was in there.'

Barton also suspected that was the most likely scenario, but his mind would remain open until the body was identified. The next questions he had were more for Mortis, but Beddows had been doing this long enough to give Barton a decent summary. Mortis would need to examine the remains in the morgue before he got his final answers.

'Right, Leigh. Assuming the Zippo started the fire, and considering what Majid said about the skip having a high level of easily burnable paper in it, talk me through what would have happened to the material inside the skip. Include the woman's fate. Give me timescales, even temperatures if you can as well, please.'

'Okay. Paper and cardboard would burn around six hundred degrees and are very flammable. It's worse in a bin like that because, thrown in, the material would have separated, so the fire had plenty of fuel and oxygen. The fire might well have taken time to get going, but once it did, it would accelerate fast. Temperatures would have headed north as the container heated up as well and bounced the heat back inside, but any metal would remain intact.'

'Majid said he used a red fire extinguisher on it. I thought that would have put it out.'

'Yes, we found the empty canister. Normally it would work, or at least bring it under control. It's too late to say for certain but I suspect the extinguisher wasn't maintained properly and he might as well have stood on the edge of the skip and peed inside.'

Barton grinned. 'Risky business, though. Will you get much more from sifting through the rest of the skip?'

'I left the collating and bagging of evidence to Sirena's team. I doubt you'll get a great deal from it. The contents will be fire- and water-damaged.'

'Okay, and the victim. How would she have died?'

Barton heard Beddows take a deep breath, and listened carefully.

'The woman would likely have taken some time to perish. We can hope she was asleep and drunk to start with. The heat may have woken her. If she was inebriated in some way, she may well have not woken until the temperatures had risen substantially. The blaze seems to have started on one side of the skip. Once raging, it could have raced across to the other side. We found some spirit bottles amongst the debris. Sirena was checking with the shop owner to see if he was able to identify them, so that's another element to help. The shoplifter is the most plausible person to have been in there so far.'

'How long would it take to die?'

'She might have been unconscious for the start of the fire, perhaps conscious for a minute. She might have only managed one scream, at which point she would have inhaled the burning toxic fumes, which would damage her airway and lungs. A lot of fire deaths occur from CO poisoning. The shock may have caused a massive drop in blood pressure and led to her becoming swiftly unconscious.'

'But?'

'You're a good man, John. I know these situations are tough to deal with. I would say she had a very painful time before her nerve endings were burned through.'

Barton cut the call. He didn't want to hear that, but knowing everything gave him focus. That had been someone's child in there. Whether the killing had been accidental or not, the culprit would pay. He'd make sure of it.

16

DI BARTON

Barton hadn't even put the phone back in his jacket pocket when Sirena rang him.

'Afternoon, John. Leigh should have rung you by now. We're just about to finish up and get the skip moved. Here are my preliminary findings to add to his. We found two empty bottles of whisky and checked them with Mr Majid in the shop. Even though the label had burned away on both, the code on the bottom of the glass on one of them is the same as the whisky that was stolen. There was also a suitcase in there.'

'Yes, I saw her with it in the shop on the CCTV.'

'It's one of those smaller ones that you could fit in the overhead storage on an aeroplane.'

'Any help with identification?'

'No, zip, which is strange in itself. Who would walk around with a suitcase full of clothes, but no ID, no bank card and no phone?'

'There was nothing at all in any pockets?'

'Nope. Mortis has taken the body back to the mortuary. It was in reasonable condition, despite surface damage. There are a couple of interesting aspects, which I'll let him explain.'

Sirena took a deep breath before continuing.

'Our victim died with a mask on, which was burnt to her face. Her hat was in her hand. I assume she pulled it off because it was on fire.'

Sirena stopped, and Barton heard her sniff. Her voice cracked slightly as she continued. Cases like this hit the responders in waves. People slipped into professional mode to process the scene, but the brutal fact was they would spend hours with this poor young woman. Barton's brain took photographs at scenes that might then pop up at any moment in his mind, blindsiding him. Sirena would be no different.

'It was mostly clothes in her suitcase,' said Sirena. 'They're in good condition and decent brands. M&S underwear and Next blouses. There's a romance novel and a trashy magazine, both in English. The boots she wore were well made, and the jeans were Levi's. She seems an ordinary woman. A young lady, John. We have to find out how she ended up in there. No one should die like this.'

'We'll do our best.'

Barton didn't know what else to say. It didn't get much worse than finding burned remains. What you hadn't seen, your mind imagined for you. Many emergency personnel resigned after seeing too many road traffic collisions where gushing fuel from ruptured petrol tanks had ignited. People became hardened to it and coped in different ways from jogging to the bottle, but each blackened body you saw took its toll.

Barton could still remember a young woman's desperate, imploring face as he unsuccessfully tried to open her mangled car door. Very occasionally, at night, he woke to her screams.

'The skip driver was helpful and returned with the booking records. He said he'll take the skip to the compound for us and help unload it, then he can have it back.'

'Great work today, Sirena. We'll catch up for a beer soon.'

Barton wasn't sure when that would be with all the recent restrictions. His new favourite pub, The Wonky Donkey, still hadn't reopened since the first lockdown. People were losing coping mechanisms all over the country. He wondered if this case would have anything to do with what was happening elsewhere, but when a woman was killed or taken advantage of, it was nearly always men responsible. Mankind didn't need a virus to behave deplorably.

Barton returned to his desk, pondering who might be guilty. He'd give up fast food if Majid was involved. The first email he read was from Mortis.

Give me a ring at five.

Barton looked at his watch and picked up the phone.

'Evening, John. Excellent timing, as always. I've completed the PM. Obviously we'll need to wait for toxicology, but I can make assumptions. Jane Doe was young, probably early twenties. Her face and hands were fire-damaged, but the clothes and coat in particular, which are all quality products, protected her torso. She was childless.'

'Any signs of substance abuse?'

'No, nothing. It's unlikely we'd notice anything at her age unless she had real problems, but there is no evidence for it. Her heart and liver are in perfect condition, although that's not to say she has had an uneventful life. Her right index finger has been broken recently and doesn't look like it's had any treatment.'

'How recently?'

'Days, I would hazard.'

'Could she have done that climbing into the skip?'

'Maybe. It's the kind of break you'd see from a fall. She is extremely thin. Not to the point of being malnourished, but I suspect she hadn't been looking after herself for a good few months. Five feet three inches. Seven stone, four pounds. One tattoo, which is a lark rising on her right shoulder. No other clearly identifiable marks or features.'

'How damaged is the face?'

'Quite seriously. Her mother might recognise her, but few others.'

'Hair colour?'

'Tricky to guess on her head, but probably blonde or mousy, judging by other parts of her anatomy. She could have dyed it.'

'Jewellery?'

'Plain stud earrings. Small ring with a red stone. A ruby, I think. A nice necklace, which had warped a tiny bit when I looked under a microscope. Makes me believe it's gold, which has a relatively low melting point for a metal, approximately a thousand degrees.'

'Definite signs of wealth.'

'Very much so. This girl wasn't a pauper. You're the detective, but I reckon she hit on recent hard times and found herself outside. It's possible she was a recent alcoholic or experienced a breakdown or break-up of some kind. She might have fallen over and broken her finger, or perhaps she wanted to warm up on a cold night.'

'No signs of internal or external assault apart from the finger?'

'One fresh large bruise on her leg. One smaller, older bruise on her torso. The former could have been done when she got in the skip.'

'Thanks, Mortis. That's a lot to consider, but nothing definite, which is a bit of a pain. The tattoo sounds like it wasn't run-of-the-mill, so if we get the info out into the public domain, we might get a hit.'

'I've been saving the best for last.'

'Go on.'

'She's had one of her front teeth replaced recently.'

Barton paused. That was good news for them.

'How recently?'

'Hard to state exactly, but it's immaculate, so I'd guess within six months.'

The police often used dental records for identification, but it was usually for confirmation. A dental implant would give little change from a thousand pounds. Saying that, Barton also knew from experience there were about twelve thousand dentists in the UK.

He smiled. It might take a long time but, combined with the tattoo, they had a strong chance of identifying her. There couldn't be too many young women having had a front tooth replacement in the local area. It was possible she used a false name, but unlikely as she would have had to pay. It was also conceivable she went abroad for the treatment, but that was less likely.

'How about domestic abuse or a fight? Tooth missing, broken finger.'

'Not for the tooth. Usually when people lose front teeth, both get damaged. It looks like this was removed and replaced professionally.'

'Excellent. Sirena said the novel and magazine in the case were in English, so it's unlikely that a foreigner who just arrived would own them.'

'I agree, although she may have been using them to learn English.'

'Good point. Okay, how did the girl die?'

'My medical opinion is that she suffocated. Her lungs and throat are damaged beyond any chance of survival. The exposed skin is severely scalded, which would occur at anything above 65°C. Even if they were able to rescue her from the fire, she would probably have died of pulmonary oedema within twenty-four hours. I always find fires fascinating. The consequences, obviously, but also the motivation.'

'Terrifying is more like it,' said Barton.

'Yes, but it is a fast death. There are many worse ways to go.'

'I'm thinking it was an accident. She climbed inside the skip. Then someone torched it because they were bored or just because they could.'

Barton heard Mortis tut down the line.

'Maybe they set fire to it for a laugh, but consider the possibility that they set fire to it because they must.'

Mortis cut the call, leaving Barton smiling at his colleague and friend's perception.

17

DI BARTON

Barton drove home at six p.m. feeling positive. Hopefully, they would identify the victim over the next few days. Then they could see where that avenue led. Barton was ready for some family time. When he opened the front door, his seven-year-old son, Luke, was waiting for him with a stern look.

'Come, Dad. This is important.'

Barton pouted his lip.

'I still prefer Daddy to Dad.'

Luke's expression darkened.

'I know. You said that already. But I'm not a baby any more. I said that already.'

Barton acknowledged that, but even though he was pulling Luke's leg he was still a little sad. The other two often called him Daddy, but only when they wanted something or were joking at his expense. He allowed himself to be guided to the kitchen, where his wife, Holly, and his other two children were sitting. He ruffled eighteen-year-old Lawrence's hair and kissed the top of thirteen-year-old Layla's head. Both grinned at him. Holly grinned at him too.

'Oh, no,' moaned Barton, slumping into a seat. 'How much is this going to cost me?'

Luke was still trying to appear serious, but his face broke into a gigantic smile.

'We're getting a dog!' he bellowed.

Barton glanced around at their expectant faces. Luke had asked for one for his birthday last year, but they'd told him to wait and think about it. Obviously, he hadn't forgotten. The other kids had half-heartedly mentioned having a fur baby over the years, but Luke hadn't let it drop. Barton and Holly had agreed that they could get one if Luke persisted. It looked as if he had.

'Okay,' he said. 'Although I choose.'

The room erupted into a cacophony of good-natured abuse.

'Dobermann or Rottweiler. Nothing else,' shouted Barton.

'John,' said Holly. 'We all think we should get a rescue dog. So, getting one of those two might not be the best idea.'

Barton gave himself a second to enjoy an image of him walking a big, strong, proud hound, then shelved his dream.

'Okay, but it has to be a boy. And no chihuahuas, or terriers, or anything I can hold in the palm of my hand.'

'That doesn't rule much out though, does it, Bearpaw?' joked Lawrence.

'I've spoken to a local rehoming place,' said Holly. 'They're permanently full, so there's a lot of choice, but because of Luke's age they'll only let us have small dogs unless we go for a puppy.'

'Puppy! Puppy! Puppy!' chanted Lawrence and Luke.

'Actually, you know what I've always fancied?' said Barton.

'Go on,' said Holly, sceptically.

'A Newfie puppy called Ferdy.'

'No way,' said Holly.

'What's a Newfie?' asked Layla.

'Hang on,' said Holly, getting her phone out.

'They're lovely, fluffy things,' said Barton.

Holly began showing the kids a picture.

'This is a full-grown Newfoundland,' said Holly.

'Holy shit,' said Layla. 'Is that a dog or a bison?'

'Hey!' said Holly. 'Language, young lady.'

'Sorry, it slipped out.'

'Come on, John,' said Holly. 'If we get something that large, you'll be the only person strong enough to walk it. Let's see what they've got. Besides, I don't want a long-haired dog moulting smelly fur all over the place.'

Layla rose from her seat and stood behind Barton, kissing him on the top of his bald head.

'Yes, Daddy, dear. One huge, stinky, hairy-backed thing is enough for any household.'

Holly laughed so loud that at one point Barton thought he'd need to ring for an ambulance.

After the kids had gone, Holly came over and sat on his knee. When they'd gone on their first date, she'd reminded him of a short Sharon Stone. She kissed him on the head as Layla had.

'I can call you Ferdy if you want,' she said.

Barton stood, picking her off his lap with one arm at the same time, and plonked her on the table.

'I'm not joking. No handbag dogs. I know who's going to be walking the damn thing.'

Holly crossed her heart and started laughing again.

'Yeah, me! We have an appointment at eleven tomorrow. You said you were off work, so we can all go together and meet a few. We don't have to get one if we don't feel a connection to any.'

Barton left the room, shaking his head. Whoever heard of anyone meeting a puppy and not wanting to take it home immediately?

When he reached the dining room, he remembered Mortis's

words about the motivation for setting fires. Barton powered up his laptop. There was a big difference between arson and what Mortis had hinted at – pyromania.

Arson was the criminal act of deliberately setting fire to property for some kind of gain, whether it be revenge, spite or something else. Barton had investigated many cases of arson in his career. The fires destroyed the evidence at the scene, but they couldn't get rid of the reasons for the crime in the first place. What the detective needed to do was look for who gained from the blaze. Often it was for insurance purposes. Sometimes it was as easy as asking the insurance company who would receive the payout.

Pyromania was a different beast altogether. These crimes were notoriously hard to solve, and they were often incredibly dangerous. Barton typed pyromania and arson into Google. He read Wikipedia and a few other sites and came to some conclusions.

A person who commits arson is an arsonist. They often use an accelerant to ignite and accelerate fires, which helps with an investigation afterwards. Pyromania is different. It's an impulse control disorder characterised by the pathological setting of fires. This often induces euphoria, and sufferers may fixate on the institutions of fire such as the fire station or the firefighters.

Barton leaned back in his seat. If they were dealing with pyromania, then discovering the motivations of those responsible would be the key to solving the case. He carried on reading.

Before the act, the person usually experiences tension and heightening emotions. A person suffering from pyromania is intensely interested or fascinated by fires and may also experience pleasure, gratification or relief. Another contributing factor linked with pyromania is stress. When studying the lifestyle of

someone with pyromania, a build-up of stress and emotion is
often present. This is common in teenagers with the condition.
Neglect and abuse can feature, too. In adults, the recovery rate
is generally poor.

Barton already knew that arson was the largest single cause of
fires in England and Wales, costing the economy billions, but to
update his knowledge he searched and found some shocking stats.
In the last decade there had been around 2.3 million deliberate fires
resulting in over twenty-five thousand injuries and more than nine
hundred deaths. The final titbit was what he was most worried
about, and the reason why he wanted the case solved yesterday.

He knew from experience that pyromaniacs' behaviour often
escalated because a small, simple fire no longer provided enough
excitement or drama. At some point in the near future, they might
have an inferno on their hands.

18

THE FIRE KILLER

I've spent the day going stir-crazy. Normally I would be at peace with myself after a fire, and that feeling would last for as long as the memories of the incident did, but I haven't had the release this time. The urge to do something idiotic rushes around my head.

I was in a huge queue at the chemist's this afternoon when I overheard someone saying that there was a woman in the skip that burned. I felt my face flush hot, as though those flames were eating me instead of her. It appears I have killed again. That's devastating to get my head around because it means it's time to stop. No more fires. Can I continue to exist knowing that I will never feel alive again? Just as fires need air to breathe, I need fires to cope.

Deep down I know there has to be one more. I'm in too much of a state not to have a last release. It's been a tough period of late, although living has never come easy. On my walk earlier, I spotted a likely target and when I got back home, I realised I could even see the line of bins from my bedroom window. I bought lighter fluid, just to be prepared, just in case.

It's midnight now. The streets are empty, and I know it's time.

My feet tingle as I pull on my boots. I can almost feel the blood speeding up through my veins. I can't help a small grin creeping onto my face. I flex my hands, and haul on a different coat from the one I wore today and yesterday. There's a full moon on display, making the evening cooler, but there are promises of unseasonably warm weather tomorrow. My life would be simpler if I could only be satisfied by the fiery sun.

I trudge through the alley to the shops, stopping to check if anyone else is about, but apart from a tabby cat stealthily hunting a wandering crisp packet, I am alone.

The skip has gone, as have any signs of its presence. Just like that, the dead are so quickly forgotten.

As always, I walk past my target before I begin and when I return, I lift the lid of the fullest bin and squirt the entire contents of my tin inside. If this is to be the last, let's go out with a bang. There is a solid wall behind the bins, so there is no chance of the fire spreading. I know it's not a victimless crime. Someone will have to pay for the bin. The fire brigade isn't free, but better this than what I really want to do.

Wheelie-bin fires are my favourites. They are the perfect receptacle to suit my needs. There's fuel and air inside, and with the lid almost down, it's hard to notice the beginning of the fire until it's too late. Then once they go, they rage. Black, hateful smoke streams from them. They are difficult to extinguish. The fire brigade will come. I will have my pleasure, and I will feel some peace.

I lick my lips and, after a final look around, light a match and drop it in. There's a whoosh as the fuel ignites. I leave the box of matches under the lid to create a small gap for oxygen to enter, then I retreat. I pause to observe my work. A long flame creeps out of the side of the bin, like a lizard's tongue tasting the air.

I pace down the passageway to my block of houses. The cat sits on the fence, staring at me in judgement, his eyes shining in the moonlight. This is our time. We are creatures of the night. I blow him a kiss, then hurry home to await the show.

19

DI BARTON

The next morning, after a lot of faffing around, Barton finally had everyone loaded up in the car and the front door locked. He clambered in behind the wheel and looked around at his family.

'Just think, guys. There could be six of us for the return journey.'

'Wow, I'm weirdly nervous,' said Holly beside him.

'Try to keep your nerves under control. You'll be in the boot on the way back. Ferdy will be sitting in your seat, and I'd hate for it to be wet.'

Holly playfully slapped his arm. Barton looked at his side mirror and found a large face filling it.

'Hang on,' he said to groans.

He wound down his window.

'Sorry, John,' said Zander. 'Strange just texted me. I'm supposed to be off today as well, but I'm going to meet her in Welland. There was another fire last night.'

Barton grimaced. It was an effort to look around at Holly.

'Five minutes, okay?' he said to her.

'Be quicker. We don't want to be late.'

Barton hopped out of the car, gently closing the door behind him.

'Where?' he asked. 'Why wasn't I told?'

'Strange found out first thing this morning when she went in. She knew there weren't any casualties, so decided it could wait, seeing as you'd been working all week. It was a wheelie-bin fire that burned to the ground before the services turned up.'

'Where was it?'

'That's the issue. It was close to the skip fire. Now, it might have been copycats or just teenagers mucking about, but mid-morning, the watch commander rang to say that a couple took their kid to the hospital last night with breathing issues. They'd been here a year from Portugal for the farm work.'

'Don't tell me the child died.'

'No, but it was touch-and-go. The boy has asthma. Strange rang the hospital and got all the details. You know the filth those plastic bins discharge when they burn. Basically, it drifted into this little lad's bedroom.'

'Bloody hell. We need to find this nutter before someone else gets hurt or worse.'

'Well, we've had some good news on that front. You remember the bloke who rang in to report the skip fire but then we couldn't get hold of him after?'

'Yes.'

'He called the station this morning. Kelly took the call and had a chat with him. He works until ten thirty at night, so he spotted the skip fire when he got home. He didn't think he saw anything suspicious, but then he was up late last night too. Someone was acting suspiciously near a wall, who then vanished. He remembers there was a person walking down there the first night.'

'Excellent. Could he provide a decent description?'

Zander shook his head.

'He couldn't even say for sure what sex they were.'

Barton rolled his eyes. 'If that's the good news, I hope there isn't any bad.'

Zander chuckled. 'The guy said there's an alleyway by that wall, which leads to four houses. The only other way out brings you back to the main road, so there's only one reason to head down that path.'

Barton smiled immediately. Now that was a lead. The thing was, he was the DI. He didn't need to go in, but he had a sense that this was important. It would take time and repetition of the facts to get someone else involved. He turned and reopened his car door to poke his head inside, but Holly had already shifted over and was putting the driver's seat belt on.

'Sorry, love,' said Barton.

She gave him a filthy sneer.

'Miss Chi-Chi the chihuahua will be looking forward to meeting you when you return home.'

She reversed off the drive and he spotted Luke scowling at him from the rear window, which made him feel as if he'd missed the winning penalty in the last few seconds of injury time. Holly stuck her tongue out and roared off.

Zander shrugged. They both knew that this was what being a detective was all about. Barton ruefully clambered into Zander's MR2, and they also left at speed.

'Is Kelly there now?' asked Barton.

'Yeah, she drove there to take a statement from the witness. I was going to call in Leicester, but it's only four houses. Maybe it's better that you and me do all of them. If anyone's nervous, they might pop with us two staring at them.'

They were soon at the scene and Barton and Zander got out and examined what was left of the wheelie bin. Up the wall, there was a big black scorch mark, which gradually ran across at an angle, but no other damage than that was visible. Zander checked his notes and pointed at a window of a house directly opposite.

'That's the one.'

Barton could see a woman taking the curtains down. There was a pool car outside a house further up the road. After a few minutes, Strange and a handsome young man with blond hair came out of the house and strode over to Barton and Zander.

'This is Domas,' said Strange. 'He's showing us what he saw.'

Domas's English was almost perfect. He confidently ambled across the road for approximately a hundred metres over to a wall that had a big tree hanging over it.

'The person was here. I didn't see them at first, only when they moved. They went into this alleyway. Come.'

The four of them walked down the alley and a cat leapt off a fence with a hiss as they passed by. After about twenty metres, they came out into a small cul-de-sac. There was a row of four identical terraced houses. The road then snaked out to the right, but there were no other dwellings for a hundred metres or more, just a grass verge. It made sense that only the residents and their visitors would come down here.

Strange thanked Domas and sent him back to his house, then she looked from Zander to Barton.

'Okay. How do you two want to play it? If you both do the calls, I'll go and have a word with the mother of the sick child. The father is still at the hospital, but she's returned to air the house. There's a Portuguese woman on Traffic today, so if I need a translator, I can call her and she'll do it over the phone. Maybe the parents know something but haven't had a chance to tell anyone.'

'Good plan,' said Barton. 'Give me a ring when you're done. There are cars outside each of these four houses. With all the restrictions, someone should be in.'

Strange handed him a printout.

'This is who's on the council tax register. Each house only has one resident listed. That's not to say nobody else lives there, but it might give you a clue on who's telling the truth if you see more than one person at the property.'

Barton nodded and loosened his tie while regretting his decision to stay formal. He felt the power of the sun on his back. Moisture collected on his forehead as he mentally prepared himself. He didn't want to miss anything. It could be something innocuous that gave the game away. The first interview couldn't be repeated. He took a final look down the passageway. It was as clear as day. If a person came through that alley, they were heading for one of these houses. They might well be about to meet their arsonist.

20

DI BARTON

Barton and Zander approached number one. The front garden was a small patch of grass leading to an expensive-looking uPVC door. The lawn had been mown recently, but there were no personal items at all. No pots, no trellises, no bench, not even a gnome. It was as though the house was waiting for its owner to arrive. Yet on the drive to the left was a pristine blue Nissan Micra and there was a much older red Volkswagen Polo parked on the kerb.

Zander and he had been doing the job for a long time. Both knew the importance of an open mind. Barton knocked on the door.

The young woman who opened it appeared to have stepped out of a teenage boy's fantasy. She had thick hair pulled back in a pony-tail, full make-up, bare feet, and a small pair of cut-off jeans. Barton's handkerchief was bigger than her T-shirt. She looked like a cross between Daisy Duke and Pamela Anderson. Barton focused on her eyes, which were a striking dark green.

'Mrs Eileen Croston?' asked Barton.

'No, that's my mother. She's in the lounge.'

'We're making door-to-door inquiries. We believe the individual we're looking for lives near here. Can we have a word inside?'

The woman shook her head. 'My mum's resting.'

'It's important,' said Zander.

'What's this person done?'

'You must have heard about the recent fires around here,' said Barton.

'And you think my mum's responsible?'

'We'd like to talk to everyone in the area. Do you live here?'

'Yes, I'm Lynette Croston. I suppose you can come in.'

Barton and Zander stepped inside. The house was small, as was the hall. The woman hadn't moved back far.

'Aren't you a big pair of beefy boys?' she said with a wink.

Barton and Zander exchanged a slightly worried glance. The woman in front of them smelled of alcohol.

'Would you like a drink?'

Barton was about to say no, but then thought it'd be a chance to look around while she was distracted.

'Sure. A glass of water would be nice.'

Lynette opened a door behind her and went into a tiny kitchen. She grabbed a big two-litre bottle of water out of the fridge and poured two small glasses. Barton and Zander took them. They were like shot glasses. Lynette seemed to notice and laughed.

'Pinkies up!' she said.

'Do your mum and dad live here?' asked Zander.

Barton watched a flicker pass over Lynette's face. There was definitely something off about her but the pristine make-up and false eyelashes made it tricky to gauge what it was, as if she were wearing a mask. It didn't seem to be guilt or nerves. Her quick eye contact and twitchy demeanour reminded him of someone who had gone through some kind of trauma.

'No, he's dead.'

'Sorry to hear that.'

'Don't be. He was a crap father, and he died in an accident a long time ago. Look, my mum's...' Lynette paused for a moment. 'She's quiet. We have a bit of a strange relationship. We lived together after Dad died, but more like strangers in a shared house. I wind her up, sometimes she laughs, other times it's as though she's in a different world.'

'That must be hard at times,' said Zander.

'Yeah, but it toughened me up.'

'Why aren't you listed at the address?'

'I've been back here less than a year. That's the thing. I had a nasty break-up. I thought me and my ex were soulmates, and, well, let's just say that he didn't. Basically, I was skint and homeless. Fucked. I left my mum's house years ago in a storm, and I was rude when I went. You know, I'm not coming back. I don't need you. All that shite. She could have slammed the door when I came back with my tail between my legs, but she didn't. I've grown up a bit now. Seen the world for how it really is, and I understand her. I owe her, and she can rely on me to look after her if I get the chance, but it's complicated. Understand what I mean?'

Barton nodded. Lynette beamed at him.

'Listen to me giving you my life story. It's the lack of human contact in lockdown, it's sent us all mad.'

She left the kitchen, brushing her ample chest against Zander's arm as she passed by, and walked through a door to the rear of the house. Zander whispered to Barton after she'd gone.

'Don't leave me here alone.'

Barton chuckled. 'I'm sure she's lovely.'

They followed her into a room that was larger than Barton expected. A set of stairs was at the back, which he assumed led up to the bedrooms. A woman in beige clothes with grey, unkempt hair that resembled a crazy halo looked up at them without interest, as though a visit from a pair of detectives was a regular occurrence. *Casualty* was on the TV and Barton guessed it was a rerun, because the main characters appeared younger than he remembered. Lynette rested her hand on her mum's shoulder.

'Mum, those Chippendales you ordered off the Internet are here. They said to remind you there's no touching.'

'Okay, dear. Tell them to keep it down.'

Lynette rolled her eyes.

'Just kidding, Mum, they think you've been starting fires.'

'What fires?' asked Eileen, straining her head towards her daughter.

Lynette turned to Barton.

'Would she go to prison if she confessed?'

'Definitely,' said Barton.

'Sweet. I've been thinking about putting her in a home. Prison's free, right?'

'Correct, ma'am,' said Zander with a bunched jaw as he suppressed a smile.

'Ah, just kidding. I suppose you shouldn't joke about things like that. The fire, I mean. Not when someone's died. I can't put Mum in a home either, because this place belongs to the council. I'd be homeless, and all I'd inherit is her collection of tea cosies.'

'Were you at home the night of the skip fire?' asked Barton.

'Yes, we both were. Wasn't it late Thursday night? We're morning people, so I reckon we'd have been in bed. Why do you think someone around here did it?'

'We have an eyewitness.'

Barton checked her reaction, but she failed to respond to the news.

'We'll take a quick statement from both of you,' said Zander.

This time, her face fell.

'Is that necessary? We didn't do it.'

'It's procedural. Nothing more.'

Lynette shrugged. Her mother picked at a loose seam on the armchair.

'Have you heard about last night's bin fire?' asked Barton.

'Nope,' said Lynette with a blank face. Her mum was watching the TV again.

The detectives took a signed confirmation from them that they were in bed, but there wasn't much else they could take from the conversation if both women said they hadn't seen anything.

'Why bother taking a statement if it says nothing?' asked Lynette as she gave him the pen back.

'It's important because most people don't like signing things that aren't true. If it came out that you lied to us, we'd know to take what you said later with a pinch of salt.'

Barton watched Lynette's response, but she shrugged it off. Making a false statement was a relatively minor offence, but it often led to conspiracy to pervert the course of justice, which was much more serious.

'Is it okay if I use your bathroom?' asked Barton.

Lynette twitched and looked over at her mum.

'I'd rather you didn't, if that's all right. I'm sure next door won't mind.'

Barton detected the briefest of smiles from her.

'Have you noticed a lot of fires around here?' he asked.

Lynette paused, then cocked her head.

'No more than normal.'

'How about the convenience store near where the skip was set on fire? Do you use it, Eileen?'

Eileen turned the sound off on the TV. She looked over at them both and sneered.

'Only when I have to.'

Lynette went to stand next to her mother.

'We call the new guy Mr Grumpy, but the old couple are nice.'

Barton and Zander got up to leave.

'Thanks for your time. Here's my card, just in case you remember something,' said Barton.

'Do they know who it was who died?' asked Lynette.

'No. Why? Do you have any idea? Have you seen anyone behaving strangely around there? Maybe a homeless person, or teenagers messing around? The woman might not have been dressed like she was homeless.'

Lynette stared again at Barton. Her eyes seemed to swirl and he found it unnerving.

'No, but I reckon it was probably a tramp. We get the odd annoying one.'

'Have you seen any homeless people in the last week or so?'

'No, not for a while now.'

Just before they got outside, Zander stopped and turned to Lynette.

'What about your neighbours? Any of them seem the fire-setting type?'

'They're all weird. Take your pick.'

21

DI BARTON

Barton and Zander stepped outside.

'Bye, boys,' said Lynette at the door with a Marilyn Monroe pout. She slammed the door shut with a deep-throated chuckle.

Barton looked at Zander.

'Well, that was an interesting experience,' he said.

'Yes, I suspect Lynette is guilty of many things, but I haven't a clue if one of those is the fires.'

'I agree, although appearances can be deceptive. It's a little concerning that she thinks the rest of the people in the street are weird.'

They walked down Eileen's path, then up the next house's path. It had a similarly unloved feel to it as the one before, but whereas the previous drive was swept and clean, this one was cracked, potholed and riddled with weeds. Barton peered through the window of a ten-year-old Skoda and decided he'd rather use a pogo stick to get to work than accept a lift in a vehicle as foul-looking inside as that one. Mr Ernie Fowler, who resided here according to the sheet, loved crisps and chocolate bars so much he'd completely filled the floor of his car with the wrappers.

Zander knocked on the door, then looked at his knuckle as though he'd got some grease or paint on it. He curled his lip.

'If you try your "Can I use the toilet?" trick so you can check out the rest of the house in this fine dwelling, don't worry about your family. I'll take care of Holly and the kids for you. Hey, we could have you stuffed, like they used to do with bears. We can keep you out the front of the station as a deterrent.'

'You're all heart.'

The man who opened the door had to be the owner. His eyebrows were so bushy, they almost concealed the mistrustful stare underneath them.

'What?'

'Police, DS Zander and DI Barton,' said Zander. 'We're here with some questions. Can we come in?'

'Can't you do it on the doorstep?'

'We need you to make a statement, so it'll take a quarter of an hour. I'm sure you'll be more comfortable inside,' replied Barton.

Fowler cursed under his breath, then turned and shuffled away leaving the door open. He appeared to be around seventy years old, but he was so unkempt, it was tricky to be certain. Zander choked on the cigarette smoke, which hung heavy in the air. Fowler turned to them in the lounge.

'Take a seat. I suppose you'll be wanting tea and biscuits next.'

Barton couldn't help staring at the man's multi-hued, light-blue cardigan. At first, he'd thought it was a pattern, but up close he could see it was a variety of stains. Fowler left and returned with a battered biscuit tin, which he dropped in Barton's lap.

'I've run out of milk,' Fowler stated bluntly, then sat opposite them.

Barton's stomach didn't have eyes or a nose though and it treacherously rumbled, and he was thirsty from the heat. Zander glanced at him with horror as if to say eating or drinking anything offered by this guy would be madness.

'It's okay, we won't be that long,' said Barton, putting the tin down.

The room wasn't as dirty as the car, but it reminded Barton of those films where they discovered a starship floating in space, and everyone had died centuries ago, leaving piles of ash. He couldn't resist putting his finger along the fireplace next to him, where the dust had to be five millimetres thick. Barton grimaced, then realised Fowler was staring at him. Fowler let out a small growl.

'Okay, Mr Fowler, or shall I call you Ernie?' asked Barton.

'You can call me Jesus or Mary if it means you'll leave quicker.'

'Okay, Ernie. We're investigating a spate of fires. I'm sure you've heard what's happened.'

Fowler glared at them from under his brows but didn't comment.

'Is that a yes?'

'Spit it out, son. I'm much older than you and don't have time to waste. What do you want to know? Did I do it, or do I know who did it?'

'Okay, yes.'

'No and no. I don't go out at night. Don't go blaming Little Bob either, just cos he's a kid.'

Zander was still struggling with the atmosphere. It was as though there'd been a gunfight in the lounge just before they arrived, and this was the aftermath, where the pistol smoke filtered around, lit up by the beam of sunlight coming through the filthy windows.

'Who's Little Bob?' asked Zander.

'My grandson. He lives with me. Long story short. His mum was a smackhead and died. My son was a knobhead and cleared out. I got Bob. He's eighteen and leaving school soon. Then he can bugger off too.'

Barton stared at a school photograph on the fireplace. He gestured to it.

'May I?'

Fowler growled again. Barton picked it up anyway.

It said 2017 on the bottom of the picture. Little Bob, who would have been about fifteen in the photo, appeared to be about six feet tall and had the frown of someone in permanent pain.

'I assume Little Bob is like a joke name,' said Barton.

Fowler growled again.

'Will he be back soon?'

'Buggered if I know. He's feral. I tried hard with him, but he doesn't want to be in the house at all. Only time he's here is when he's using his computer upstairs. Never stops eating, that boy. Draining my pension worse than the government.'

Barton detected a slight shift in the man's demeanour. Ernie liked the lad, but Barton reckoned he struggled with those kinds of emotions. It was tough for some of these old-timers to show they cared. Barton's dad had been similar. Quick to punish, but slow to show love. You had to look at their actions to understand how they felt. Fifty-hour weeks in factories, no treats for themselves, making do with hand-me-downs, affection from afar, always making sure there was food in the cupboards.

'He looks like a good lad,' Barton said softly.

'Well, he isn't. He's feral.'

Barton wasn't sure if Zander was breathing his last or laughing.

'Where is he?' asked Barton.

'Out with the cats. If you want him, he'll be back for his tea at seven. We watch *Wipeout* together.'

'Do you use the shops?' asked Zander, rising and moving towards the door.

'Yes, if I must. I was hoping the person in the skip was the manager of the store, but I saw him yesterday. I told him that I forgot I put that chocolate bar in my pocket, but he still called me a thief. Idiot has taken all the baskets away because of the virus.'

'Okay, Ernie. We'll come back at seven if you're sure Bob will be here,' said Barton. He'd ask them together if they knew anything about a woman acting unusually in the vicinity.

'Yeah, he'll be back. Bob never misses *Wipeout*. We love it when the women flop into the water.'

22

DI BARTON

Barton stopped outside house three while Zander ran to the shop to get them a couple of bottles of water. This terrace also had an impersonal air like the first house, but the Mercedes on the drive was almost new, and the curtains looked clean and modern.

Barton still smelled smoke around him. Lynette was right, Fowler was weird. He didn't strike Barton as an arsonist, though, but who knew? He might have lobbed a match in the skip after lighting a fag as he walked past one night, despite his protestations about not venturing out after dark. Or maybe he threw his lit Zippo in deliberately. Barton could check the shop CCTV to see if he ever appeared on it in the evening. He'd know then Fowler was a liar, even if it wouldn't be proof he'd done anything.

Little Bob, on the other hand, was more promising. For children, there was, and always had been, a fascination with fire. Your average beat copper spent plenty of his time involved with that sort of thing. Fireworks and bonfires in unsuitable places were extremely common. It had been a while since he'd considered the psychology of that side of things. Major Crimes only tended to deal with the more serious cases such as big insurance claims or violent acts of retribution.

Barton thought of Mortis. He'd give him a ring. Mortis's nickname came from his fascination with the stages of decay after death and fire affected those stages; therefore, Mortis would know a lot about it. Barton would just need to be prepared for having an encyclopaedic amount of information drop on him all at once.

Barton had been hoping for better intel from the first two houses than they'd gathered so far. They didn't have much from the fire at all, other than the tooth and tattoo. Mortis would send them an accurate description of the work. Malik was tasked with making sure that information was sent to local dentists with a requirement for a negative result. Basically, each dentist had to reply either yes or no as to whether they'd done the work, but it would take time, which Barton was beginning to suspect they might not have. He needed a break.

If the woman was a local drunk or someone down on their luck, then you'd have thought she would have been noticed. But that was the curse for unfortunate souls like that. People chose not to see them. Charity wasn't easy when it was breathing fumes in your face.

Zander returned and handed him a bottle of water.

'Didn't they have any cold ones?'

'It's from the boot of my car. Majid was shutting the shop for good, remember? There's a sign saying it will be open tomorrow to see if he can clear some of the remaining stock.'

Barton took a sip of the warm water and swilled it around his mouth with distaste.

'Who's next?' asked Zander.

'Garth Henson. Lives alone, allegedly. He's probably got the seven dwarves in there.'

'Let's hope he's not barbecuing them,' replied Zander.

Zander gave the door a meaty knock. The resident took a long time to open it, but he seemed relatively normal when he did. He was late thirties, heavily muscled, but wearing nice jeans and a smart, ironed, red shirt. His trainers looked as if they had come out of the box that morning.

'Mr Garth Henson?' asked Barton.

'Yes.'

'We're police.'

Henson had wavy auburn hair and was handsome. But when he ran his hands through that lustrous hair, Barton could immediately detect it wasn't vanity but nerves.

'Can we come in?'

Henson nodded and stepped aside, avoiding eye contact as they walked in. Barton and Zander looked around with surprise. It was hard to believe this state-of-the-art man cave was an identical house to the other two they'd visited. Henson didn't say anything. Instead, he perched on the edge of the red leather sofa as though he was worried the sofa would swallow him.

Barton took an armchair opposite, got his pen out, and chuckled to himself when Zander sat on the sofa just a little too close to Henson.

'You live here alone, Garth?' asked Barton

'Yes.'

'Lived here long?'

'Yeah, years.'

'Own it?'

'Council.'

'Do you set fires?'

Henson leaned back, clearly surprised. He looked at Zander next to him, imperceptibly edging away up the sofa.

'No, of course not.'

'Do you know the woman who died?'

'I don't know who died.'

'Do you go to the shops much?'

'Which ones?'

'The ones next to the skip fire?'

'No, not really. Occasionally, if I'm desperate, but I eat clean. That's not really their thing.'

Barton recalled the rows of crisps and booze he'd walked past in the aisles of the store, and the fridges packed full of plastic cheeses and salamis. The Chinese takeaway looked shabby. He nodded in agreement.

'Have you seen a girl around here? Maybe homeless or troubled. Perhaps dressed reasonably well with nice boots.'

A trickle of sweat rolled down the side of Henson's head. His huge biceps bulged as he shifted in his seat. Barton could see an edge of darkness at the armpits of the red shirt. Henson shrugged.

'Anything you'd like to tell me?' asked Barton.

Henson swallowed and shook his head.

'So it's only you here?'

'Yes.'

'Girlfriend?'

'No.'

'Boyfriend?'

'No.'

'Friends over?'

'Not often.'

'Why are you so nervous?'

Henson checked around the room as though he might find the answer written on the wall. Then he shrugged again.

'You're the police. Isn't everyone nervous when you lot turn up?'

Barton considered that for a moment. It was the familiarity of dealing with the police that dispensed with the fear for a lot of repeat offenders. Although even they were shifty when they'd recently been up to no good.

'Will you sign a statement to say you know nothing about all this?' asked Barton.

'Yes,' whispered Henson.

'Have a think and see what you remember. I'll come back tonight and you can update me.'

Henson clearly didn't like the sound of that, but agreed nonetheless.

Barton scanned the walls and surfaces for photos as they were leaving, but the place was clinical and bare beyond the plugged-in electronics. It had been years since Barton had spoken to someone so obviously ill at ease. Henson appeared large but incredibly compact and therefore presumably enormously powerful, but there wasn't a whiff of aggression or danger about him. His face was red and damp when they left.

'I'll be back,' said Barton as Henson closed the door. It was then that he realised what it was that was distracting him.

The house reminded him of a show home. Aesthetically pleasing and modern, but devoid of anything personal. More hotel than home. It was the kind of place you could leave at a moment's notice and never look back.

23

DI BARTON

Barton and Zander walked up the path to the final house. There was an eight-year-old estate car parked in a bay surrounded by a high brick wall. Both had seen better days, but there were pots of flowers outside and a trellis with some kind of purple climbing plant on it.

'I'll be back,' said Zander in an Arnold Schwarzenegger voice.

'Oh quiet. I didn't mean to say it like that. Anyway, Arnie's cool.'

'Did you know he's only five feet seven?'

'No, he's not. He's over six feet.'

'I read it in the *Daily Star*. He's shrunk. I think he's seventy-three now.'

'The *Daily Star*?'

'That's right.'

'Do they still have front pages about Martians?'

Zander scowled. 'Sometimes.'

'I rest my case.'

Barton knocked at the next house and they heard someone grappling with some keys. The man who opened the door was extremely pasty, but had dreadlocks. It looked as though he'd just woken up because he was naked except for a loose pair of cut-off tracksuit bottoms. Barton idly recalled that he'd been about nine when his own ribs had disappeared, but he could count Mr McBride's.

'Mr Clive McBride?' asked Barton.

They got a nod in reply.

'Sorry to wake you, sir,' said Zander.

'No, it's okay, man. I was just chilling. Are you, like, Jovos?'

Barton and Zander looked at each other. If there were ever two people who looked less like Jehovah's Witnesses, Barton had never met them.

'No, we're police.'

'Oh, shit, sorry.'

Mr McBride started laughing. It took him a little while to stop.

'Sorry, dude. You know, lots of different people knock on my door. I don't mind if you are. That kind of groove is a bit heavy for me, though.'

Great, thought Barton. The last house contained a pothead who'd started early.

'Can we come in?' asked Zander.

'Yeah, yeah, mi casa and all that. Look, it's just one plant. I don't know who told you. I write music, and I think some people are jealous. They all seem to know I smoke weed around here. God knows how, but I often get people wanting to buy it.'

They followed him into what appeared to be a normal lounge compared to the others they'd been in so far that day. There was a comfy, grey fabric sofa, pictures of family and a Banksy print. The cream carpet was thick and looked new.

'Any of your neighbours buy it?' asked Zander.

McBride chuckled again.

'I told the old guy I could roll him one once. Said it would help with his arthritis.' McBride broke into a deep, loud laugh, displaying pronounced laughter lines. 'Man, he was really rude.'

'What about Little Bob?' asked Barton, trying to put them back on track.

'Yeah, he came around one time. I don't sell any, man. Nothing. It's only for me, you know. It helps.'

'You mean when you write music?' asked Zander, with a smirk.

McBride tipped his head back and guffawed again. Wiping his cheeks afterwards, he dropped onto the sofa and sprawled out.

Barton and Zander exchanged another glance, raising an eyebrow each in unison.

'No, brother. I can't write anything when I'm fucked. I just like to get high. I need to relax.'

'Is your life stressful?' asked a now grinning Zander. But Barton could see it was a good question.

McBride smiled. 'Not today.'

'Do you know anything about the fires around here?' asked Barton.

'What fires?'

'The blaze in the skip. The bins next to the wall of the flats.'

'When were they?'

'Last few days.'

'No, it's lockdown, and I don't go out much, anyway. I work from home, and I get my shit delivered.'

'A woman died in one of the fires.'

'No way, harsh. Was it suicide?'

Barton hadn't even considered that. This guy was thinking out of the box. Zander would be recommending a bong for the staff meetings next.

'We're at an early stage in the investigation so we're interested in all scenarios. Have you seen anyone looking out of place around here? Someone begging for money?'

'Hard to say. When are we talking?'

Barton gave him the estimated time and date of the fires.

'No, as I said, I don't venture far,' McBride replied after a long pause.

'Do you visit the shops much?'

'No, just for Rizla. I'm always running out. Tesco don't always deliver them. Those Syrian dudes have the liquorice papers too. They're the bomb. You know, I reckon they're both blazing away in the storeroom when no one's looking. They are so chilled and polite. The new guy is a stress-head, though. I have to be really mashed to use that Chinese.'

'Then you do go to the shops quite a bit,' said a clearly exasperated Barton.

'For Rizla, yeah. And the munchies, of course.'

McBride laughed again. He signed a statement with a flourish a few minutes later with a signature that seemed to be a big M. Barton decided that was enough of the merry-go-round to nowhere that he'd found himself on, and Zander and he walked towards the exit. Barton heard a noise upstairs.

'What was that?'

'My dog. He's old, so he sleeps on the bed. You can stroke him if you like, but he's old, moults like hell, and does the worst farts.'

Barton sensed Zander grinning like crazy next to him, but didn't give him the pleasure of looking at him.

McBride was just shutting the front door on them when he shouted out.

'Wait!'

Barton blew out his cheeks, but still turned around.

'Yes.'

'I did see a girl. She was crying. It was a few nights back.'

'The night of the fire?'

'I don't know. Whenever the football was on ITV. I was watching it, and I remember nipping out at half-time to get some Pringles. She had nice boots on.'

Zander got his phone out and checked the TV schedule on the Radio Times website. He nodded at Barton.

'There was an extra football match put on the night before the skip fire.'

Barton got his notebook back out.

'What did she look like?'

'Erm, big coat, hood up, nice boots.'

'Tall, thin, pretty, young?'

McBride squinted into the distance.

'Yeah, yeah, that's it. I can't remember exactly. It was a good game, though, and I was really licked. But I do remember thinking at the time she looked familiar. You know, you recognise someone, but you can't think where from.'

Barton suspected that was a regular occurrence for Mr McBride. Probably happened when he met his parents.

'It's really important we identify this lady,' said Zander.

'Let me have a ponder. I was about to have a kip before you guys arrived because I've got a deadline. I tend to write at night because it's more peaceful.'

'Do you think you might remember more details then?' asked Barton.

'The mind does wonderful things when you sleep, so who knows? But at least I won't be stoned.'

'Okay, we're back here around seven, so shall we knock then?'

'Definitely, definitely. It's been nice chatting.'

A minute later, Barton and Zander were back in Zander's car.

'Interesting couple of hours. I assume we're ignoring the plant comment,' said Zander.

'Yep, for the moment. It looks like Lynette was right. They are a peculiar bunch, her and her mother included.'

'Hey, maybe they all did it together. It's the Peterborough equivalent of *The Wicker Man*.'

Barton didn't chuckle. 'Don't even go there.'

24

DI BARTON

Barton and Zander spent the early afternoon of Saturday doing admin in the office. It was rare for Barton to take statements and door knock nowadays, but he didn't mind doing the basics every now and again to keep his eye in. He hadn't spent much time with Zander recently either, and they always had a laugh together or at the very least set the world to rights.

At three p.m., Barton said he was going home for a bit because he suspected it might be a while before he had any time off. He wanted to join in with the dog enthusiasm too. He'd always longed for a puppy, even though he knew from others that the lovable furball stage didn't last long, but it had never seemed the right time. Zander dropped him off at his house, agreeing to pick him up at seven that evening to continue the morning's interviews.

It was a warm afternoon, and Barton grinned as he stepped through the front door and out of the sun. Or perhaps it was excitement. He had a flashback to his youth and the joy and pleasure from anticipating much-wanted presents. His ears strained for the sounds of barking or the patter of tiny furry feet, but the house was silent. Holly was sitting at the table in the kitchen, reading a magazine with a cup of coffee. She smiled up at him.

'Are you back for good?' she asked.

'No, I've got to go out again at seven.'

'Okay, I was going to cook, but I'm too hot. I'll do sandwiches in a bit.'

She looked down at the glossy pages.

'Where is he?' asked Barton.

Holly spoke without raising her head.

'Lawrence is out. Luke's showing Layla something about an evil Piggy on Roblox.'

Holly sneaked a peek up at him.

'You big softie. Did you think the dog would be here already?'

'No, of course not.'

'Yeah, right. I almost ran off with one, but they don't just let you have him there and then. They need to do a home check first. Make sure we have a home for a start, and confirm there aren't any other bad-mannered pets in the place already, so probably best if you make yourself scarce when they come.'

'Very funny.' Barton clicked his fingers. 'Ah ha! You and the kids saw one you liked, and it's a he!'

'Yes. He's kind of a puppy. Six months old. He wasn't wanted because he had a slightly withered back leg when he was born, but it's strengthened now and is no problem.'

Barton found himself hopping from one foot to the other.

'Go on, then. What is it?'

'They printed a picture off for us to show you. You do need to be here for the home visit. They already have someone in the area on Monday night, so I'll confirm if you're planning to be back for six thirty. Then, if we pass the inspection, we can collect him the following day.'

Holly passed him a piece of A4 paper with a photograph on it.

Barton picked the sheet up, his eyes slowly widening.

'What the hell is this?'

'That's Runty.'

'It really is. Is it alive?'

'His name is Runty. He's been neglected, that's all. He was probably bred for coursing, but with slow growth, the breeders abandon them. A farmer found him hiding in one of his barns.'

'He's all teeth and looks a bit like a gremlin. And that's after the incident with the microwave.'

At that moment, Lawrence returned. He walked straight to the fridge, took the milk out, then drank straight from the bottle. Holly's teeth clenched.

'What's a gremlin?' asked Lawrence.

'You know, the film from the eighties. Your dad says Runty looks like one. And how many more times do I have to tell you to use a glass?'

Lawrence cocked his head to one side.

'Yeah, I've seen clips on YouTube. It's funny. There's a cute Gremlin called Gizmo in it. Let's call him that.'

Barton read Runty's profile. He'd never considered a greyhound, but at least it wasn't a female Shih Tzu called Bunty. His phone rang: Mortis.

'How are you, John? On second thought, don't answer. I don't really care.'

Barton laughed.

'Good timing. I've got a couple of questions about arsonists and pyromaniacs.'

'Okay, just to confirm what I said about the body first. We haven't found out anything particularly surprising. Only that new tooth is unusual, especially for someone so young. Paperwork's done for that. Her alcohol readings, however, were off the scale. She consumed a lot of that whisky, but there's no proof that she drank that level of alcohol on a regular basis, or if she did, then it was a recent thing.'

'Okay, noted. We haven't got much closer on her identity, which is annoying, but we've had some interesting discussions with a few types in the vicinity. We're back there tonight, but I wanted to ask you about kids and fire.'

'Okay, I do know plenty about it, but ring the investigator from yesterday. Leigh knows more. He's a kindred spirit, so be prepared to learn. He'll give you a profile of what the person is liable to be like. Remember, John, crimes like these relate to human nature. These disorders are characterised by a failure to resist impulses, which we all suffer from, but generally are able to control. Some people buy more clothes than they could ever hope to wear or pay for, others drink gallons of beers or vineyards of wine until their health fails, but the person who you're looking for might cope with life by lighting fires.'

Barton said goodbye, cut the call, and rang Leigh Beddows.

'Hi, Leigh. Sorry for ringing you at the weekend. I was wondering if I could get a profile for people who set fires. I've got a few suspects, but there's nothing clear. It's been a while since we had something like this, and I just wanted a quick refresher.'

'No problem. We deal with these cases regularly. Are you sitting comfortably?'

Barton grabbed a bottle of water from the fridge and sat down.

'I'm all ears.'

'The average suspect is actually quite young. They're usually a white male, age seventeen to twenty-six. There's often an unstable childhood. One or both parents would have been missing from the home. Maybe abuse and neglect were present. The other indicators from that kind of upbringing are well known and things you'll be aware of already.'

'Poor academic performance, antisocial behaviour and a criminal record.'

'Correct,' replied Beddows. 'If the parents are still around, or the primary caregiver is, they might have a cold or aggressive relationship with the suspect, although the mother could be overprotective.'

Barton thought of Little Bob.

'I assume they might be loners, maybe single,' he said.

'Very much so. If they are in a relationship, it's likely to be unbalanced and not in their favour.'

'Okay.'

'If they're single, it's also likely they'd still live at home with their parents.'

'So there's often a lack of stable interpersonal relationships combined with weak social skills.'

'Exactly, John. Add poor employment prospects to the mix, too. They're probably unemployed or working in a low-paying, unskilled job such as labouring or warehousing.'

'Or, something that's less common nowadays, but if they were in the military, they were likely to have been released early.'

'Excellent.'

'Although of course, our fire-starter could actually be anyone of any age, or even a group of people.'

'Yes. I'm afraid so. The best indicator is an obsession or fascination with the fire service. It could be any aspect of it that motivates them. The big red vehicle, the firefighters themselves, a thrill that all this drama and all these people are there for something they created.'

'Intelligence levels?' asked Barton.

'Mixed, I'm afraid. Many studies have found arsonists to be of limited intelligence, but that's probably because they were the ones we caught.'

Barton laughed.

'Yes,' said Beddows. 'It helps if they're still stood next to the fire with a lighter in their hands.'

'I assume other negative indicators would be common like alcoholism or substance abuse.'

'Yes, marijuana in particular could be an indicator. There's definitely expected to be some kind of mental health issue present, such as personality disorders, depression, schizophrenia, and, of course, suicidal tendencies.'

'That's quite a big list.'

'Yes, I'm sure you know that arson is still one of the hardest crimes to solve if it's just done for fun. There can be a weak connection to the choice of target, so if they flee the scene and aren't seen, you have nothing.'

'Okay, like kids setting fire to a cornfield near their house. All we really have is the fact the kids might live nearby.' Barton considered any last questions. 'Any final thoughts on anything, such as the difference between arsonists and pyromaniacs?'

'With pyromaniacs, it can be about a buzz from the control, but the most common reason they do this is unadulterated thrill-seeking. It's compulsive, but the suspect also relishes the chaos created by the arson. Setting an uncontrolled fire is an incredible exercise in obtaining, demonstrating, maintaining, or acquiring lost power. Don't focus on the mental illness, though. A schizophrenic may still set a fire out of anger and revenge. They could be psychotic or deluded, but they don't have to be contributing factors. Pure pyromania is rare. After all, if you're going to light a fire and ruin someone's day, you might as well make it the house of someone you hate.'

'Or at least one in walking distance.'

'Yes, nothing beats convenience.'

'It's a lot to think about.'

'I know. The perpetrator may even seem relatively normal right now, because they've set a recent fire. They could be at peace, but it won't last.'

'I reckon you've described half the city.'

'Yes, but I believe you'll catch this dangerous person because they might be escalating.'

'A skip to a bin isn't escalating.'

'No, but if they were responsible for the previous bin fires and escalated to the skip, it would be. The fact that another fire was set so soon after might mean that they need a bigger buzz, or they might have finally lost complete control.'

'So they might have reached rock bottom.'

'Yep. You don't usually glide down there, you hit it with a bang. If you don't catch them soon, they may well expose themselves by doing something verging on the insane. I wouldn't be surprised if, when that happens, more people die. Nothing kills the innocent like fire.'

25

DI BARTON

At a quarter to seven, Zander knocked and Holly came to the door with Barton so she could say hello.

'Nice to see you, Shawn. How are things?'

'Good. I was expecting a woof.'

'Hang on.' Holly returned to the kitchen, picked up the photo, and passed it to Zander. 'This is Gizmo.'

Zander just managed to conceal his surprise.

'He looks like someone's told him his new home is haunted.'

'He's been through a tough time. We'll look after him.'

'There's a lot of love in this house. I'm sure he'll be happy, assuming John doesn't eat him, of course.'

Barton barged past him.

'I'm glad you're interested,' he said. 'You'll be having him when we're on holiday.'

Zander and Barton got in the car and drove to the block of four houses, with Barton updating his detective sergeant on the conversation he had with Beddows.

'Sounds like he agrees with my Wicker Man theory about it being a group effort,' said Zander.

'I've got a feeling at least one of them knows more than they're telling us. We can always bring people to the station to apply more pressure.'

'Yes, although bringing Lynette back to the station would be dangerous. She reminds me of one of those Instagrammers.'

'Do you mean influencers?' asked Barton. 'Layla's started talking about them. Needless to say, I usually become the villain in any discussion.'

'It's a brave new world where everyone's got an opinion,' said Zander.

They were soon at the cul-de-sac, and this time parked directly outside the row of houses. All the cars were still present. Just as they were about to get out of their vehicle, Zander and Barton watched in amazement as a head rose above the far wall to the left of the terrace. Then a body appeared, and a leg was slung over. A very tall teenager dropped to the floor, like a falling spider. He looked around, then trotted to the door of number two and let himself in.

'Bollocks,' said Zander and Barton, as they realised at the same time that whoever set the fire could have known about that route away from the scene. They were contemplating that fact when the door for number one opened and Lynette left her house. They stayed in the car and watched to see what she would do.

'Wonder where she's heading, dressed like that,' said Barton.

'It can't be too many places. Certainly not hiking.'

'She wasn't the average type of person we meet.'

'I noticed she has unusual eyes,' replied Zander.

'Yes, I focused mostly on them, or at least I tried to.'

'I looked it up once. Did you know only two per cent of the world's population have green eyes?'

Barton turned to look at Zander. 'Must be nice to have a lot of free time.'

'Yeah. It's because seventy per cent of the world is non-white. But eighty per cent of people from Iceland have blue or green eyes.'

'I hope this is going somewhere.'

Barton returned his focus to Lynette as she strolled up her path, swinging her handbag, while Zander blathered on.

'The article reckoned those with green eyes were passionate, mysterious, devious and jealous.'

'Case solved, then,' sighed Barton.

'Although it did also say that most scientists think those assumptions are a load of old bollocks.'

Barton let out another big breath, although Lynette still had his attention. She had walked past her own car towards theirs and stopped. She leaned on Zander's bonnet.

'Evening, boys,' she mouthed to them, clearly but silently.

Barton stepped out of the car.

'Are you supposed to be going out?'

Lynette pulled her skirt down as she stood upright in a struggle to maintain decency. She smiled and spoke normally.

'Sorry, I get cheeky when I'm bored. My boyfriend's a key worker, so I pick up groceries and essentials for him.'

'Fair enough. Lynette, I was wondering what your views were on firefighters.'

'Sexy, although I must admit that I had a bad experience with one once.'

'Yeah.' Barton paused for a moment as he wondered how to ask for the details. In the end, he decided just to ask. 'Do you mind sharing it?'

'Not at all. A kid near here got stuck up a tree and couldn't or wouldn't come down. There was a big drama, so his parents rang 999. When they arrived, I stared into the windows of the truck and a guy gave me a massive, flirty smile. He looked like a film star. But when he stepped down, he was shorter than I was. I love my men how I like my heels.'

'Tall and thin?'

'Correct, but don't forget dangerous.'

She winked at him and click-clacked away to her car. Barton stared at the row of houses lit up in the evening sunshine and suspected it was going to be a long night.

26

DI BARTON

Barton knocked at number two. The tall lad opened the door, dressed exactly how you'd expect a teenager to dress, down to the backward baseball cap.

'Bob Fowler,' said Zander.

'That's me. Grandad told me the Feds were coming. Enter at your peril.'

Bob walked through the hall into the lounge, leaving them to shut the door and follow. He stood next to the stairs at the back of the property as though he was ready to flee up them. Ernie Fowler eyed them suspiciously from an armchair. The room still had an unloved air, but the windows were open and it smelled fresher.

'Evening, Bob,' said Barton. 'Do you mind answering a few questions?'

'It wasn't me.'

'That's okay. We just wanted to ask you about that wall you climbed over.'

Bob's eyes narrowed.

'What about it?'

'Do many people climb over there?'

Bob shrugged.

'Me and a few of my buddies. There's a little wood back there where we hang out occasionally when we're bored with gaming, which isn't often.'

'Is that where you were?'

Bob blushed and suddenly looked all of his age. 'Yeah.'

Barton decided to keep his suspicions to himself because he didn't want the lad clamming up.

'What do you think of your neighbours?'

The cocky attitude instantly returned.

'Ah, ha! You're talking about Jugs next door. I saw you two dirty old gits checking her out. You're as bad as Grandad. Hell, man. At least he isn't on duty. Although, I suspect he'd like to be, if you get what I'm saying.'

'Shut it, you saucy little git,' said Ernie, but Barton detected a twinkle in his eyes.

'Answer the question, please,' asked Barton.

'I don't really talk to my neighbours.'

'Do you visit the store much?' asked Zander. 'The manager says people are always thieving from him.'

'Jeez. It's the corner shop and we're kids. Of course we steal his shit.'

'Right, son,' said Zander. 'Change your tone and show some respect. This is serious. A woman died in that skip fire.'

Bob's face reddened further. He nodded.

'Can we have a look upstairs?' asked Barton.

'Yeah, no worries. Come up. My room is different.'

Ernie glared at them as they followed Bob up the stairs and into his room, but he didn't comment. Bob's bedroom was like a modern oasis in comparison to downstairs, not dissimilar to Henson's place next door. Barton noted that Ernie had given Bob the bigger bedroom. The walls were bright white and there was a large flat-screen on a bracket, with some gaming consoles on a shelf underneath. The bed was made. The carpet, clean.

Bob smiled at them, proud of his domain.

'He can't hear us up here, so you don't need to close the door. It's his house, so he can do what he wants, but this is my room. I live in here most of the time because of the smoke. I sometimes watch a bit of television with him. He likes *Wipeout* of all things, which is pretty weird for someone his age.'

Most of the energy had dropped from Bob's voice.

'Do you get on all right with him, Bob?' asked Barton.

'It's Rob, actually. He calls me Bob. Has since he first took me in. But yeah, we're cool. He's a bit grumpy and cantankerous, but aren't all you old guys?'

Barton ignored the insult, mostly because it was true.

'Where were you, really?' asked Zander. 'You can tell us.'

'I wasn't doing anything dodgy. I've been seeing someone from school. He lives around here, so we meet there and hook up.'

'You think your grandad would mind?'

'Nah, I doubt it. He'd be fine if we came here, but the walls are thin. I often hear Jugs up to no good next door.'

'I hope you don't call her that to her face,' said Barton.

'No way, man. She scares the hell out of me. I only say that stuff about her chest because it amuses Grandad. You understand how it is with old-school heterosexual men.'

'No,' said Barton. 'How is it?'

'You can only show affection by being rude to each other. You're too uptight to say it to each other's faces, so you wind each other up instead, burp, and watch the football together.'

For the second time that day, Barton chose not to look at Zander.

'And of course we don't nick stuff from the shop,' said Rob while looking out of the window.

Barton suspected that was the first lie that he'd told.

'Have you or any of your friends threatened the manager of the shop? Maybe said you'd burn it down.'

'No, of course not. None of my mates would do something like that.'

'What do you really think about your neighbours? Be honest. I bet you're out at all hours. Have you seen anything strange, or seen anyone hanging around you didn't recognise?'

'Lynette always chats to me. She's nice, but I think she's a bit messed up. I make her laugh to distract her from whatever her troubles are. I told her we should get some gear off the hippy two doors up and she can teach me how to roll in bed.'

Barton chuckled.

'What did she say to that?'

Rob laughed freely for the first time.

'She always says, if you can wrangle any out of him, come over, but it's unlikely I'd survive the experience.'

Barton's chuckle died in his throat.

'Have you ever got any?'

'Sex or weed?'

'Either.'

'Neither off anyone in the street. I smoked ganja once that my mate got from his brother, but it made me paranoid. That's the joke, see. The hippy won't sell or give it to anyone because he reckons our brains aren't developed yet. He says that his dope is so strong that if you're under twenty-five and smoke it, you're likely to develop schizophrenia.'

'There is a link,' said Barton, with his smile returning. 'So you all get on well?'

'Yeah, if we spot him getting out of his car, we all shout, "Sell us some weed", really loud. He always runs away, you know, laughing, saying "Shhh", and pretending he's looking for the police. It's okay here. The muscley guy's dead quiet. Doesn't talk to anyone. We rarely see him. He must have a good job because he has the sweetest cars. He had a Porsche for a while. I should ask him what he does because I'm leaving school soon and I haven't got a clue what I want to do.'

'Nothing untoward, then?'

'Nope.'

But Barton noticed a thought register in Rob's mind.

'What is it?'

'You know, it has been much busier down here lately. I know everyone gets their stuff delivered nowadays, but it's been more than that. I see more people walking along the street or talking outside. There was a weird girl with purple hair I saw a couple of times. Then I heard a massive argument and a crash not too far back.'

'Like a car crash?'

'No. The hippy's shed collapsed. Maybe he was trying to fix it.'

'Can you describe the people involved in more detail?'

'To be honest, I take no notice. Obviously purple hair isn't common, but I have seen a motorbike here a few times as well. I remember that because it was sat outside for hours like it was waiting, but the rider never took their helmet off.'

'Why was she weird, or was it just the hair?' asked Barton.

'She was walking up and down the street talking into her mobile, but when she removed her hand, I don't think there was a phone there.'

'It might have been a little Bluetooth,' said Barton.

'Maybe.'

'What about the motorbike, small or big, tourer or sports?' asked Zander.

'I'm not into that sort of thing. Medium maybe, not flashy.'

'Whose house was it near?' asked Zander.

'It was on the opposite side of the road, but kinda in between ours and Garth's.'

Barton asked a few more questions, none of which gave them specifics, then mentally put Rob near the bottom of his list. Rob was walking them out when Ernie came out of the kitchen with a plate of biscuits.

'Oh, I was having a few,' he said, 'and wondered if you wanted one. Bob hasn't had his tea yet.'

Barton and Zander both took a biscuit, not wanting to seem rude, and Ernie shuffled back to the lounge. At the door, Barton paused and cleared his throat to get Rob's attention.

'You know, you could hoover and clean the house for him.'

Rob gave him a look of amazed disdain, then closed the door.

27

DI BARTON

Next up was the hippy, as Rob had called him. After their previous visit, Barton wasn't hopeful, and his earlier optimism about swiftly identifying the body was fading. The shed might be interesting though.

Clive McBride answered the door in exactly the same attire, but his eyes were noticeably clearer. He ushered them into the conservatory at the back and asked them both if they wanted a cold beer. Barton politely declined, despite being so hot under the glass roof that he'd have exchanged a kidney for one if drinking on the job hadn't been a sackable offence.

'No problemo,' said McBride. 'Water, juice?'

'A glass of water, please,' said Barton.

Zander had sat in the chair opposite him and was staring at the plant next to it. You didn't need to be Bob Marley to know what it was. Although Barton didn't see marijuana at that moment. He saw leverage. McBride returned and passed them each a glass. It was chilled to perfection, and Barton nodded in appreciation.

'Did you remember anything, then?' asked Zander.

'Yeah, as the song says, it's all coming back to me now. Me and the lady's eyes connected, you know, when I walked by in the street. She recognised me. Normally, I'd chat, but it's nervous times, and she looked kind of down on her luck. Anyway, I didn't speak to her the only time we met, which was when she was with her boyfriend when he knocked on my door once.'

Barton and Zander both leaned forward in their seats.

'Brilliant,' said Zander. 'Who is he?'

'No idea, man. I prefer to focus on people's positives. Peace to everyone, and all that, but he was a little trying.'

Barton blinked with confusion.

'You mean he was arrogant?'

'Who knows? Maybe he'd received some bad news earlier that day.'

'What did he want?'

'To score some weed.'

'Like from that plant next to Sergeant Zander?'

'No, that's not ready yet.'

'That's interesting,' said Zander. 'The young lad down the road said he tried to buy marijuana off you to smoke with the woman at number one.'

'What? You mean, Rob? He didn't say it was for that. He was the one who told me Ernie had arthritis.'

'Did you sell him some, anyway?'

'No, man. I certainly wouldn't give any to a child.'

'I meant did you sell any to the girl and her boyfriend when they came around and asked for some.'

'No, and that was the first and last time I saw them, until the other day when I half-recognised her.'

'Have you ever just given it to anyone?' asked Barton.

'No, I told you. This stuff really affects some people. Kills their ambition and energy, ruins their memories and minds, and it's bad for kids.'

'How's your ambition?' asked Barton.

'Just fine. Smoking chills me out and I can deal with it. I made over a hundred grand last year. I don't need to sell drugs.'

That grabbed Zander's attention.

'No offence, but why do you still live here if you're earning that sort of cash?'

'No worries, that's cool. I like this area. It's real. It's moody, and it can be scary. The people are struggling, they don't have much, but they're trying. I dig all that and put it in my songs. Besides, moving would be a massive hassle.'

Barton stood up.

'We'll be on our way, then. I don't suppose you can remember what car he was driving.'

'Nah, I was a bit freaked out because he was on edge, so I looked out of the window, but he just went back inside next door.'

Barton's ears perked up at that. Then they twitched as a floorboard creaked loudly upstairs.

'That's a big dog you have up there.'

McBride looked sheepish.

'It's a friend. She's up there with the dog.'

'Was she there when we were here earlier?'

'Maybe. I think so. She comes and goes.'

'Is it your girlfriend?' asked Zander.

'No, no, no. We lived together as a couple here ten years ago, but it got a bit complex, so we're pals now. I've known her since school.'

'Can you ask her to come down?'

McBride shook his head.

'No, man. She wouldn't like that. This vibe, no. She's had a tough time. Ceri came from a broken home.'

Barton gave McBride a smile.

'It's okay. You don't have to ask her to come down.'

'Sweet.'

Barton walked to the bottom of the stairs.

'Ceri!' he roared up them as though he were trying to wake the dead.

A young woman with short black elfin hair appeared at the top of the stairs.

'What?' she whispered.

'Police, we'd like a word.'

There was a hint of gothic to her hairstyle and make-up, but she wore a loose long white dress that made him think of girls in Woodstock clips with flowers in their hair. She glided down the stairs.

'We're here about the fires,' said Barton.

Ceri merely nodded.

'Do you know anything about them?'

She stuck her jaw out, then shrugged.

Barton's cool was vanishing rapidly. He spoke to Ceri, but his voice was loud so McBride could hear as well.

'We're in the last chance saloon. If you two don't immediately start being more co-operative, you will be arrested and you'll spend the night in custody. In separate cells. Clear?'

Ceri and McBride both mumbled yes.

'Ceri, were you aware of the skip fire?'

'Yes.'

'How did you know?'

'Clive told me.'

'Do you know about any other fires, or have you seen something around here out of the usual?'

'Nope.'

Barton knew he was wasting his time.

'How often do you stay here?'

'None of your business.'

'We'd like to take your phone number in case we need to speak to you again. What's your address and phone number?'

'I don't have an address. I sofa surf all over. This place has gone bad, so I'll be elsewhere. And I don't have a phone. My email is Ceri@danzefloor.net. Now, I don't feel very well. See ya.'

Barton watched her swish back up the stairs. She didn't even acknowledge McBride. Barton growled.

'Mr McBride. You don't have a dog, do you?'

28

DI BARTON

McBride raised a shoulder and looked sheepish.

'Let's talk outside,' said Barton.

Barton walked to the door of the conservatory, turned the key in it, and stepped outside. There was a small, listing, badly repaired shed at the bottom of the garden with its door hanging open. Barton walked over the grass and looked inside. The walls inside had silver foil on them. There was a big pot in the middle of the room with the remains of a dead plant in it. The lights on the ceiling were intricate.

Barton had been pondering what to do about the marijuana. He'd believed McBride about not dealing it, and he'd eventually been helpful, but it was still illegal and his open use was also legitimising it for the kids around here.

'Can you explain this?'

McBride held out his hands. 'I need to grow it in the winter too. I only do one plant at a time.'

'What happened to the shed?'

'A few months back, some guy came around wanting to talk about buying weed off me. I said I don't deal. He just brushed past me and walked through my house. Then he walked out the back of the conservatory like you did and went to my shed. He was a bit freaked when he saw a single plant. I think he expected more.'

'Then what happened?'

'He had a backpack, which he opened, and pulled out a small hammer. I shit myself, but he just smashed the window and the lights, knocked the door off its hinges and kicked a panel through. Then he left without saying anything else.'

'What did he look like?' asked Zander.

'Black jacket, mask, jeans, strong, thirtyish, that's it. I was too scared to look at him directly.'

Barton smelled a rat.

'And yet you still live here?'

'Yeah, he never came back, but it was great material. I got a sound song out of it, based on the fear, you know.'

Barton didn't know.

'Why would strangers come around your house looking for drugs?' he asked.

'I don't know, man. Maybe one of the kids said something.'

Barton made a quick decision. He needed time to think about what he was going to do, if anything. The shed was neither here nor there, and a single house plant was a waste of time for the courts. Ceri was more concerning. She seemed distant and bohemian at best.

'What's the score with Ceri? Why does she live such an unconventional life?'

'She doesn't like men much. I let her come here as she pleases. Sometimes she's here all the while, other times rarely. We all seem to let her down. She's a dancer when she feels like it, brilliant. I recommended her sometimes, but she's a bit flaky and doesn't always turn up.'

'Does she pay you rent?'

'No, no way. I owe her.'

'Why?'

'My best song was based on her. Loneliness. Everyone knows it.'

Barton wasn't sure if the song was called Loneliness, or if that was the theme. He'd had enough, but McBride was his best link to Ceri if he wanted to speak to her again.

'Why lie about the dog? We could arrest you for obstruction.'

'There was a dog like that, but he passed six months back. I was protecting Ceri. She's fragile. I won't see her again for ages now. She'll vanish.'

'Can you get in touch with her?'

'She does answer my emails, so yes.'

Barton suspected Ceri wouldn't reply to one from the police and he'd have no idea where she was.

'We'll see you again, Clive. We might need you to look at some photographs for identification purposes. I strongly recommend you purchase some different plants in the meantime.'

McBride glanced at the plant with a confused expression.

'Hey, I thought you were allowed to grow it for personal use.'

'Not true. Get rid of it. Perhaps it *is* ruining your mind after all.'

When they'd left McBride's, Barton took a deep breath.

'Can this day get any weirder?'

'I really hope not,' replied Zander.

'I liked him, though, despite his mushy brain.'

'Maybe he was too helpful. He's the only person we suspect has had contact with the deceased girl. Perhaps him saying this bloke knocked on his door is bullshit, and she came alone. He invited her in, got her unconscious, and ended up slinging her in the skip after having his evil way with her. At which point, he set fire to it.'

Barton knew that was possible, and why it was best practice to interview in pairs, but even so the theory seemed a stretch.

'The shed thing is odd. Cox said some organised crime types had been here last week, but she didn't know what for.'

'McBride said all that was months ago. Let's focus on identifying the girl first. We can see where we are after that.'

Zander checked his phone after a beep. He shoved it back in his pocket, then stomped across the grass to house three.

'Everything okay?' asked Barton

'Yeah. Pigs cancelled our date tonight. We were going to catch a late movie, but she's cried off.'

'Is that a big deal?'

'Not really, but my head's all over the place. Perhaps I should just get a cat and be done with it.'

'Or a gremlin?' asked Barton with a smile, but Zander merely pounded on Henson's front door.

Through the frosted glass, they both noticed a shadow move, but nobody came to the door. Zander thumped it again.

After a minute of silence, Barton swore under his breath. There was no law that said you had to answer the door and talk to the police, and Henson could evade them forever if he wanted to, if they received no further intel. Right now, all they had was waffle from a less than reputable witness, which meant they had no hope of a warrant to obtain forced entry. No magistrate on earth would give them one on what they had so far. Shame it wasn't 1973 and he could put his shoulder through the door.

Zander and Barton went back to the car and saw that Lynette's vehicle had returned. Barton turned for a final stare at the houses.

'It's been a long day,' he said. 'We'll come back tomorrow first thing and catch Henson. If he doesn't let us in then, I'm going to be very suspicious.'

The sky was turning a bright burnt orange. He hoped it wasn't a sign of things to come.

29

THE FIRE KILLER

I watch the detectives leave. It's hard to say if they're on the ball and I wonder if they know what they've got on their hands. Will they understand me? I doubt it.

But it's unlikely those men are fools. They will be back. I need to practise how to answer their questions convincingly. I wasn't ready before because the pressure is already building again, and I'm finding it hard to concentrate.

I can't stop thinking about the poor woman who died. I've been a selfish fool, but will I ever be able to stop? Unless the police put an end to it all. Is that what I secretly want? To think I can deny who I am is stupid. I know I'm self-centred and totally worthless.

The confusing part is that people are attracted to me. Isn't that typical of life? The ones I push away pursue me more. What I want, I don't get.

Life confuses me. It's biscuits and cigarettes! When I was young, I used to love both, but now they're tinged with regret and guilt. When even the simple pleasures are gone, it really is time to worry.

Drama rules now, not peace, so is it time to act, or is it time to confess?

30

DI BARTON

Barton woke the next morning on his own to the sounds of tweeting birds. It was warm already and his T-shirt was clammy and stuck to his back. He rubbed his eyes, feeling the greasy skin around them. Holly came in with a glass of orange juice.

'Everything okay?' she asked.

'I feel a bit like I've been in bed for ten hours but not really slept.'

'You were rolling about all night, which is dangerous for me when I'm so small. Plenty on your mind?'

Barton sat up and yawned. 'You could say a lot of suspects on my mind. There's something about this case that's starting to concern me.'

'A young girl being burned alive isn't concerning enough?'

'Well, of course, that's obviously tragic, but there's something else at play here. I don't know if it's more serious or less. Alarms are going off left, right and centre, but because I've seen so many potential suspects in close succession, I'm not entirely certain which one of them they're ringing for.'

'You'll solve it. You usually do, but don't try solving it tomorrow at seven when we're having our home inspection, or it will be your last investigation.'

Holly narrowed her eyes and wagged her finger. Barton pulled her onto the bed and gave her a cuddle, which turned into a kiss. He was glancing over at the alarm clock to see if his luck was in, when his youngest son appeared.

'Wrestle!' roared Luke.

He clambered onto the edge of the mattress, leapt high into the air, and came down on Barton's back, knees first.

'Argh!' roared Barton.

Holly, underneath him, merely whimpered.

After a quick breakfast, Barton made a flask of coffee, grabbed a packet of Bourbon biscuits, then stepped out of the house when he heard a car pull up outside. Zander had gone into work and booked out a powerful pool Volvo this time. He must have had the same alarm bells ringing that Barton did. Barton only received a grunt in reply when he got in and said hello.

'What's the plan?' said Zander after yawning profusely while he drove.

'Rough night?'

'Couldn't sleep.'

'Ditto.'

'Right, we need Henson to talk, but we can't make him do that if he doesn't open his door. Sadly, the days of dressing up as delivery men are over.'

Barton shook the flask to mix the coffee, but the close heat didn't make the thought of it as appealing.

'First, good call on the car. I was going to suggest taking a different vehicle. Let's park up for a bit down the road. See if there's any movement, comings and goings, that kind of thing. Perhaps discuss your personal life.'

Zander curled his lip.

They parked fifty metres away on the curve of the street so they could see the front doors of all four properties. Barton poured the coffee into plastic cups while Zander opened the biscuits. After some munching, Barton focused.

'Why is Garth Henson nervous?' asked Barton.

'He's done or doing something illegal,' replied Zander.

'That would be my guess. What kind of illicit business do you think he's involved in?'

'Whatever it is clearly pays well. Look at his car and his clothes, although, if he's loaded, why does he live here?'

'It's possible he's flying under the radar. He doesn't seem the type for heroin, so maybe more the recreational side of things. Might even be steroids.'

'I'll ring the station.'

While Zander rang to see if Henson had any previous, Barton made a mental note to check if any other residents had criminal records. Henson could be nervous because he knew the girl who died and nothing more. Barton would be surprised if he'd done time. Most people who'd been inside had a certain recognisable way about them.

He thought of McBride and smiled. He won't have been behind bars either. Maybe it was Henson who told some heavies that McBride was a dealer. Barton didn't think so, though. Henson wouldn't want the risk of living next door to a dope farmer.

'Clean as a whistle,' said Zander after finishing his call. 'Not even speeding.'

'He's in there. The bathroom light came on.'

Barton checked his watch, then cracked his window. It was just before nine, and the car had already become unpleasantly hot. He was about to tell Zander to turn the engine back on for the air-con when Lynette came out of her house and got in her vehicle. As she drove past, she gave them the finger.

'Once they've trained you in undercover ops, you never lose it,' said Zander.

Barton guiltily put the biscuit packet in the glovebox, having eaten six.

'Lynette isn't fazed by our attention. I wouldn't be astonished if she has a record.'

This time Barton rang the station, but the call was longer.

'Okay, email it to me. I'll read it on my phone,' he said before finishing the call.

'Don't tell me she's done time for arson?' asked Zander.

'Nope.'

'Murder?'

'No, harassment without violence. Five years ago. Community order because it was her first offence. Not serious, but still concerning. It looks like a bloke split up with her, and she didn't agree with the decision.'

'I bet the bloke she harassed would describe it as serious.'

Barton nodded. For that sort of case to get all the way to court and result in a sentence, there was usually some extreme behaviour over a significant period of time. Rejection sometimes drove the scorned person to a level of madness that they themselves would never have thought possible. They had a case last year when a woman told the police that her ex's new girlfriend had attacked her thirteen-year-old son.

Luckily, Strange had recognised the mania in the accusation and they'd managed to stop it rolling too far. It was a sad situation with no winners. The young lad had ended up with an aunt, the boyfriend had decided life was easier single, and the rejected woman had finished up in a psychiatric unit from which she still hadn't been released.

'Shall we give it a knock?' asked Zander. 'Henson's probably hidden a girl in the basement, another in the loft, four in the boot of his fancy motor, and has three severed heads on the top of his runner-bean canes.'

Barton got out of the car. He didn't have the time or the authority for surveillance. You could get away with an hour or so, but police rules stated you needed authorisation to set up an observation post. TV taught you that special officers could be brought in on a whim, but it wasn't true. The costs were significant.

American movies also showed the FBI using the latest technology that would enable them to hear the perp brushing his teeth while watching him on infrared. Peterborough was a provincial police force in the UK. It would more likely be a civilian guy from technical support with thick glasses who would install a conventional video camera that would capture some slightly blurred film of the front of subject's house. There'd be no sound.

Getting permission for any such intrusion on anyone's liberties was hard work. Maybe Henson would let them in and apologise for being shifty yesterday. Zander also got out of the car and as they began walking towards the house, the door opened and Henson came out. He fumbled with his keys, dropping them once.

His shoulders drooped as he walked up the path, and he kept his eyes on the ground. It was only when he reached his car that he looked up and saw the approaching officers. Henson's expression changed to one you'd expect if a wild stallion had raced around the corner and was heading straight at you. His keys slipped from his hand again and jangled on the floor. Then he sprinted in the opposite direction.

Zander stampeded after him, while Barton retrieved the dropped car keys, knowing Zander had about as much chance of catching a stallion as he would the fit young man. Barton peeked through Henson's lounge window. It looked normal inside. Glancing back, he observed Henson leaping up the wall that Rob had climbed over yesterday in one smooth move, but then he stopped. Henson peered over his shoulder, slumped back down, and stepped towards Zander.

Barton was about to rush over, expecting the worst, but Henson began to say sorry for running. He and Zander walked back together. Barton selected a Yale key from the set he'd picked up and opened the front door.

'Shall we?' he asked Henson, who slipped past him like an errant schoolboy.

They sat a deflated Henson down in the lounge.

'Would you care to explain that?' asked Zander.

When Henson's gaze rose, his eyes were wild with fear, and something else.

'I've done something terrible,' he said. 'And I panicked. I'm not a bad person, it's just, it's just...' He leapt to his feet and started to pace the room. 'I think I know who the girl was in the skip.'

Zander got his notebook out.

'What's her name?'

'Joss, no Jess, one of them. Jess, I think.'

'Surname?'

'No idea. We only met three or four times. She was with a bloke who came around.'

'A friend of yours?' asked Barton.

'Yeah, kind of. I've been keeping my distance. I prefer a quiet life, but he was popping around all the time, so I stopped answering the door, and he didn't like it.'

'And this Jess was his girlfriend?'

'Yes.'

'What's his name?'

This time, the pained expression was even more evident.

'I'd rather not say.'

Barton had had enough.

'She's dead. Tell me who he is.'

'It's nothing to do with him any more. They split up.'

'I don't get it. Why are you so upset about this woman you barely know dying, when she isn't even going out with your mate now?'

Henson slumped back onto the sofa with his hands over his face. He seemed genuinely distraught. Zander opened his mouth, but Barton shook his head at him. A minute passed before Henson glanced at them. His eyes were rheumy.

'She came here that evening. The weather was bad. It was really windy, if you remember. She was desperate for help. I, I, I said no.'

'What did she want? Money?'

Henson wiped his eyes.

'No, she just wanted to stay the night. She said she'd sleep on the sofa and be gone in the morning. I closed the door on her. I'll regret it for the rest of my life.'

Zander and Barton were decades into their police career, and they were as cynical as each other. There was something not right here.

'Why didn't you let her stay?' asked Barton.

Henson seemed to struggle to remember, then the same shadow passed over his face that had appeared when he saw the police earlier.

'She was a bit, you know, crazy.'

'In what way?' asked Barton.

'Just clingy and weird. I couldn't trust her.'

'Trust her to do what?'

'Not steal.'

'Was she on drugs? Drunk?'

'She smelled of drink, but she was cold and desperate. God! Why did I say no?'

'Look, it's very sad,' said Zander. 'But you don't even know the girl's surname. You hardly knew her. What aren't you telling us?'

'If I'd let her sleep here, she'd still have been alive today. I let that girl down.'

Barton sat opposite the young man, whose shoulders were heaving.

He still didn't get it, which usually meant someone was lying, but Henson seemed genuinely devastated. After a minute of Henson's sobbing, Barton rose and rested a hand on his shoulder.

'It's unfortunate, but you weren't to know. I'm not sure I'd have let her stay at my place, either. Sometimes, events are set in motion, and the end result is terrible, but it's nobody's fault.'

Henson's sobs turned to weeping. Barton thought about the steroid angle again and wondered if Henson had ruined his mental health by injecting strange substances into his body. He wanted information, though, and he suspected it was now or never.

'What's your friend's name?' he asked.

Henson looked up, as if he was ready to talk, then set his jaw. Zander frowned and stepped towards Henson.

'Now, Mr Henson,' said Zander. 'Or my next action will be to put you in cuffs and take you down the station.'

Henson seemed to realise who he was speaking to all of a sudden.

'Okay, okay, but don't tell him how you found out that it was me who brought his name into it.'

Barton considered that for a moment. He couldn't see the immediate harm in agreeing to that if he got answers now, but he couldn't guarantee he wouldn't need to mention his source in the future.

'Okay,' said Barton. 'I don't think we need to at this point, but I might change my mind on that.'

Henson nodded. 'So I don't have to go to the station?'

'No, we can take a statement here. You may need to come in further down the line.'

'That's fine.' Relief came off Henson in waves.

'Who is it, then, you're so reluctant to name?' asked Zander.

'Stefan Russo.'

Barton half expected him to name someone famous. He looked at Zander, who shook his head.

'Should I know him?'

'No, I just don't want him to hear it was me who said he was involved.'

Involved with what? thought Barton.

'Where does he live?' asked Zander.

'The new estate near the train station. Ninety-eight Marchmont Square.'

It was only a ten-minute drive there, if that. The houses were gigantic. It was strange to think of someone living there dating a girl who ended up so desperate she had to sleep in a skip, but Barton had seen virtually everything.

Zander went into the kitchen and made Henson a cup of sweet tea while Barton wrote out a statement. Half an hour later, they were ready to leave.

Barton almost felt like pulling Henson into the old Barton bearhug, the man looked so wrung out, but there was too much out of balance here. Barton suspected Henson was holding back some very important information.

First things first. Identify the girl. Barton had a feeling he would be back here soon, but the next time he saw Henson, he would probably be arresting him.

31

DI BARTON

The two detectives got back in the pool car. Barton looked out of the window as Zander drove them through the empty streets. It was going to be another glorious day. He relaxed in his seat and, after his poor sleep, felt himself almost dozing off to a Beautiful South song when Zander turned the music off.

'I guess I'll give it a proper go with Pigs. Do you think I should tell Strange?'

Barton cocked open an eye. 'You want dating advice from me?'

'I find it's best to gather a range of opinions.' Zander chuckled.

'Is it really that hard to choose? Don't you get the sense that you want to be with one of them all the time?'

'I think I'd be happy with either. Does that make me a bad person?'

'Very. Next lightning storm we have, I'd get inside fast.'

Zander drove through the entrance gates to an area that reminded Barton a little of the posh part of central London. Big mock-Georgian houses were perched on comparatively small plots. He guessed to afford one of these you'd need to work long hours and not care too much about the size of your garden. They found the house they wanted and got out of the vehicle. Barton rang the bell, which was a fancy one that recorded any movement in front of it, then looked at Zander.

'Strange knows what's going on, and she hasn't spoken to you, which I'd have thought she would if she was that bothered. It's your call, but make your mind up, then properly commit to whatever you decide.'

At that moment, the door opened. Barton was expecting the owner to look highly groomed and wealthy, but he wasn't expecting him to be as old as himself. He had to be mid-forties at least.

'Morning, gentlemen, how can I help?'

'Are you Stefan Russo?'

'I am.'

'Detective Inspector Barton and Detective Sergeant Zander. Cambridgeshire Constabulary.'

Russo didn't appear fazed by a visit from the police, which made Barton suspect he was used to it, or expecting them.

'I think I have some tough news for you,' he said.

'Oh. How so?'

'Do you mind if we come in?'

'I do, actually. I'm just leaving, so spit it out. I'm a big boy.'

'We have reason to believe your girlfriend has been involved in an accident.'

'That would be a surprise, seeing as I'm single.'

Russo locked the door and edged by them. Barton heard a beep, and the garage door came to life. Another beep sounded, then the boot of a yellow sports car popped open. Russo strode towards it, took an expensive-looking leather briefcase out, then the boot closed. That time, Barton saw Russo press the fob in his hand.

'Work on a Sunday?' asked Zander.

'My career *is* in London, but I'm going there for pleasure today. I'm meeting a truly beautiful woman.' He smiled at the two detectives as though it was a joy they would never experience. Barton forced himself to keep calm. There was something perky and over-confident about Russo, overbearing even, that was really rubbing him up the wrong way. Still, he could just be an innocent man, looking forward to a hot date.

'Maybe it was your ex-girlfriend. The woman in question was wearing black boots with heels. Nice quality.'

Russo had strolled to the edge of the driveway. He stopped and turned, giving them a dismissive shake of his head.

'Is that Peterborough's equivalent of DNA profiling?'

He gave them a tiny smile, then walked away.

'She recently had a tooth implant,' shouted Zander.

This time Russo halted mid-stride, as though someone had pressed pause on the world. He stayed like that for three or four seconds. He half turned and spoke to the side without looking back at them.

'Jessica. Was her name Jessica?'

'We still haven't confirmed that,' said Zander.

'Why not?'

'She didn't have any ID on her.'

Russo turned around fully.

'Is she in a coma or something?'

'It's easier if we talk about it inside, sir,' said Barton.

Russo's eyes blinked fast for a few seconds.

'She's dead?' Russo asked, flatly.

'I'm afraid so.'

Barton could almost hear Russo's brain whirring as it caught up.

'Blonde hair, mid-twenties.'

'Yes, we think mid-twenties and she probably had light hair.'

Russo shook his head. 'Why can't you tell?'

'The body was damaged by fire.'

Russo walked towards them.

'Jessica had a tooth replaced recently,' he said.

'Which tooth did Jessica have replaced?' asked Zander.

'Front incisor,' said Russo, tapping one of his front teeth. 'It was a good job.'

Barton and Zander both nodded.

'Christ,' said Russo as he trudged past them. 'You'd better come in after all.'

They followed him into the house and Barton and Zander took their shoes off at the door, even though Russo didn't ask them to. It was that type of carpet. Russo headed straight into the lounge, where he quickly made his way to a drinks cabinet that reminded Barton of the one at Southfork in Dallas. Russo poured himself two fingers from an intricate bottle into a glass that could have been crystal and gulped it back. He gasped. Then he repeated the process, wheezing the second time as the whisky went down. Barton moved towards him to stop him going for a third gulp, but Russo had dropped the glass with a clunk on a table and slumped onto a pale-blue velvet sofa next to it.

'Bloody hell. She can't have been twenty-five.'

'Yes, it's tragic.'

'She was a lot of fun. Well, she was at the start. I assume it was a car accident, you know, then a fire?'

Barton could tell it was a genuine question, which immediately removed Russo from his list of suspects. Barton already wasn't surprised that Russo didn't know how old she was.

'No, she died in a skip.'

Russo stole a glance back at the drinks cabinet.

'What the hell was she doing in a skip?'

'We were hoping you could help us with that.'

Russo ran his hands through his hair. It was thinning slightly on the top, but there were no signs of grey. Barton's wife, Holly, always said she could tell if she was going to fancy a man by looking at his shoes. Apparently, Barton himself had only just passed the test. She'd be head over heels with Russo if she could see his fancy brogues, which were on display now his chinos had ridden up. Barton stared at Russo, who seemed to relax as the alcohol took hold. Zander wandered behind him, out of sight, peering at photographs and pictures.

Barton's gaze drifted out of the window. The rear garden was only six metres wide and about ten metres long and was devoid of any furniture except for a four-piece rattan set in the far corner and a large hot tub, which rested on its side next to the garage wall. Barton felt Russo's eyes on him.

After a few seconds, Russo cleared his throat.

'I'm just about to refill my hot tub. I had some friends over and there was a spillage. It's the weather for it. Now, is there anything else you want from me?'

Barton's eyes widened. Although grief affected people in different ways, his manner was unusually cold.

'What was her surname?' he asked.

'Craven. Can I ask a question?'

'Sure.'

'How did you get my name?'

Barton paused for a moment. 'We had a few lines of inquiry. Looks as though we were right to come here. We'd like you to identify the body.'

Russo looked at his fingernails as he thought.

'I'd rather not be involved if you don't mind.'

'Really, why not?'

Russo looked up and held fleeting eye contact as he spoke.

'We split up a month ago. We had a lot less than a year together, so she isn't really anything to do with me. I don't particularly want to see her burnt remains, or anyone else's for that matter.'

'I understand, but it would help us, and it means we could notify her relatives as soon as possible. Perhaps consider it a last kindness,' replied Barton with a small smile.

'No, thanks. Sounds like it's a job for a relative, I would have said. The relationship didn't end well, but I'm sure one of her friends would help.'

Barton took out his notepad.

'Fair enough. Could you give me the names, numbers, and addresses of her family and friends?'

'Sorry, I don't know any of them. She said her brother was in New Zealand.' Russo clicked his fingers. 'Neil! She mentioned he was in the capital but wasn't sure what it was called, so probably Wellington. I think she hoped to visit one day, because they'd both had a tough upbringing. They weren't close. I got the impression that Neil wanted to get as far away from this country as possible. I never met any other friends of hers. She was a bit of a fuck-up. Pretty, but damaged.'

'Date of birth?'

Russo squinted.

'When was the FA Cup Final last year?'

'I don't know, mid-May?'

'Whenever that was. That's when I first bumped into her in the Solstice in town. We were watching the football, and she came in for a drink to celebrate her birthday with her friend, Sasha. They were pissed as newts, but they were both stunning.'

Barton was about to ask if he was with Garth Henson, but that would give the game away. His brain scrambled for a moment before he responded.

'Who were you with?'

'Just a mate. Can't remember which one. He cleared off with Sasha, and crazy times commenced.' He winked at Barton.

'Did you split up because of her behaviour?'

'In a way. To be honest, I like my birds a bit fruity, but she was too out of control, even for me.'

'Drink or drugs?'

'It's probably easier if I start with what she didn't do. Now, gentlemen, sorry to seem heartless, but I have a train to catch. I've already missed my reserved seat and might have to sit in economy now.'

Russo stood and walked to the door. He beckoned for them to follow. Barton rose slowly and wandered over to Russo. He looked down at him.

'I agree. That is heartless. Would you rather answer my questions at the station?'

'No, of course not. But we'd split up.' He frowned. 'Okay, I'll give you all I know. She lived in Greenham when I met her, off Bretton Gate, but she practically moved in here for a few months. It got too much, so we separated. She wasn't happy, but what could she do? Jess pestered me for a bit. I have a place in Docklands where I often stay, so I kept out of her way. It's a damn shame, but I haven't anything more to tell you.'

Zander came over.

'Did she have any enemies?'

Russo avoided his gaze and stepped backwards to the front door.

'No, she was just a lonely girl, who was a complete mess. We had some fun. I didn't really know her well.'

When they were outside, Russo locked the door again.

'May I go?'

'Can we have your number?' asked Barton.

Russo grudgingly gave it and when Barton nodded at him to leave, he scuttled up the road sharpish.

'Nice guy,' said Zander.

'Cracking,' replied Barton.

People never failed to amaze him, but it didn't make them guilty of murder.

32

DI BARTON

Barton considered Russo's behaviour, which, although dismissive, was on the edge of normal. Barton returned to the pool car and grabbed the radio to call Control.

'Hi, DI Barton here. Can I have a voter's check for ninety-eight Marchmont, and check the PNC for anything interesting, please?'

While they waited, Barton went back through the conversation in his head. He supposed there was no reason for Russo to be involved further if he didn't want to be. Besides, they knew where Russo lived if they wanted to get hold of him. His house wasn't anywhere he could leave at the drop of a hat, and it would be no effort to find his place in London.

Control confirmed that Russo was the only person registered to the Marchmont address and there was nothing else of interest.

'Okay, can you check for a Jessica Craven, please? Possible address, Greenham, Bretton. Date of birth middle of May, about 1995.'

Zander started the engine, but didn't pull away. He stared at the grand houses.

'This is turning into an onion case.'

'I agree,' said Barton. 'Each layer being more bizarre than the last. There have been too many unusual responses, Russo's included. I bet we get to the address where Jessica lived and find ourselves with another mystery.'

'Yes, and our weekend is vanishing without us having solved anything.'

Zander's phone beeped. His face fell when he read whatever the message was.

'Bollocks.'

Barton groaned. 'I'm not sure I want to know.'

'I've just got the heave-ho from Pigs.'

'Dumped? How do you feel?'

'Gutted, but a bit relieved.'

'Perhaps that's your answer,' replied Barton.

Control came back on the line. Barton took out a pen and wrote down the address and the rest of the details. He tutted after he put down the phone.

'She's got previous. A couple of drunk and disorderly offences from her late teens and a possession of class A, namely heroin, from a few years ago. No jail time, and the fines were tiny, which would indicate that she was unemployed and possibly even homeless.'

Zander nodded. Magistrates' court fines were based on your earnings. He put the car into gear and pulled away.

'Let's sum up, then,' he said. 'Jessica dates Russo, moves in, quits her bedsit to do so, then he lobs her out, leaving her homeless and skint. There's a substance history. The night she dies, it's cold, she's withdrawing or high, she heads to Henson's for a chance to stay somewhere warm for the night. He refuses and, with no other option, she steals a bottle of whisky from the shop, perhaps not for the first time, then clambers in the skip to keep out of the wind, where she passes out.'

'Then someone sets fire to it and she dies.'

'Yep. It's all we've got, and it seems reasonable.'

Barton couldn't help shaking his head. 'That sounds plausible, but why have there been inconsistencies from nearly everyone we've interviewed, apart from Russo, who should feel guilty and didn't? Not only that, but why was Russo, a city slicker, dating someone like Jessica, who appears to have come from the wrong side of the tracks?'

'He said he prefers them a bit lively, and he said she was pretty.'

Barton still didn't like it.

'Maybe a resident at her old address will know something, or perhaps she had managed to move back in. Her provisional driving licence is registered to Greenham, even though she isn't on the council's register. That address rings a bell. Isn't three-nine-eight Greenham one of those big blocks of flats full of bedsits with shared kitchens where they put people who've been homeless as a step off the streets?'

'I can't remember, but it makes sense if Jessica was staying there. It still doesn't help us with finding out why the fire was started though.'

'Perhaps we never will find out why. It doesn't have to be a crime. It could have been a discarded cigarette and a dreadful run of events.'

Even though he was the one who said it, Barton thought in his gut it was unlikely.

* * *

They pulled into Greenham. The area had a bit of a reputation in the past, but it had improved over the last decade. He remembered a house fire there many years ago, but it had been caused by a chip pan. Barton tried to dredge his memory to see if there was perhaps anything dodgy about it, but it was too long ago.

They stopped outside the three-storey building. A sign on the wall said it was managed by a local housing association, which was good to learn because it confirmed Barton's recollection of the place. The front door had reinforced glass and was locked. Barton rang the buzzer for flat C, but if it worked still, there was no reply. They waited ten minutes, which they spent arguing over who should walk down the path to see if the shop that used to be around the corner still existed. There was an increase in both temperature and humidity as the day went on and both men removed their ties and jackets.

Finally, two women arrived at the property but one of them took a glance at the two detectives and was off on her toes before Zander and Barton could open their mouths. The other appeared too stoned to contemplate running.

'I'm clean,' she slurred.

Barton's nose wrinkled as she passed by, suggesting she was lying on many levels. She rooted around in her coat pockets next to the door.

'We're looking for a young woman called Jessica,' he said. 'I think she was in flat C.'

The girl looked at them, then wiped snot across her face with her sleeve in the same way his youngest son did. Her eyes cleared slightly. She didn't appear much more than sixteen, despite the husky, dry voice.

'I'm in D. I moved in a year ago. The person next door left around the same time. Her stuff was bagged up under the stairs, but it was junk, you know, nothing much. It had Craven written on it, so maybe that was her surname, or something.' She sniffed loudly. 'Don't suppose you got any food. You look like the type to have some with you.'

Zander snorted next to him, which startled the girl.

'Sorry, I didn't mean to be rude. I'm hungry.'

'Yeah,' said Barton. 'Dope will do that to you. What about a woman called Sasha?'

'That might be the girl from B. She disappeared a bit after that. She left a load of stuff too. It's all gone now. The folks who run the place took it away. Probably bin it. Women here don't have much. It can all be left behind, so they often just chip. There's always somewhere better than here. You know, down the road.'

If Barton hadn't seen the words falling out of her mouth, he could have imagined them coming out of an old timer's toothless maw, sitting on a porch, having long accepted his fate.

'Okay, thanks for your help,' said Barton.

Zander's hand came forward, and he slipped a brown note into the pocket of the girl's coat. Barton and Zander walked away, leaving the girl blinking in the bright sunlight.

'You need to stop doing that,' said Barton.

'Yeah, yeah. I hear you. People will think we're soft. I would never have contemplated it years ago, but after my son died, I sometimes have this strong urge to help a little. Last time, eh?'

Both men were smiling as they got back in the car.

33

DI BARTON

Zander drove out of Greenham and onto Bretton Gate, towards the police station.

'Home, Jeeves?' asked Zander.

Barton looked at his watch. It was nearly two p.m. His quiet weekend with the family was rapidly diminishing. Soon it would be gone, never to be returned. He pushed those thoughts away. This was the life he had chosen.

'No, let's go to the housing association. Their head office is only in Woodston. They're a big organisation, looking after thousands of homes, so they're bound to have at least a skeleton crew at work on a Sunday. We could get more joy today if it's just one bored person sitting around without any managers about.'

'What are you hoping for?'

'I'm hoping that this Sasha hasn't vanished as well, or we might have something else to worry about.'

Zander's face fell as he considered the implications of that.

'She left her things,' he said. 'Would she have bothered leaving a forwarding address?'

'She might have done. People like them often leave stuff behind.

The lovely young girl we just spoke to there told us that it was just rubbish. Obviously, back then, when she had a quiet moment, she must have kindly looked through the bag to make sure there was nothing important left behind.'

'Very decent of her.'

The two men laughed together.

'But,' continued Barton, 'further down the line, people like this Sasha and Jess realise they need a reference, or they might want to get in touch with people they met there. It's worth a shot. Knowing Jessica's name and date of birth isn't going to be any good if we can't find out anything about her. If she has no family and few friends, this Sasha will be our best chance.'

'Fair enough, but I'm starving.'

'That's okay, I know a nice little place that sells a wide range of tasty snacks and beverages.'

Five minutes later, Barton pulled into the Esso service station on Oundle Road. Zander filled the car up while Barton perused the aisles. He returned with two large sausage rolls and two tins of full fat Coke. Zander looked at it mournfully.

'No fruit?'

'None that I could see,' said Barton shiftily.

'You do realise, I'll be able to sue you later when I die an early death.'

'Your family will be able to sue me.'

'Right.'

Zander started the car and they continued to Woodston Business Centre. The administration office seemed closed, but Barton spotted a young man tapping away on a computer. Barton knocked on the window. The lad rose from his seat and strolled to the window where he mouthed 'Come back tomorrow' at them.

Barton pressed his warrant against the glass and mouthed 'Open the door' in reply.

A few moments later, the door opened. Up close, Barton realised the kid was wearing Crocs and swimming shorts, combined with a running top. A 'K' had been shaved into the side of his crew cut.

'We aren't open at the weekends,' said the lad as Barton and Zander walked past him.

'What's your name, son?' asked Zander.

'Kenny.'

Barton explained what they were after, trying to tempt Kenny to check his records. Unfortunately for them, Kenny was on the ball.

'Data protection prevents me from giving out personal information, unless of course you have authority from the courts.'

Barton's long day was getting to him.

'I'm not asking you to give me the specifics, just let me know whether you have anything on record.'

'What's the difference?' asked Kenny.

'Quite a bit,' said Zander slowly, 'if you want to stay healthy.'

Barton gave Zander a look, but his veiled threat did the trick.

'Okay, okay, I'll see if we have a mobile number for Sasha. If we do, I'll ring her and if she picks up, I'll explain that two nice policemen are here who would like to speak to her.'

Kenny went back to his computer and after a moment picked up the phone, cocked an eye at Zander, then dialled a number. Barton smiled. He liked Kenny. The call was answered, and Kenny did as he'd promised. Barton watched him as he wrote down an address.

'Okay,' said Kenny, putting the phone down. 'Sasha only lives over the road in one of the flats on the edge of Botolph Green. She's happy to chat to you because she's been trying to reach this Jessica.'

'And she's okay for us to go over now?' asked Zander.

'Yes,' said Kenny, pushing the address over to Barton, but looking at Zander. 'I didn't mention how impolite you've been.'

Barton had breathed enough car air, so, after leaving the office, the two detectives grabbed their laptop bags and walked, but he was regretting it before they were halfway there.

'This day is turning into purgatory. A never-ending wild goose chase in punishing conditions.'

'I know,' replied Zander. 'It feels like my clothes are steadily shrinking. I'm pretty sure my voice has already gone up one octave.'

They reached the flats and looked around. It was a far cry from Greenham. Had Sasha won the lottery?

Barton pressed the bell for her flat, and the door buzzed a few seconds later so Zander pushed the door open. The stairwell smelled of fresh paint as opposed to the usual damp and mould, or worse. They found their way up to number six on the second floor and the girl who opened it could have stepped out of the centre pages of a lifestyle magazine.

'Sasha Yates?' asked Barton with a raised eyebrow.

'No prizes for guessing who you are. Come on in.'

She beckoned them in with a grin and a swirl of her floral dress as she turned. Inside was pleasantly decorated and simply furnished. The flat was tiny and open plan, but with the curtains gently billowing in the light breeze, it felt modern and light. Barton introduced Zander and himself, then explained what had happened. Barton kept the details of the skip fire brief, but even so two big tears rolled down Sasha's cheeks at the news of Jessica's demise.

'And it's definitely her?'

'Yes, well, we're ninety-nine per cent sure anyway because she had a tooth implant as well as a tattoo on her shoulder, which was quite unique.'

Sasha focused for a moment.

'Really? Was it her front tooth?'

Barton nodded.

'That must have been new, because it was going brown when I knew her.'

'Right, we think it was recent.'

'Jessica was skint, though. I had a quote for one of mine ages back and it was thousands. I'm surprised she had the money.'

Barton instantly suspected that Russo paid for it, but he decided not to mention him.

'And the tattoo?' he asked.

'Was it a lark?'

Barton nodded. Sasha's chin wobbled, but she rapidly pulled herself together as though she'd been expecting bad news.

'Can you remember the last time you saw her?'

Sasha got up with a quizzical expression, then wandered towards the kitchen. She opened the fridge, returned and threw them both a bottle of water, which, judging by their battered condition, looked as if they were refills.

'I'm not sure but it was around six months ago though. We both had a bad run of things. Jessica had a very similar history to mine. We'd both gone to London to work for modelling agencies but the business is so competitive and we're average builds, so we struggled against the thin, leggy types. I lived on blueberries and rice cakes for months, but every now and again I'd blow out and have a Big Mac. I'd feel so guilty afterwards.'

'John's very much the same,' said Zander with a straight face.

Sasha lit up with a huge smile. She tossed her hair, and it instantly reminded Barton of Julia Roberts in *Pretty Woman*. Modelling would have come naturally to her.

'Yeah, so I ran out of money. I ended up living with a boyfriend, who treated me like shit. I had to leave in a rush and the council put me in that place at Greenham.'

'Where you met Jessica?' asked Zander.

'Yes, she was lovely, so funny, but in a right mess.'

'Drugs?'

Sasha looked from one to the other.

'Will I get her or me in any trouble?'

'No, we're just after her background.'

'Yes, she struggled like I did. Nearly all the models took coke, because it's everywhere and it dulls your appetite. It's kind of fun, too, at the beginning. Jessica liked it too much, and she started on other stuff. Cocaine's expensive. Heroin isn't. Her tooth started to go brown, and she looked like shit, so she got binned by the agency and ended up back in Peterborough as well.'

'Is this where she grew up?'

'I don't believe so, but she rarely talked about her childhood. She always joked that she was an orphan. Peterborough was where the train staff chucked her off because she didn't have a ticket. She was tough, though. I dread to think what she did for her habit. Anyway, there's a homeless street patrol in this city and they got her a room at Greenham. To cut a long story short, we hung out.'

'Was she still using?'

'A bit, I think. We were hoping to get ourselves back on our feet, but neither of us had much work experience, except modelling. It's hard to explain how we felt. When you're down and out like that, it's like waking up each morning at the bottom of a well. You can't get out by yourself, which is terrible if no one knows you're down there.'

'So living at Greenham was a chance to get started again.'

'Yes, it was good to have a safe place. Jessica was thinking about doing escorting, but I was trying to persuade her not to. I know it tends not to stay at escorting for long, and the lifestyle churns you up, and that's without considering the danger. She was desperate to get her tooth fixed and couldn't afford it. She was still stunning, but it affected her confidence.'

'Then you met Stefan Russo,' said Barton.

'Yeah! How did you hear about that wanker? Is he involved in all this?'

'That's what we're trying to find out. What can you tell us about him?'

'Well, I only met him once properly, and he picked her up a few other times in his flash sports car.'

'You first met him in the Solstice,' stated Barton.

'Yes, how do you know that? I'd got a lucky break. A commercial I did for a national retail park got repeated. They put it on TV. Out of the blue, I was sent a cheque for three grand. Me and Jessica raced out to celebrate with a day of drinking. It was her birthday as well, and we ended up in the Solstice. It was packed with blokes watching the football, but these older men kept staring at us. One of them wandered over, Stefan, and asked if we'd like to join them. He bought us drinks, then champagne. We got steaming, then he gave us a wrap of coke each. We couldn't believe our luck and finished up staying till chucking-out time.'

The hairs popped up on Barton's neck.

'Russo gave you the coke?'

'Yeah, he had loads. Then he invited us both to his place.'

'Wait, so all four of you went back. You, Jessica, Russo and his mate?'

'That's right.'

'Can you remember his friend's name, or what he looked like?' asked Zander.

'Of course. Garth was well fit.'

34

DI BARTON

Barton smiled as his luck turned. No wonder Henson was nervous.

'Was it Garth Henson?'

'Yes, that's it. He gave Jessica his card to get some drinks in. She read it and thought it said Gavin Henson, like the rugby player. To be honest, he was a bit quiet, but he was probably fitter than a rugby player. He could have been a model himself.'

'And he went back with you all as well.'

'Yes. Stefan's place was massive.'

'Did Henson take drugs?'

'No, he wasn't even drinking. Garth seemed quite nice. I liked him, but Stefan was a knobhead. He'd just filled his huge hot tub up and wanted everyone to jump in, even though we didn't have swimming costumes. Stefan creeped us out by saying he had spares. Anyway, being models means you don't embarrass easily, so we got in with just our knickers on.'

'Then what happened?'

'Do you know what? I don't have a clue. I woke up alone at midday in a spare room. Garth had disappeared. Jessica and Stefan were naked on the sofa together, passed out. And I felt like shit. I just wanted to get out of there, so I sneaked out and left. Before I vanished, I poured half a bottle of red wine into his hot tub. I couldn't get out of bed for two days afterwards, which was disturbing, because I'm used to partying.'

'What did Jessica say when you saw her next?' asked Barton.

'Honestly it was a bit strange because I hardly spoke to her again. She came back a couple of times for a night or two, but stayed in her room. Then he'd pick her up and I wouldn't see her for weeks. I thought they were loved up so it was fair enough, I suppose, but he reminded me of all the shady characters in the modelling business. Jessica reckoned he was great because he gave her a credit card to use, but I bet he did that to control her. They basically just fuck you for a while, show you off, then dump you. I could see what was going to happen. She looked as though she was back on the powder big time, too. The weight she'd gained at Greenham dropped off her like mad.'

'You don't know when she left Greenham?'

'No. That night at Stefan's house freaked me out. It was a total blank and really scared me. That money from the advert came at the right time. I managed to find a part-time job at a gym cleaning and helping out, and had enough cash for a deposit on this place. I was considering modelling again and got in touch with my old boss. He was planning on starting up this online make-up blog, where people can pay for private tuition. He'd forgotten about me, but remembered my lips when I rang and thought I'd be perfect.'

'And it's going well, I see,' said Barton with a smile.

'You know, I feel so lucky, with all that's happening in the world. And yes, it's going great. We even need more models and tutors because it's really taking off, and I told my boss that Jessica would be ideal.'

Barton considered that for a moment.

'Wouldn't she have been a bit of a liability?'

'Maybe, but I wanted to give her a chance. When I first went to Greenham, I was at rock bottom. She picked me up. I don't know where I'd have been without her. It's a shame that she'll never get the opportunity. She was always too trusting and kind, and nearly everyone took advantage of that.'

'Mostly men?' asked Zander.

'Everyone. She had such a good heart. I tended to keep clear of most of the people at Greenham. Jess was always helping them with their benefits, writing letters to family for them, letting them use her phone, or borrow toiletries. They all ripped her off at some point, but she never gave up on them. She said they'd had tough lives and someone had to start trusting them for them to change.'

Barton suspected Jess could have done great things with a different start to life.

'Do you think Stefan or Garth might have hurt her in any way?' he asked.

Sasha nibbled her finger while she thought. Barton considered what he'd say if his daughter, Layla, said she planned to go to London and model in a few years' time as these girls had. The water bottle crinkled in his grip.

'No, I never saw Garth again, but he didn't seem the type to hurt anyone. At times, he looked kind of scared of Stefan, who was clearly the one in charge. I would have said no about Stefan, but when I got home that afternoon and took a shower, I found something odd.'

Sasha looked upset as she recalled the memory.

'Go on,' said Barton.

'I found his business card in my purse. I don't remember putting it in there. On the back he'd written "call me".'

35

DI BARTON

Barton couldn't say he was too shocked after what he'd heard about Russo.

'Do you think he wanted you instead of Jess?'

'I'm not sure. He was all over her like she was the finest girl in the world and I didn't actually talk to him that much. The rest of the night was a blur.'

'Can you remember how it ended?'

'No. We did way, way too much coke. So much that I felt low enough to be suicidal. I stayed under the sheets once I got back and swore never to be in that position again. Do you reckon he deliberately gave us too much?'

'It's hard to say. If you were out of it, he could have done anything to you,' said Zander.

'Gross. Do you think he killed Jessica?'

'We don't have any evidence to suggest that. She ended up homeless though.'

'I hope he fries in hell for it. He put her in that skip one way or another.'

Sasha told them she had a one-to-one session with a client at four. She agreed to have a thorough think about everything she knew and would visit the station the next day at five to complete a full statement.

Barton wished her the best and said he'd be in touch if he didn't see her tomorrow. They stepped out of the flats and trudged towards the car. Zander and he looked fondly over at the beer garden of The Botolph, but it was empty. The pub still hadn't reopened since the lockdown was partially lifted. They had another trip to make, anyway.

'Back to Welland, then,' said Barton. 'Mr Henson's stock has dropped in value.'

'Yeah, you know what, he was pretty furtive. Maybe he was high when we spoke to him. He probably had a big bag of it in the drawer next to his sofa.'

'Hmm,' mused Barton. 'We should have asked him what his job was. I didn't ask Russo what he did either.'

'Judging by their cars, both have money to burn.'

'Yes, although Henson didn't seem as happy with his wealthy life as Russo did. Some people with money let it go to their heads and somehow still manage to spend too much.'

'Maybe he's an investment banker and burning out or something similar.'

Zander grimaced.

'That would explain the stressed behaviour, the high-tech equipment and the nice cars, but if he earns a wedge, why is he living there? Maybe Henson works in London with Russo? Even if he wasn't loaded, a guy like Henson seems more likely to have a flat within walking distance to the station for trains to London, not one over in Welland.'

'Whatever. He's got some explaining to do, as has Stefan Russo.'

'It looked as if Russo's not going to be back until late, if at all. We could ring him, but let's wait until we hear what Henson has to say first. If we're lucky, he might drop Russo in it.'

Both men squinted as the sun began to dip. Barton just wanted to go home and sit in the garden with an ice cream before the daylight vanished completely. They drove in silence and pulled up outside Henson's house.

'I'm going home after this call. I'll get Strange to take Sasha's statement tomorrow with Pigs. Hang on, I'll check they're both working,' said Barton

Barton rang the detectives' office and after a few rings, DC Pignatiello picked up.

'Hi, Nicola, are you in tomorrow?'

'Yes, I am.'

'Can you ask if Kelly is?'

'Sure, give me a mo.'

There was a pause, during which Zander frowned at Barton. Pigs came back on the phone.

'Yes, she's in. Between us we've devised a new system for filing, so we'll let everyone know about that tomorrow. And, sir, call me Pigs, everyone does.'

Barton smiled, but didn't reply. He was beginning to feel awkward using nicknames in this day and age. It was a sign of the times. Some people were easily offended even if it wasn't really anything to do with them. Nicola and her nickname Pigs would probably be a legend in thirty years' time, where people quaked at being in front of her.

Barton explained he'd like Strange and Pigs to do the interview with Sasha and asked them to complete the necessary paperwork to urgently connect with Wellington Police and locate Jess's brother. Zander growled next to him as soon as Barton took the handset from his ear after finishing the call.

'I didn't realise that they were both in today.'

'The filing cabinet needed sorting again. It's a good way to learn, so Strange was taking Pigs through it this afternoon.'

'You don't reckon they've been discussing me, do you? Funny how I got dumped out of the blue today.'

'Women, talk? No, very unlikely.'

'That makes it your fault that I've been ditched.'

Barton broke into song.

'I'm only human, after all. Don't put the blame on me.'

Zander was shaking his head as the sound of a motorbike came into range. It idled behind their parked car, then raced past and turned around in the cul-de-sac. The rider was small, casually dressed in denim and leather. It could have been a man or a woman because the black helmet with a tinted visor obscured the driver's face.

The rider looked to the left at the row of houses, then right directly at them. Before either Barton or Zander had a chance to comment, the motorbike accelerated hard past their car and raced out of sight. Barton exited the vehicle and watched it leave in a trail of fumes. He would have taken the number plate but it didn't have one.

Barton and Zander didn't have to say anything. They both remembered Rob saying he'd seen a motorbike dawdling. Zander rang Control and reported the incident. Riding without number plates was illegal, but that wasn't what they wanted to talk to the rider about.

There was little point in turning around because a bike like that would be long gone. Control would ask Traffic to track it down. Some of the more feral kids in the city didn't care if they were caught without a plate or insurance. Yet it was another layer to the nervous behaviour of some of the people around this street.

Barton checked the parked cars on the drives. They were all present. The young lad, Rob, came out of number two, gave them a brief wave, then jogged towards the wall and dragged himself over it.

Barton and Zander walked towards number three and knocked on Henson's door. After a minute of waiting and no sign of movement, they gave the door one last thump. Stepping away, the detectives stared at the houses. All of them had windows open upstairs. Curtains swayed in the very slight breeze, giving them the impression that they were being spied upon. Maybe they were.

Back in the vehicle, Zander exhaled deeply.

'We don't have enough for a search warrant?' he asked.

'Definitely not, nor surveillance. I wouldn't mind a look at his bank records though. Hopefully Jess's brother won't be hard to trace. I'm pretty sure the New Zealand Police would be able to find him.'

Zander frowned as he thought.

'Russo?'

'I don't want him to know we're suspicious just yet. I'd like to watch his face when we pin some of this on him. Let's come back here tomorrow night after eight, then see Russo after. Give them both a chance to get home from London if that's where they are. Although, I wouldn't be surprised if both end up being evasive.'

'Okay. I can't believe after all this we still don't have anything solid.'

'My head's spinning. Let's call it a day. We can escalate all of this tomorrow. Let's get CCTV for the roads around here for the nights of the fires, and maybe the day before. Perhaps Russo's vehicle will turn up.'

They drove back, chatting about politics and sport with both men wanting a break from work matters before they got home. Barton heaved himself out of the car outside his house and wandered in, feeling like Beau Geste returning from a difficult mission. He found Holly tidying the kitchen. Sometimes she pulled his leg around missing out on family life, but he knew she would see the weekend had drained him.

Barton picked up the tub of Neapolitan ice cream, which was on the table. He almost sobbed, knowing it had to be empty.

'Don't suppose there's another one of these?'

'No, all gone.'

Barton pouted.

'We've saved a Magnum for you, though.'

Barton took his ice cream and wandered out the back. He sat on a low garden wall and let the weakening sun bathe him. A couple of bottles of beer sounded appealing, but he'd resist. Tomorrow would be a long day. The fire investigator's words echoed around in his mind as he bit through the chocolate coating with a crunch.

'If you don't catch them soon, they may well expose themselves by doing something verging on the insane. I wouldn't be surprised if when that happens, more people die. Nothing kills the innocent like fire.'

36

THE FIRE KILLER

I stand behind the curtains for a long time after the officers have gone. I'm kind of contemplating what's next, but I'm also thinking of what's past. I can't help thinking most of the good stuff in my life is likely to have been in my past. I want new experiences.

There was a film on the other day with such a brutal war scene. Legs, arms and heads were being lopped off by the heroes, but I'd seen it all before. I prayed the bloody goblins would win for a change. I wanted the trolls to bite the fucking heads off the humans and stamp their bones to dust. I want to say wow again.

I can't cope with much more of this boredom, but what do I do, and who to? Ideas and plots flash through my mind. Some are appealing, others horrifying. Some are reckless. Do I care?

The walls of this small house move inwards, just as the investigation will close in on me.

Alcohol would normally numb my buzzing brain, but there's nothing in the fridge. I don't want to wake up tomorrow not feeling straight anyway. Tough decisions are ahead, and at least one more release.

I walk to the back door, slip on some old trainers, then step outside. I stand there until the sun begins to set, perhaps not just on the day. There are a few wisps of cloud and an auburn hue against the roofs of the houses where the red globe descends behind them.

There's a route I take around this estate, which is kept mostly lit. Pointless lives are lived in these streets, but it's like nobody can see it. I wander past the now-boarded-up shop and wonder if that too is a sign. I suppose it was my fault.

Around the corner, Mavis is leaning against her front gate again, smoking as usual. I cross over to say hello. She's a strange fish. I don't think she said anything to me for years. It's only now, as dementia takes hold in her nineties, that she smiles and sometimes waves. I feel so young when we chat. A woman arrives behind her, who looks like how Mavis probably looked before the sands of time emptied.

'Evening, Mavis,' I say.

She doesn't look at me, but stares up at what must be her daughter, as though looking for permission. The younger woman points inside the house and Mavis wanders back down her path. I marvel at the line of newspapers and magazines that I can spy piled in her hallway. Mavis is a hoarder.

'Do you know my mum?' asks the younger lady.

'Not that well. We say hi if we see each other.'

'I'm Beth Doran, her daughter. My partner and I are taking her to live with us in London. She can't cope. Keeps leaving the fire and the oven on, and she's started to wander.'

'When's she's going?' I ask.

'Tonight. I've come to pick her up.'

'Good luck. I'll miss her friendly face.'

'I'm sorry to intrude, but may I ask a favour?'

'Sure.'

'Can I give you my card? The house is a wreck inside and out, and my mum has misplaced the back door keys. I'll secure it properly next weekend. If you see anything unusual this week, would you be able to ring me?'

'There won't be any valuables in there?'

'No, we've packed anything of value in her suitcase.' The woman smiles, blinking rapidly to save her mascara. 'It's sad when your life can go into a suitcase.'

Mavis appears again, tugging on her daughter's sleeve like a child.

'Is my programme on?' she says. 'I always watch my programme.'

'Of course,' I say to Beth. 'I'll let you know.'

'Thank you,' says Beth.

I watch her take Mavis's hand and guide her into the house.

'Come on,' she says. 'I'll put the TV on for you.'

'You aren't leaving, are you?' says Mavis.

'You and me are going on holiday.'

They disappear back into the house. Continuing my walk, I stare towards the darkening horizon where the fireball sun will soon vanish. There's a warm amber glow to the sky. It's going to be flaming hot tomorrow.

37

DI BARTON

Barton arrived in the office early on Monday morning and got stuck into his work. He had received an email from Wellington Police, so rang the number. After being bounced around a bit because it was after hours in New Zealand, he was finally passed through to a Sergeant Tavo and Barton confirmed what had happened and who he wanted to contact.

'Your case is a suspicious death, then?' said Tavo.

'At this point, we really don't know. It might be a terrible accident.'

'And this brother, Neil, is the only relative you're aware of?'

'Yes, she doesn't seem to have kept in touch with anyone else, but we know she had the odd interaction with Neil.'

'Okay, bro. Hold the line.'

Barton smiled at the Kiwi accent. He was pondering whether it was still expensive to ring down under when Tavo returned.

'We've got an address here in the city for him. We're pretty crammed in the centre, mate. In fact, he's not far away. Do you know if they were close?'

'No, the friend said they weren't, but I'd still rather he didn't hear about his sister's death over the phone.'

'I've got your email addy and work telephone number. I'll get one of the liaison officers to knock on his door. Tough call, but you're right, it's always better face to face. It's evening here but we have a guy on call seeing as it sounds urgent. We'll let Mr Craven know to ring you for further details if we can get hold of him. Obviously he might not want a bar of it. Will you be available over the next few hours?'

'Yes, I'll give you my mobile.'

'Sweet. I'll email when it's done. I'm on nights this week, so use me as your contact, although I might need to pass this on if there are further developments. All the best.'

'Thanks. And of course, when the investigation is over, we'll obviously inform the brother. I'll also email you at the same time, but at this point I'm not sure where this investigation is going to end up.'

'No worries. I understand.'

Barton finished the call and leaned back in his chair feeling the lack of confidence in his closing comment. At the moment, they didn't have enough proof to look at Russo's bank account or his phone records. And with no clues, to solve this case, they were going to need someone to talk.

Barton smiled as he remembered a London cop drama that Holly was watching last week. A detective was sitting in a van, tapping away at a computer, pulling up a variety of individuals' call histories and credit-card statements. It was pure bullshit. There were rules to protect people's privacy. To obtain permission for that, he would need strong evidence that the person in question was involved in something that could lead to at least a five-year sentence. Even then there would be a paper trail as long as the Great Wall of China. Despite what script writers thought, unfortunately, he wasn't allowed to log in to his computer and check anything he liked willy-nilly while eating a cheese sandwich.

Still, Zander and he would talk to Russo and Henson tonight and if either proved elusive, Barton would suspect the worst.

It was nearly eleven a.m. when Barton's mobile rang. The screen said 'International', with the number withheld. He found an empty office and pressed answer.

'DI Barton speaking.'

'Hi, this is Neil Craven. I've just had a visit from the police to say that my sister has passed. They said I could ring this number for more information.'

'That's right. I'm sorry for your loss, and I apologise for having to do this over the phone.'

'That's okay. I understand. Even though I haven't seen her for years, it's still a shock. How did she die?'

Barton explained with as little detail as possible, saying that Jessica wouldn't have suffered. Neil was quiet after he'd finished talking.

'I can't say I'm too surprised that this is how her story ended. She was pretty crazy as a kid. There's five years difference between us, so we didn't have much of a relationship. I was about nine when she started staying out all night. She kind of grew up too fast.'

'Do you mind if I ask a few questions? I truly hope the fire was an accident, but some of the people she was involved with have weak stories about their relationship with your sister. I'd like to get to the bottom of it all.'

'Go ahead. I doubt the news will hit me for a while. I spoke to Jessica about six months ago. She was upbeat, saying that things were great, and her and her boyfriend would fly out and visit.'

'Did she mention his name?'

'Steven, I think. I didn't bother trying to remember names because she was up and down like a yo-yo. Each new relationship was fabulous to start with. Then they all went tits up. You know how some women are attracted to totally the wrong type of person for them. That was Jess.'

'And she'd been modelling in London?'

'Yes. She did a few decent shoots, but she wasn't as skinny as the other models. She'd get called fat at auditions, then go on mad diets. And as for boyfriends. Well, the main problem was she fell in love hard and would commit fully and then she'd get discarded and be left with nothing, including her self-esteem. After, she'd pull herself together and repeat the process. It was like she had a big sign on her forehead saying gullible. The drugs didn't help either.'

'Had she been using for years?'

'Her habit was nothing too bad, but it didn't help. The last communication I got from her was a text message saying she'd been dumped, again.'

'By this Steven?'

'Yes, we had some email tennis about it. She used to do promo work. You know, like those darts girls who walk the players in at the championships looking sexy. They used to stick her in a tight top and the drunk blokes would go wild, but all that kind of work dried up recently. It's funny. She always said she got paid *so* much for just wandering around in a short dress and high heels that she thought she was the one doing the exploiting.'

Barton recalled his earlier thoughts about the world changing, but kept quiet and the brother continued.

'Losing well-paid work wouldn't have helped. She wasn't great with money. Anyway, she was staying with this guy, Steven, but she had to leave town for a job for a few days. When she got back, he'd put her stuff outside. That was it. No note, no nothing.'

'Could his name have been Stefan?'

'Hang on, I'll check my text messages.'

Barton waited a minute before Neil returned.

'Yeah, Stefan, that's right. He's the one who lobbed her out.'

'Which left her homeless?'

'Yes, apparently he'd changed the locks.'

'Bastard,' said Barton without thinking.

'Yes, that was the word I used too. I told her to forget him, that she was fine on her own, or she could meet someone new, someone kind. I've sent money before but she never learns. She reckoned she was going to win him back.'

'I take it she didn't.'

'It doesn't look like it. Jessica was daft when it came to relationships. She glossed over how she hooked up with him.'

'Which was?' asked Barton.

'She met him in the pub on her birthday. But from what she told me, he was already living with another girl who he dumped without a second thought to be with Jess.'

'The same way he then dropped Jess when the time came. What a guy.'

'I know. If being a shitbag was a crime, I'd string him up myself.'

'What about your parents?'

'Our mum was one of those who sat around on Valium. Pretty useless, but she tried. Cancer took her not long before Jess moved out. Our father was a cold fish. He was some kind of biology researcher but I never really understood his job. After Mum died, he was rarely at home. I finished school, got the best-paying job I could, saved up, and got a visa to work over here. I wanted to get as far away as I could. It's like a different world and I love it. It feels as if I've left my old life behind.'

'Will you come back for the funeral?'

The line was quiet for a few seconds.

'No, I don't think so. The borders are closed and I'd struggle to get home. I assume you'll be looking for someone to pay for it.'

'The council will, there's no need for you to contribute. Look up public health funerals online. We can talk to your dad if you have his details. You might like to order a plaque or something to remember her or have the ashes sent over. Scatter them somewhere beautiful.'

Barton held the line while Neil quietly wept and Barton wiped a tear off his own cheek. Life was brutal at times. He was getting the feeling that this Jess had lived a hard existence, made harder by selfish men. Neil finally pulled himself together.

'No, my father passed a year ago. I only found out through Jess. I'm not certain how she knew. He gave all his money to Cancer Research before he died. I'm still not sure if that makes me happy or angry. Neither of us contributed to his funeral, either. He couldn't be bothered with us in life, so why should we bother with him in death?'

Barton couldn't argue with that.

'Thanks for your time, Neil. Have you got someone to be with?'

'Yes, thank you. Let me know if you find any of her possessions.'

'I will do. Take care.'

After Barton had finished his call, he opened the office door and called in Zander and Strange and filled them in on Jessica and her brother's background.

'Sounds as if she had it tough in life,' said Strange.

'Yes, poor girl, and it ended tough, too,' said Barton. 'When her friend Sasha comes in this evening at five to give her statement, Kelly, if there's anything new, can you please ring me before I pick Zander up at eight tonight?'

'No problem.'

'Zander, while I think about it, did you catch up with Traffic about that motorbike with no number plate?'

'Yup. They picked it up on CCTV on Fulbridge Road, but it vanished after that. There are thousands of houses in that area. Someone could have just driven it into a garage. A quick respray and it's a different bike. I wouldn't be surprised if it was teenagers messing around.'

'Okay, but that's a lot of unusual visitors around McBride and Henson's houses.'

'I agree. Malik visited the Chinese Sunday night but the manager obviously didn't want to get involved. Malik said the chow mein was good. Leicester spoke to the manager of the chemist, but he had little to add. She lived above the premises and has done for at least a decade. She also said there had been a significant number of small-scale fires over the last ten years.'

'Okay. Let's get the system updated and the paperwork cleared away. I've got a few meetings first thing this afternoon, then I'm going to go home early in preparation for this visit tonight from the rehoming shelter. I've already lost my weekend. Let's hope Henson and Russo spill some beans this evening to make it worthwhile.'

Strange smiled. 'Very exciting. Zander told me there's a new creature in town.'

'We'll feed Gizmo up. You know I'm all about charity,' said Barton. 'Taking a stray in should secure my place in heaven, whereas you two have plenty of work to do.'

The two sergeants left, grinning at each other, leaving Barton wondering if there was hope for their romance yet.

38

DI BARTON

Barton pootled home at six p.m., typically not having left work early as he'd hoped after all. Something had been toying with his subconscious since the afternoon meetings and he was just about to let himself in the house when the dots finally connected: the drug link. Sasha had told them that Russo had plenty of cocaine on him, so that could just mean he had a rich man's habit, but it was also possible he was dealing and that was where his money came from. He said he worked in the city, but Barton knew he'd lied to them already about Henson coming back to his place the night he met Jess so maybe that was a lie too.

That would also explain Henson's nervousness. Perhaps the two men were in it together. Barton hoped tonight would make everything a bit clearer. The other Major Crimes team tended to deal with any big drug investigations in the county, so he'd check with them in the morning.

Barton thought about Cox's warning about one of the Bates brothers being tracked to Peterborough. The motorbike could be a link to that angle. Drug couriers often delivered their products on scooters and motorbikes all over the city. Encrypted apps like

WhatsApp meant you could order drugs as easily as ordering a pizza. Even when the couriers were chased, they usually had escape routes planned and the vehicles and wares were discarded if the police got close. The ones they caught knew to say nothing and were mostly underage. Dealing like this wasn't easy to prevent when kids loved having the use of a motorbike and getting paid quadruple the money they'd earn from working at Subway.

Barton tried to remember what type of bike it had been. He wasn't knowledgeable about motorcycles, despite wanting one when he was seventeen. The problem was that, due to his size, when he'd had a test drive on a small one, he'd looked ridiculous. The bike he and Zander had seen was small too – it had looked lightweight and fast, but not particularly expensive.

The helmet covered the rider's face, but there was a sense of confidence from the way he or she held themselves. He didn't think it was a young teenager, but kids grew up quick these days, so who knew? Ernie Fowler's grandson had mentioned seeing a regular bike around that area as well.

He considered ringing the station to see if anyone was in to ask about the drugs angle, but it could wait until tomorrow morning. The door opened and Luke stood in front of him with his arms crossed.

'Evening, Luke,' said Barton. 'Can I come in?'

'My friend at school, Colin, said that detectives spend all their time sleeping in their cop cars and eating doughnuts. Is that true?'

'Pretty much,' said Barton.

'How many doughnuts have you had today?'

'Twenty-six.'

That seemed to impress Luke as he stepped aside to let his dad in. Layla, Lawrence, and Holly were sitting at the kitchen table.

'Ah ha!' said Holly. 'He's here. Sit down and chew your finger-nails with us.'

Barton had to admit that he felt illogically nervous. Their house was fine, but it seemed that Gizmo belonged to them already. If something went wrong at this late stage, they'd all be devastated.

At a quarter to seven, the doorbell rang. Luke raced to the door and came back with a short-haired elderly woman who had a small briefcase with her and a big grin on her face.

'Hi, everyone. I'm Lydia, and I bet you're all excited.'

'We are,' said Holly. 'Would you like a drink?'

'No, I'll get on if you don't mind.'

Lydia had a quick look in each room of their home. She checked the garden for anything that could hurt an animal or if there was a route for a dog to escape. There was neither, so she sat them all around the table. Barton and Holly had a sneaky smile at each other with the kids on their best behaviour.

'Now, Runty has had a tough start to life.'

'We want to call him Gizmo,' interrupted Luke.

'You can name him what you want, but give him time to learn he has a new name. Let me explain a little about what your new dog will be like. People think greyhounds need a lot of exercise, but they don't. Obviously, there are exceptions, but an hour's walk, or even half an hour with a fast run, will probably be plenty. After that, greyhounds love nothing more than dozing. Be careful with temperature, because they have very low body fat and a thin coat and skin, so they feel the cold and heat more than other dogs. There's a heap of information online for you to access.'

'You said he was abandoned?' asked Barton.

'Yes, we believe so. It's pretty common for this breed. He's quite nervous at the moment, and he isn't house-trained.'

'He'll fit in here a treat,' said Holly, giving Barton a sly glance.

'Will he sleep in my bed?' asked Luke.

Lydia smiled. 'Given half a chance. He's not very big for a greyhound, but he'll grow.'

'Why would anyone abandon a puppy?' asked Layla.

'He's fine as a pet, but greyhounds are often bred for a purpose such as coursing or racing. With his weak leg they wouldn't have bothered training him. He'd always have been too slow.'

'Sounds a bit like Lawrence,' said Layla with a mischievous grin. 'Perhaps we should send him to a rescue centre.'

'That's enough, Layla,' said Holly.

'That's okay, Mum. She's just in a foul mood because her boyfriend dumped her.'

Everyone froze, even the woman from the rescue centre. Layla leapt out of her seat.

'Twat!' she shrieked in Lawrence's face, then sprinted from the room.

Holly ran after her while Barton sat wide-eyed and confused. Lydia rose from the table.

'Splendid. Such a lovely age,' she said. 'Nothing I haven't seen before, so I'm delighted to say you've passed. From everything I've seen, any dog would be lucky to join your family, so all that remains is for you to come tomorrow and pick Gizmo up.'

'Result,' bellowed Luke.

'That's wonderful, Lydia,' said Barton. 'Are you sure you don't want a drink? I feel like one.'

She laughed. 'Dads are often the last to know. Sorry, but I've got another call.'

'I'll show you out,' said Barton.

He pumped her hand at the door as if he'd won on a gameshow, but was thinking of Layla when he returned to the kitchen table. Only Luke remained. Barton slumped in his chair, not having known his daughter had been dating. Luke stared at him, then shrugged.

'Yeah, she got dumped.'

Twenty minutes later, Holly remained upstairs talking to Layla, so Barton left the house without a chance to say goodbye to his wife, and walked to his car. As he drove to pick Zander up, he couldn't help feeling rueful. Then he smiled. Being a detective was a full-time job, but even if he'd been at home, he doubted his daughter would have been discussing her love life with him. Still, it was a reminder his children were getting older and their lives didn't pause just because he was busy.

Zander was pottering around in his front garden when Barton arrived, but they were soon racing around the parkway. Their first stop was Garth Henson's house. His car was still on the drive, but there was no answer at the door.

Barton wandered around to the rear of the property in case Henson was sitting in his garden and went through his back gate. Barton quickly noticed the back door was slightly open. He walked towards it, swung it wide with his elbow, and shouted through.

'Mr Henson! Police!'

But before he could go into the house, a mark on the patio caught Barton's eye, and when he crouched down, his heart dropped when he realised it was a splatter of blood.

39

DI BARTON

Barton raised a hand for Zander, who was following behind, to stand still, then pointed at the ground. Zander nodded. They both took a deep breath and stepped inside the house.

'Garth Henson!' shouted Zander. 'We're walking into the rear of your property.'

The men paused. There was the sound of subdued talking coming from the front of the house. They stepped into the lounge. Barton gestured to the right of the sofa, where a laptop had been knocked over. There was a cup on its side on the floor, with a big puddle of coffee around it.

'Doesn't look good,' whispered Zander.

Barton was staring at the coffee table, which had a credit card, a furled-up ten-pound note, and a smattering of white powder on it. He shook his head once, but the time for caution had passed. He strode towards the kitchen, making a loudhailer with his hands.

'Mr Henson, we're entering the kitchen. Shout out if you can't move. Let us know if you're upstairs.'

Barton put his hand on the door handle. It was times like this that he couldn't help thinking of American police. They must expect someone to be holding a gun every time they approached a door. Still, kitchens had knives, so he opened the door a crack, then gave it a shove while stepping back and crouching. A Boney M song began playing quietly on the radio in the empty room. Once they were sure there was no one downstairs, the two detectives went upstairs, but after a thorough search it was soon clear that the house was uninhabited.

Back downstairs, Barton crouched and touched the underneath of the coffee cup, nodding to confirm it was still warm. Barton felt a presence behind him and spun around. There was a tall figure standing in the rear doorway.

'Hey, man. Is everything cool?'

It was Clive McBride from next door. Barton recovered fast.

'Yes, why do you ask?'

'I was cleaning upstairs and heard a van pull up. I thought it was my Amazon delivery, so I glanced outside, but the two blokes in it came to Garth's. I didn't think any more of it, but a minute later, the van pulled off fast, you know, screeching, so I looked out the window again. They left in a real rush, man. And then I saw you guys turn up.'

'Okay, can you go out to the garden for a moment? And please don't touch anything.'

Barton and Zander followed him outside.

'Tell me about the people and the van. Describe them.'

'The van was just a regular Sprinter, white. Sorry, I know that's not very helpful.'

'And the men?'

'They both had peaked caps on and blue medical masks, which covered their faces, so I've no idea, but they were big. Not tall, but wide. Blue jeans and black bomber jacket on one, jeans and white T-shirt on the other.'

'As you say, that's not massively helpful,' said Barton.

McBride raised both eyebrows.

'Remember my shed.'

Barton twigged that it was the same description that McBride had given them of the man who'd wrecked his shed.

'How long ago was this?' asked Zander.

'Literally five minutes. It seemed weird, which is why I was still peering out the window when you dudes turned up.'

'Did you see your neighbour enter the van, or get taken to it?' asked Barton.

'No, I only saw it driving away. I got most of the reg number.'

Barton studied his face. Even though McBride spoke calmly, his eye movement was rapid.

'Can I give you some advice? If something like this happens again, mention the number-plate part immediately, okay. What was it?'

'HK19SUN or HK10SON, something like that. As I said, they left pretty sharpish.'

Zander already had his phone out.

'Control, this is DS Zander. We need an immediate BOLO for a white Sprinter van, number plate Hotel, Kilo, one, nine, Sierra, Uniform, November, or Hotel, Kilo, one, zero, Sierra, Oscar, November, or variation thereof. Run an owner search, please. Be advised, do not engage at this point. Send two patrol vehicles to our location on Fig Tree Lane.'

Barton just about made out the reply.

'ETA for patrol is one minute.'

Barton clicked his finger when he thought of where the motorbike was last seen and shouted so he was heard.

'The van may be heading to, or in the vicinity of, Fulbridge Road.'

Zander finished the call.

'I'm concerned for Mr Henson,' he said.

'Yes,' replied Barton. 'I'm betting that van was stolen recently.'

'That kind of muscle means it's a significant operation. Run-of-the-mill criminals aren't so organised and efficient. It seems Mr Henson has upset the wrong people.'

Barton realised McBride was still standing with them.

'You think it was the same man.'

McBride nodded.

'Could they be organised crime?'

'How would I know? He must have got his wires crossed.'

Barton studied McBride's face, but he sensed no deceit.

'What about Ceri? Does she have any disreputable friends?'

McBride was no actor.

'What is it?' asked Barton.

'She emailed me. Said she was keeping off the beaten track. She said she'd see me at Christmas.'

'And you have no way of knowing where she is?'

'Nope.'

Barton had to forget that line of enquiry and deal with what he had.

'Have you seen any strange or suspicious behaviour around here? Late night drop-offs, that sort of thing?'

'No, nothing. Garth's dead quiet. The street is chilled. There's no reason for anyone to come down here.'

Satisfied he'd got all he could out of him, Barton sent McBride back to his house. They spent the next hour setting up a crime scene with the uniforms who turned up. Strange and Pigs had also arrived. Zander must have called one or both because they were due to finish earlier so must have come from home. CSI were on their way. Barton was grumbling to himself about the lack of concrete facts. But that was this case all over. For all they knew, Henson could have nicked his chin shaving and gone for a ride with his mates. Zander's phone rang.

Zander answered and nodded grimly as he listened. He cut the call.

'Stolen vehicle?' asked Barton.

'Yes, from Walthamstow, reported this morning. ANPR cameras picked it up on the A1, so we knew it was in the area, just not exactly where.'

'Isn't Walthamstow in East London?'

'That's not the important news. They've found the van. It's in a field on Fulbridge Road.'

'Excellent.'

Zander shook his head.

'It's on fire.'

40

DI BARTON

Barton glanced at his watch. The process of coordinating multiple scenes out of office hours was a nightmare. The first constable to turn up at Henson's house said it had been a quiet night, so at least they had that to be thankful for. But Barton assumed that was all about to change if his suspicions were right – he felt horribly sure that when they put the van fire out, they would find a body inside. Barton racked his brains for anything he should do that was imperative now.

If this case was what he believed it was, then the public were at little risk. Barton's guess was that Henson was the local operator for someone big in the drugs world, probably based in London, and more than likely with the surname Bates. They'd probably uncovered a county line. Even though the gangs usually used teenagers, there was no upper age limit and Henson might well have been a small-time dealer and got taken over by a bigger organisation.

If Barton's theory proved right, this latest fire was a scary progression in the case. That motorcycle the other night could have been sent to check out the situation and if they had reported back to the person in charge that the police were outside Henson's property and had been sniffing around all day, that could have led to Henson being taken out. Dead men couldn't break under questioning. No wonder Henson had been nervous.

Barton remembered Stefan Russo. What was his part in this, if any? Sasha said that Henson seemed scared of Russo when they were out, and he was clearly the one in charge. Was it conceivable that Russo was part of a Peterborough operation? Barton had met ruthless gangsters before, and they often looked like everyday people, but Russo had already had a visit from Barton and Zander. Russo would have suspected that Henson was the one who named him, so he must have also known that he'd be the first person Barton would visit after he heard of Henson being on the wrong end of some bad luck.

Russo didn't strike him as reckless or stupid, although he could have ordered someone else to actually do the killing. Barton had a nasty thought. It was also possible that if Russo wasn't involved, then he might be the next to disappear. Without Russo, the chances of Barton and his team getting anywhere with this whole case would be tiny. He called Zander and Strange over.

'Zander, drive to the van fire. Assume control if necessary. Ring me as soon as the fire brigade make it safe and look inside. I've a bad feeling about this, and if I'm right you're going to find Henson's body. Go in Strange's car so I have the one we came in. And take Pigs. Strange, can you hold this scene for us while we try to work out what's going on?'

'Okay, where are you heading?'

'Russo's place. I'm hoping to find him at home for many reasons.'

Zander nodded to say he understood. Barton looked at Strange.

'Did Sasha come in this evening to provide a statement?'

'Yes, she was thorough and happy to help, but gave us nothing we didn't know already. She mentioned Russo was amazing to

Jessica to start with. He paid for everything. Jess didn't need to work. He let her use his car. The works. Sasha remembered the last time she spoke to Jess on the phone it sounded like Russo's enthusiasm had faded. Same old story. He got bored, and she probably got clingy, which would have hastened the end. Apparently, one of Russo's previous girlfriends turned up at the house when only Jess was there. She warned Jess that Russo had discarded her at the drop of a hat, and he still had her passport in his safe. That worried Jess.'

'I don't suppose Sasha knew the ex's name?'

'No, I did ask, but she couldn't remember if she'd been told or not. Otherwise, it was just general stuff. The other girl tried to encourage Jessica to leave Stefan because the same thing would happen to her, but Jess loved him, and she thought he loved her. The other girl might have been lying to get him back, I suppose. Sasha's ringing us tomorrow morning after double-checking the date she moved into the room at Greenham. I'll see if she's remembered the ex-girlfriend's name then. I'll read up on all the notes of the case so far again to see if there's anything else I should query or double check.'

'Good work, I'll chat to you afterwards.'

Barton left the scene and got in his car. This was getting really serious. Jess Craven was a known drug user so maybe she became involved with the drug dealing as well, in exchange for some free drugs. Perhaps they deposited her in a burning skip as punishment, or simply because she was a liability to the people at the top of the organisation.

Barton pulled over and rang DCI Cox's mobile number; even though it was late he knew she would answer, and sure enough his senior picked up on the second ring.

'Evening, John. Ringing for a bedtime story?'

Cox became all business as he updated her.

'That doesn't sound good. It's a poor time to begin an investigation.'

Barton didn't need to be told that. Most people would have finished for the day, but he could tell she was clicking into work mode.

'Okay, John, I'll return to the station. If there's a body in that van, I'll set up a command centre. Visit this Russo character, then come in too, will you? We'll see what we need to do about resources. Any obvious danger to the public?'

Barton's mind ticked over. 'No, only to Russo. We don't have the manpower at the moment to do detailed house-to-houses at the van fire. Pigs and Zander will knock on the nearest homes in the hope of getting lucky, but media tomorrow is probably our best chance to get an eyewitness to come forward. As for the drug angle, is the other detective team investigating anything at the moment you think could link to this?'

'No, but I understand there's a lot of various product around. Cocaine in particular. I've been talking to the Met. The county lines thing has exploded this last month. I'll ask them in the morning if any of these characters have appeared in any of their investigations. I suspect events like these are exactly how the Bates gang operate. The van coming from Walthamstow is a strong link.'

After finishing the call, Barton put his phone back in his pocket and continued on to Russo's property. The lounge light was on, but that was it. Barton got out of his car and knocked hard on the door but there was no answer. He went around the back and opened the gate. Russo's hot tub had been placed upright, but remained empty. Barton stared into the lounge through the French windows. There was no sign of anyone, and the TV was off. The place, garden included, had a strange vacant air to it.

Barton took his phone out and rang the telephone number that Russo had begrudgingly given him but it went straight to voicemail.

There was no message asking him to leave his details. Barton walked back to the front of the property just as a big Daimler pulled into the street from the main road. Barton waved it down.

The tanned face of a gentleman around Barton's age appeared as the window moved down.

'Can I help you?'

Barton showed his warrant.

'It's important I speak to Mr Russo as quickly as possible, but he's not about. Any ideas for me?'

'The chap with the girlfriends?'

'That's the one.'

'My house overlooks his garden. My wife's always telling me off for looking at the hot-tub action. My name's Derek. Derek Skinner.'

The man's face fell as he realised what he'd said to a detective.

'It's okay,' said Barton. 'Have you seen him today?'

'No, he'll be in London. He's rarely here during the week. I sometimes see his girlfriends, but it's hard to keep up. He changes them faster than I change my underwear.'

Barton tried to think about what else Skinner might be aware of that could help his investigation in any way.

'Can you tell me anything about him?'

'His girlfriends are young and his friends all drive impressive cars like he does.'

Barton rubbed his chin.

'Do you know what job he does?'

'Of course. He's always name dropping.'

'Eh?'

The Daimler driver gave him a toothy grin and pointed at his teeth.

'Stefan is dentist to the stars!'

41

DI BARTON

Barton wrote down the neighbour's name and number and said he'd be in touch. He took a quiet moment in his car. If his brain churned any faster, he'd have a meltdown. Russo being a dentist was a good thing. Chances were, he would be in his bolthole in the city and Barton would find that tomorrow. He got his mobile out and typed in Russo's name and 'dentist'.

Sure enough, the top pick was for Dentist to the Stars. He clicked on it and went through to a flash, slick website with an address in Kingston. Russo's grinning chops splashed all over it. There were numerous accolades including a declaration of a first-class honours degree from King's College London. Barton copied the contact details of the surgery into his phone.

Now Barton had a better idea of how Henson earnt his money, the most likely scenario was that Russo was just a weekend cocaine user, which meant Henson was probably his supplier. Barton could feel the investigation bending back to the girl in the skip – she was still the key to all of this. He turned the engine on and returned to the station. When he got to the office, DCI Cox was waiting for him. In a blue business suit, she looked fresh and professional, which was, he expected, very different from how he appeared. He updated her.

'I suppose if your boyfriend's a painter, you'd get him to paint your house, so our victim's new tooth makes more sense now,' she said.

'Yes, I guess so. It seems to be Mr Russo is one of those men who is in love with falling in love, or lust at least. Then as soon as something new and shiny comes along, he ruthlessly disposes of his current partner. And that's obviously quite a shock to the old girlfriend, especially as they become instantly homeless.'

'Yes,' agreed Cox. 'I'm betting that he encourages them to rely completely on him as a control thing, maybe encouraging them to leave their jobs and lose contact with friends and family. It sounds as though he likes vulnerable women, perhaps even seeking them out.'

'Yes, that would all fit. Strange told me earlier that Jess felt guilty when she realised Russo had just lobbed his previous partner out after meeting Jess on Cup Final day last year. Then history repeated itself.'

'Do we know the previous girlfriend?'

'Not yet, Strange is double-checking though. She's speaking to Sasha Yates in the morning, but I can't see a spurned lover attacking the current lover nearly a year later, especially as apparently she tried to warn Jessica. I wonder if Russo has moved on to a new woman in London. If so, perhaps she's involved somehow, but that would be a leap.'

'You men really are a strange bunch. So you don't think Russo's responsible directly for the murder? No suspicion of domestic violence?'

'No. My guess is that Russo is a weekend party animal who bought his drugs from Henson. I suspect Henson was a small-scale dealer who got involved in an operation that was more serious than he expected, but liked the money. It's possible he didn't even have a choice. He's probably been taken somewhere for a serious chat about why the police have been sniffing around.'

'I presume you're going to want to see Henson's bank accounts and mobile records.'

'Yes. He has a lot of money, judging by how his neighbours talk about him, but we don't know what job he does. There was the evidence of cocaine being snorted in his lounge. The house search will probably turn up further evidence of drug use. It's worth looking into who his next of kin is, even if we find him safe and sound. I guess he could have inherited money so he doesn't need to work.'

Barton's phone rang. He and Cox shared a look as he pulled it from his pocket.

'Yes, Zander.'

'The firefighters have put the blaze out. The vehicle's completely burned up, but they managed to open the back door. It's bad news, I'm afraid.'

'Henson?'

'It's hard to tell, because what's inside has been cooked. There's clearly a motorbike in there and what looks like two adult bodies.'

42

DI BARTON

Barton told Cox the news.

'Russo and Henson?' she said.

'Zander said the bodies are too charred to say with any certainty. The watch commander thinks they were doused with some kind of accelerant and plenty of it. Whoever they were, it seems they've basically been roasted within the van.'

Cox was a tough professional who didn't bat an eyelid at the gruesome thought. Instead, she was straight to the important questions.

'The skip death might have been an accident, but now we have at least two murders. Let's get the ball rolling in here, so we're all set to move in the morning. We'll break in a couple of hours, so we're fresh tomorrow. Ask Zander to control the scene until CSI arrives, but then he needs to leave fast when it's done and get some rest. If you meet him at the scene tomorrow first thing, we'll go from there.'

'Understood, and I agree I need some sleep. I've got so many pieces of information floating around in my head that I'm struggling to see the big picture.'

'We can't do much at this time of night. We'll get Mortis out asap, too. Although you'll probably want to ring Barney.'

Barton agreed. With something like this in a residential area, it was often simpler to wrap the vehicle up after the initial searching and photographing, then put it on a low loader. Barney was the owner of a local garage that was set up to provide this service, and once he'd brought it to the station, they could examine the vehicle and its contents in peace. They didn't want Joe Public watching as they emptied the van.

Before he left to start setting up, Barton explained his theory concerning the drug angle to Cox. She drummed her fingers on her knee while she thought.

'Right, carry on establishing the incident room,' she said. 'There have been rumours of a county line coming to Peterborough from London for years but nothing seemed to come of it. I'm going to call the Met, just to make sure we aren't stepping on any toes.'

Barton smiled after she'd disappeared to her office. Cox hadn't been promoted for nothing. If this was the Bates operation, the Met would need to be involved.

At midnight, Barton was starving and tired. He rang Zander, who was still at the scene despite Barton texting him to get off home as soon as possible.

'Anything new?' he asked.

'Not much. We've left the remains in situ until tomorrow. Mortis can be here when we remove them. The watch commander said he should be able to allocate Beddows to the case again in the morning. He's emailed him because it's late. The smell was terrible. It looks like the bodies were stripped beforehand. I've never seen anything like it. We're probably going to need DNA or teeth for confirmation, although one of the people inside seems larger even with the muscles shrinking from the intense heat. With what we know, it's likely to be Henson.'

'There have been more revelations tonight. I found out earlier that Russo is a high-end dentist, so it might be easier to confirm that than you think. Russo's number is straight to voicemail, but I checked the opening times of his surgery. If he isn't at work tomorrow morning, it's probable he was in that van.'

'Okay, I'm off home. There's a constable here to guard the scene, which is something I wouldn't fancy doing. Imagine if a cat got under the vehicle and started making scratching noises.'

Barton couldn't help laughing. They needed gallows humour at times like this. Tomorrow was going to be a tough day. There would be death messages to deliver and terrible images to observe. All in a day's work for the police.

Barton drove home and quietly let himself into the house. He opened the fridge and stared longingly at a four-pack of cider. Instead, he picked up the packet of ham, which had five slices left, and ate them one by one in single mouthfuls. He found a box of doughnuts on the side and chuckled. Holly must have bought them as a joke. He ate two very quickly and climbed the stairs.

People often asked him how he could do a job like this, but there was something they didn't understand. When death surrounded you, life took on new meaning. Barton poked his head in each of the kids' bedrooms. Smiling, he undressed and got into bed next to Holly. He was fast asleep in seconds.

43

THE FIRE KILLER

I check the clock for a final time as it ticks towards midnight. For a moment, I think the second hand has stopped, but then it plods on. I ease open the back door and walk to the shed. There are two canisters containing petrol inside. They're heavy for me so the lighter one will do because I won't need much. I pick a small hammer off a hook, just in case.

It's too mild for a coat, but I put my large gardening one on anyway and pull the hood up, even though it doesn't matter if someone sees me this time. I want to be in the middle of it. Big fire-fighters will be forced to brush past me as they race to douse the flames. I need to smell everything that burns and feel the heat on my face. They can arrest me, haul me to jail, throw the book at me, whatever they want. This is the end.

I reach Mavis's house without seeing a soul. There's a small path to the left of her terrace, which must lead to the back. I open a low gate, which threatens to fall apart when I push it. The paint is peeling and the nails are loose. It's unloved – I know how it feels.

These old houses have wooden doors at the rear entrance and

Mavis's is half window, half a garish yellow panel. Beth said it would be open, and it is. I place the hammer on the side now it's not needed. The house is dark and quiet, and it smells musty. I trip over piles of boxes and cases, causing magazines and newspapers to slide off their unsteady stacks. The door to the right is open and leads into the front parlour. I enter and flick the light on, closing the door behind me.

The little sofa is ancient. It's 1960s orange and when I stand next to it, I can see long black burns on the arms and fabric where someone has left a cigarette to burn and forgotten about it. Tacky-looking figurines line the mantelpiece. The wallpaper is peeling at every edge. The TV is boxy with a screen that's small for its size. On the fireplace rests a packet of Mayfair cigarettes. There's a cheap yellow plastic lighter next to it. I smile, even though I brought my own. It's all so familiar.

My mouth dries as I return to the sofa. There are more newspapers and magazines under it. I pour the fuel over everything. The fumes make me gag, but the effect on my nerve endings is instantaneous. They light up like a skyscraper at dusk. This is a final present to myself. With a flick of a finger, the lighter ignites, then the sofa goes up with an enthusiastic whoosh.

The heat hits me like a blast of desert wind. Petrol never lets you down. I perch on the armchair and stare into the flames. It's time to leave, but perhaps I'll stay this time. This is how it began when I was a child so maybe this is how it should all end too.

After a minute, the smoke in the room stings my eyes and tickles my throat. That's when I hear a creak above me. My ears strain for more noises, but the fire has lit the walls now and the paper crackles and spits as the glue burns.

Beth said Mavis was leaving yesterday. Who can be upstairs? Perhaps it's an old house breathing its last. I pick up the empty petrol canister and open the lounge door. The heat behind me rises and gives a roar in appreciation. I pull the door to, and the spitting and popping quietens.

Sitting next to the stairs is a suitcase.

44

THE FIRE KILLER

I flick on the two switches next to the door and rush up the stairs. It's eerily quiet and a dim bulb without a shade casts gloomy shadows along the cluttered landing. Smoke filters into the beam of weak light. I open the first door and find an empty bathroom from avocado hell. The second door is ajar, but bangs against something when I push it. It looks like the room is full of rubbish. I try to poke my head around the side, but can't quite see into the whole room.

'Get out,' I shout through it. 'Fire!'

There's no movement or sound. I turn to the final door and give it a firm push. It opens and I can just make out a double bed with a body-sized lump under a duvet. There's a strong smell of smoke in the room. I shuffle across the warm carpet to the side of the bed and look in. Mavis is awake and blinking. She coughs and I drag the sheet off, then grab her furthest wrist and pull her towards me. She rolls out of the bed and we stagger to the door. The hallway is much clearer of fumes, and we're able to stand. Mavis has a long off-white nightgown on. In the smoke, bent over, hacking, she resembles a spectre.

I manage to guide her downstairs, past the smoking lounge

door and out the back door. We stumble down the path, up the alley, and reach the front of the house. I half expect to see a throng of people and emergency vehicles, lights flashing, but the street is empty.

Mavis and I stand in the middle of the road. A light opposite comes on, then another. Mavis rubs her eyes next to me, face damp with streaming tears. I pull up my hood and lurch away as fast as I can.

Halfway down the street, I drop the canister into a wheelie bin. My legs are heavy as I continue my escape, but surely, I'll have been seen.

45

DI BARTON

Barton awoke to a relentless beeping. The alarm clock told him it was six a.m. He lay there, rubbing his eyes as he did the last time he went abroad and got up at two a.m. to catch a flight. The previous day's incidents appeared in his mind. He let them wash over him, hoping to see something he had so far missed.

If the murders were due to a county line from London being shut down, then his chances of solving this case were slim. The people who knew the answers he wanted were probably dead, and anyone left was unlikely to talk. Maybe what he had here were two jigsaws next to each other to solve as opposed to one. There was the fire and there was also the drug trade. He heard another distant beep and realised he'd left his phone on the kitchen table.

He rolled out of bed, feeling a thousand years old, and plodded downstairs. There was a message from Malik.

Came in at six this morning, there's been a house fire last night. No casualties, but it's on Welland Road, not far from the wheelie bin and skip fire.

Barton rubbed the grit out of his eyes and texted him back as he poured some of his younger son's cereal into a bowl.

Any witnesses or suspects?

He'd eaten the Frosties by the time Malik replied.

An elderly woman has been rushed to hospital having inhaled smoke. No witnesses other than that. There's uniform on the scene and the fire crew are damping down. The fire's long gone out. It could have been bad, but it was mostly contained in one room and the brigade were there before it spread.

Barton took some deep breaths to try and wake up. He took a big bottle of water out of the fridge and drank the entire contents, spilling quite a bit down his hairy chest, before replying.

Okay, meet me at the house. I'll be half an hour.

Barton stomped up the stairs. After grabbing a fresh towel, he stood under a cold shower for five minutes. He was already warm by the time he returned to the bedroom and pulled on his suit trousers and a white cotton shirt. He nudged Holly's shoulder and her eyes pinged open.

'I'm awake,' she said. 'As I'm sure are all our neighbours. A drunken brontosaurus would make less noise.'

'I've got to go. There's been another fire last night.'

'Do you have to leave so early? Come on, John. The kids were looking forward to us having breakfast together and discussing picking up Gizmo. You're missing the best bit, the anticipation of it all. You're losing out.'

'I know. Trust me, I know.'

Holly didn't answer and rolled over. Barton grabbed a tie from the wardrobe and left the room feeling worse than he did when he woke up. Standing in front of the hall mirror, he paused with the tie in his hand, realising for the first time in his career that he really didn't want to go in.

He was close to having his fill of death and misery, and all the terrible things people did to each other, often for very little. What he craved to do was slip back into bed and cuddle his wife. He wanted to laugh with his children over eggs and bacon about how great their new family member was going to be. Let someone else stare at burned bodies and ruined lives. Let his sleep be peaceful.

Barton analysed his face in the mirror. He had the blank expression that people like him ended up with after years of trawling the city's gutters. He threw his tie on the stairs, set his jaw, and watched his expression creep into a small smile. If not him, then who else? His children and their friends slept well because men and women like him were prepared to endure nightmares. That was why he was proud to be a policeman, but he also knew he couldn't do it forever, because each death left a mark.

After a final rueful glance upstairs, Barton grabbed an apple and a banana from the kitchen. He left the house, got in his car, and ate both while he raced around the quiet parkways. Through experience, he knew it was unlikely he'd want to eat anything for quite a while after visiting the scene of the van fire.

Welland Road was usually a very busy street, so the fire crew had left one side of the street open even though traffic was currently considerably less than usual.

Barton recognised the firefighters who were talking in a huddle. They were the volunteers from Bourges Boulevard. Dogsthorpe's full-time crew would still have been at the van fire. The firefighters split off when Barton arrived, leaving the watch commander smiling at Barton.

'Morning, Vic,' said Barton.

'John. Nice to see you. Lucky escape with this one. There was a lot of fuel in that building. Another minute and we'd have been worrying about the houses next door, but we're finishing up now. No terrible harm done.'

'Any early thoughts on the cause?'

'We've been around the back, and it's not a kitchen fire. This time of night, I'm guessing a cigarette was left burning. There are butts all over the place in the garden. It's too hot for anyone to have had a fire on inside.'

'No obvious signs of arson?'

'Nothing at this point.'

'Did you see the woman who lived here before she went to the hospital?'

'Yes, she seemed very confused and upset. Kept asking for a cigarette. She's clearly had a bad experience, but it looked more than that. Maybe dementia.'

'At least she managed to get out okay.'

'That's the funny thing. She said she prayed to God for help, and then an angel came.'

46

DI BARTON

Barton frowned.

'Was she delirious or did she mean she was saved by someone?'

'Who knows what she meant? A passing taxi driver spotted the fire and rang it in. The woman was by herself in the road when a neighbour finally noticed. There was nobody else around.'

Barton shook his head.

'These last few days have been a nightmare. We don't have the resources for this many investigations.'

'No, nor us. I heard there were two bodies in that van that was set on fire.'

Barton nodded grimly.

'We're expecting Beddows at that scene this morning,' he said. 'I suppose we should start there. This could be just a coincidence.'

Barton could believe that it wasn't directly related to the burnt van, but it was likely related to the skip blaze, and that fire somehow linked to everything else. When Malik arrived, he asked him to speak to the immediate residents and find out if any of them saw anything or if they had the new type of doorbells, which filmed when people were near them. Malik would also try to locate the taxi driver who called in the fire and take a statement.

Having left his colleague with plenty to do, Barton returned to his car and drove to the location of the van. It was seven thirty when he arrived and already a bright day. A police traffic 4x4 was leaving the scene towing a trailer with floodlights and a big generator on it. CSI couldn't work in the gloom. Barton recognised Mortis's car parked along the side of the field. There was a patrol SUV in front of it and a Police Forensic van in front of that. The van had been driven down a path, past a small playground with a slide and three swings, two goalposts, and what looked like a maintenance shed, to the bottom, where it had been set alight. Barton glanced around him. It was a mostly built-up area, but trees surrounded the field.

The blackened van, scorched earth and miles of police tape looked alien amongst the fresh greenery. Barton stepped over a low fence and walked through the plush, thick grass. A month of sunshine and showers, then all this hot weather had turned the trees into huge sentinels, laden down with leaves. Birds tweeted within the branches and swooped overhead. The smell of summer was everywhere. He suspected the light breeze must be blowing the other smells from the van away from him. It was hard to fathom what had happened here.

Mortis was talking to a young uniformed officer at the tape and they were both drinking a Subway coffee. Two CSI technicians were photographing the scene and scouring a path towards the rear of the van. No doubt they were double-checking what they'd done in the false light. He watched one of them drop a pen or pencil of some kind into an evidence bag. The other happened to turn and notice them. The person waved. He recognised Sirena behind the mask before she returned to her task.

'Morning, gents,' said Barton to Mortis and the PC.

'Morning, John,' said Mortis. 'I bought you a coffee, but I gave it to this young man. He's had a long night.'

Barton smiled.

'Fair play.'

'Anything to report?' he asked the PC.

'No, sir. It's been a spooky, long shift, knowing what was in the van. I'm not sure if the nasty smells have died down or I've just got used to it, but I'll be glad to get out of here.'

Barton felt the same way. Mortis nodded in the direction behind Barton, and he turned to see Zander trudging through the grass. As Zander was passing the maintenance shed, they heard a motor starting up. The shed door opened and a sit-on lawnmower came out and trundled towards Zander. Barton smiled again as he watched Zander remonstrating with the driver and pointing in their direction. The mower spun around and went back into the shed.

Zander made his way over to the grinning group, chuckling as well.

'The driver said he wondered what all the police tape was for,' he said.

Sirena came over to them.

'You can approach and view inside the rear of the van now. Keep on the plates, like good boys, but I think we have everything we need from outside the scene and we've analysed inside but not touched the corpses. We'll have the van towed away when you're done.'

'The two of us will look first,' said Barton to Mortis. He glanced at the PC. 'Excellent work. You can clock off. Zander, have a word with the maintenance guy to see if he's seen anything. Judging by the observation skills he's displayed so far, that's probably going to be a negative.'

Mortis had a full CSI suit on but Barton only needed gloves. The van's back door had been jemmied open and now hung about two feet open. Through the gap, Barton and Mortis could look through to the blown-out windscreen. Barton eased the doors wide and they made a creepy, creaking sound. Both bodies lay on their backs, feet towards the front seats, heads to the rear. The bigger body had the rear wheel of the motorbike on its chest, the other had the front wheel resting on its groin. Barton hoped for their sakes that meant the victims had been dead before the van was torched.

The slight breeze now blew the aroma into their faces through the front of the vehicle, but thankfully it was a burnt-out smoky wet smell, like most scenes after the fire brigade had left, as opposed to barbecued human flesh.

'Any details you need to know first?' asked Mortis quietly, before pulling up his mask.

'We think the bigger guy on the right is a well-built man called Henson. The one on the left might be a middle-aged man called Russo. Anything you can tell me will help.'

Mortis climbed into the back. Barton turned away from the charred scene. He gave the dead a bit of dignity by half closing the van door but still gave Mortis some natural light to work by, but he blocked anyone else's view with his bulk. Zander was still outside, staring at the van.

'You all right?' asked Barton.

'Yes, doesn't get any easier, does it?'

Barton shrugged, but didn't reply. They could both hear the sounds of Mortis's tools being removed from his bag. Barton let his mind wander to the skip fire while he watched Zander stroll away to talk to the maintenance man. Barton's phone rang. It was DCI Cox.

'Morning, John. I need you back in the office. There's a detective chief superintendent from the Metropolitan Police who wants to explain their case to us straight away. They have a team heading to where you are to take control.'

'So the case is related to drugs?'

'Yes, she didn't want to repeat the conversation, but she said they've been tracking a county line to this area, but they lost it when it reached here. They had no idea where the product was ending up, or even if it hadn't continued up north.'

'Nice of them to let us know.'

'To be fair to them, it seems they only found out who the person receiving the drugs was a few nights back.'

'Who was it?'

'She said she'd clarify everything when you arrived.'

'Okay, I'll finish up here and be back in half an hour.'

Barton looked into the van, but Mortis's white back blocked his view so he walked back along the plates to Zander and told him about the call.

'The Met are on the way,' said Barton.

'Have we been gazumped?' said Zander.

'Something like that. What did the maintenance bloke say?'

'He reminded me of Forrest Gump. He said he noticed the van, but thought the tape was to keep the public out. The only thing he mentioned of any importance was that he asked a man to move a white van from the entrance in the last few days as it was blocking access.'

'Driver description?'

'Male, sunglasses, younger than him, but he said he'd struggled with guessing ages since he hit seventy. He told me with enthusiasm that the van he saw was similar to the burned one, but now this one was mostly black, he couldn't say if it was the same vehicle.'

'You must love a strong eyewitness,' said Mortis, who'd exited the van and caught the back end of the conversation. He beckoned

Sirena and they were silent while she walked over. Mortis gave vivid descriptions, which would make this unpleasant to hear, so Barton braced himself. At this point, they all knew the key was to focus on the facts, not the people who until yesterday had lived and breathed.

'Ready?' asked Mortis. 'Two bodies, both cooked, not charred, if that's a helpful explanation. There's no thermal or other amputation of limbs. We'll have no problem getting at fluids and DNA inside the body cavities. No obvious injuries that I can detect. No handcuffs, although any plastic ties would have melted, and no clear sign of a struggle or struggling. I suspect our victims were dead or unconscious when the fire was set because the bike is on them and they would have pushed it off, or at least tried to if they were conscious.'

'Age and sex?' asked Barton.

'Both male, although the genitalia have mostly burned away. One has noticeably more remaining muscle if that helps with the case. Hard to say with regards to age, but neither very old would be my guess. No jewellery on either, but of course it could have been removed ante-mortem. The weight of the motorbike has kept parts of their bodies flat to the van floor. There are noticeable differences to the skin of each man, but I would say one is white and the other smaller victim is non-white.'

Barton raised an eyebrow. 'Russo was white and middle-aged.'

'How tall was he?' asked Mortis.

'Nearly six feet, at a guess.'

'I've estimated both femurs, and this guy's shorter than that. His teeth also look like those of a younger man. I don't think that's your guy in there.'

'Good to know,' said Zander. 'We need Russo to chat to us.'

Yes, thought Barton, but what Mortis had said didn't mean he wasn't dead elsewhere.

'How long before you can give us conclusive analysis?' asked Barton.

Mortis blew out his cheeks.

'Heat-related fractures are easily differentiated from traumatic fractures. Bullet damage will look the same. Old injuries and tattoos might show under a microscope. Teeth are all present in both. I might need to get a CT scan done, but I'll be finished by tomorrow night.'

'Excellent. The Met are going to manage this aspect of the case, so you could be reporting to them. They'll arrive soon. Zander, if you stay and liaise with them. I'm heading back to base to talk with their head honcho. I was planning to ask for more resources but we might only be focusing on the skip fire, and possibly the house fire from last night.'

Zander nodded.

'Anything you noticed or found, Sirena?' asked Barton.

'No, this field is well used by dog walkers, drinkers and picnickers. There's stuff everywhere. We might be able to confirm a suspect was here from their shoe prints, fingerprints or DNA, but the ground is hard and the fire was hot.'

'Yes, and the van was stolen from down south. Perhaps the Met will have more detail on that too, but it seems this end of the county line has been erased, so we won't need to have any involvement. Did you hear about the house fire?'

'Yes, busy times.' She began to walk away.

'Was the house blaze suspicious?' asked Zander.

'There was a troubling and complicated aspect to it. The resident was found in the street saying an angel saved her.'

'Maybe a passing woman pulled her from the fire,' said Zander.

'It doesn't have to be a woman,' said Sirena, stopping in her tracks and turning around.

'Aren't most angels women?' asked Barton.

'Can you name a female angel?' she said.

The men were quiet for a while.

'I can't name any angels,' said Zander.

'Gabriel,' said Barton.

'Male,' replied Sirena. 'Trust me, I'm from a religious family. Every reference to angels in Scripture is male. The Greek word for "angel" in the New Testament, angelos, is in the masculine form. The feminine form isn't present at all.'

'What about Seraphim and Cherubim?' asked Mortis.

'They're just types of angels,' she replied.

'Great, even the Good Book can't help us,' said Barton. 'I'll get someone to talk to the owner of the house if she's up to it today, but she might have dementia. Any issues, ring me.'

'Hey, maybe it was Jessica Craven. She died in the skip fire and now her ghost scours the city, saving those at risk of a fiery end,' said Zander.

'I always wondered how you ever got promoted,' said Mortis with a smile. 'One quick thing to add before you leave, John,' he added. 'The girl in the skip. Tox screen indicates recent heroin use.'

Barton trudged back to his car, wondering if that knowledge helped. He was about to drive away when his phone alarm, which he'd set for eight thirty when Russo's dentistry opened its doors, went off. He found the number and rang it.

'Dentist to the Stars,' answered an enthusiastic female voice with emphasis on the 'Stars'.

'Can I speak to Stefan Russo, please?' said Barton.

'He's unavailable.'

'It's important. When will he be available?'

There was a pause.

'Whom shall I say is calling, and he'll get back to you as promptly as he can?'

'Not good enough. I'm Detective Inspector Barton. Major Crimes. I'm concerned for his safety.'

'Oh, sorry. I thought you were a client. We've had to cancel a lot of appointments due to the pandemic, and it's made many of them cross. Mr Russo is out of the country in France at a business meeting concerning stock acquisition.'

Barton just about stopped himself from swearing.

'He's not answering his phone,' he said through gritted teeth.

'Maybe he's in the tunnel.'

Barton considered her reply for a moment and wondered whether she was protecting her boss. 'He needs to ring me as soon as he can. Pass that message on to him.'

'Will do,' she sang, then hung up.

'Bugger,' said Barton to the dead line.

He drove for a few metres, then pulled over abruptly, causing a driver behind him to beep his horn. Barton ignored her and rang the Force Intelligence Bureau at HQ.

'Sam Dench speaking.'

'Sam, could you check as quickly as possible for me if someone's left the country?'

'Sure.'

Barton gave Russo's name and address.

'I'll email when I hear back. I should be able to fast-track it.'

'Cheers, Sam.'

Barton put his phone down and continued on to the station. If Russo stayed abroad, he was untouchable with the little they had on him at this point.

47

DI BARTON

When Barton got back to the station, Cox beckoned him into her office. Barton had only recently joined the police when he first had to talk to someone from the Met. That case had been about a child abduction that ended badly. For some reason, he'd half expected the person to be whippet thin and beautiful, and wearing a wind-cheater and baseball cap emblazoned with the Met on it in yellow like the FBI. Instead, Karen Townsend had worn faded jeans and an ill-fitting blouse. She had been middle-aged, peroxide-blonde, and spoke with a Geordie accent. It was another lesson learned.

'Morning, John,' said Cox.

Cox was still power-dressed and exuded energy, but the grey-haired woman next to her was in a worn suit and looked near retirement. Barton laughed when he saw it was the very same Karen Townsend. She smiled too.

'John, great to see you. What's it been, twenty years?'

'Feels like a hundred.'

'Speak for yourself, but I know what you mean. I'm glad we don't meet often.'

'Yes. They tell me the stats are improving, but I seem very busy.'

'Well, we'll take this one off you. We can have a good talk about it, but if you take a seat, I'll give you a brief outline.'

Cox had organised coffee and biscuits. They had theirs in front of them, so Barton helped himself. When he was seated, Karen explained their position.

'Many county lines have been set up by a notorious East End villain named Justin Bates and his brothers, Simon and Tony. They have a reputation for extreme violence and a careless disregard for their employees.'

'Meaning their employees go missing?'

Karen nodded at him with the hint of a smile.

'Yes, they've been involved with drugs for a long time now. Simon took a twenty-year sentence to save his brothers. He's still inside with four to go. We've struggled with the other two. It seems they've learned their lessons. Phones are encrypted. Lines are set up and closed rapidly. They use teenagers from London to bring the drugs up. One of those was a character by the name of Omar Elmi Dihoud. We think this particular Somalian ended up in your van.'

Barton nodded for her to carry on.

'What we understand now is that Justin and Tony would visit the town they wanted to operate in, then ask around to find out who was the main supplier. As you know, since the days of The Snow Killer and the Chapmans, Peterborough's drug trade has been extremely fragmented. That's perfect for them. Justin and Tony then sell their wares through these different dealers.'

'And one of these was Garth Henson.'

'Correct, and we think he is the other body in the van. The relationship starts off cosy with good profits for all sides and it's really hard to track down at that point. Of course, like many criminals, they then become greedy, and Justin and Tony increase their cut. Henson gets squeezed but can't get out. He knows they'll kill him if he tries.'

'How do the drugs reach Peterborough?'

'Dihoud rents a small car in London and drives it here to a rented house. He gets use of a motorbike and delivers the product by hand to Henson and another guy who we found in a canal in London three days ago. They had an operation in Brighton too and that ended a month ago with a lot of gunfire.'

The deceased motorcycle rider had a name, thought Barton.

'Right,' he said. 'The Bates brothers conduct their business for a while, but when they feel like their operation has been compromised, it's the end of the road, for those at the end of the line.'

'Yes,' replied Karen. 'It's a complicated story, which I can't get into after how things finished in Brighton.'

She paused at that moment. Barton had been in the job long enough to assume that the Met might have obtained an informant from the investigation. Nobody ever revealed if they had a CHIS, which stood for Covert Human Intelligence Source – in other words someone who was a regular informant, grass or source for the police.

'We linked Henson and Dihoud by phone messages and calls,' continued Karen. 'Someone sent Henson a text from an unregistered phone saying CR. Henson forwarded it on to Dihoud's phone with an H after it, who then sent it to another burner with an O on the end of that.'

'Could the R be for Russo?' asked Barton.

'Maybe, but then wouldn't Dihoud have used a D. Obviously the O could be for his first name. We know the Bates brothers deal in codes. The C could just mean cocaine. Perhaps it stood for compromised or take care.'

'But the next thing to happen,' said Cox, 'is Henson and Dihoud are dead.'

'Which is unlikely to be a coincidence. Can you link this back to the brothers?' asked Barton.

'Yes, I believe we have enough evidence now,' replied Karen. 'We have CCTV footage of the brothers talking to two known gangsters, who we then followed up here. We lost them once we hit Peterborough, unfortunately, but then all this happened, and we caught them on their return journey to report their progress. They're currently in custody. We think they'll talk.'

'Are they muscular?' asked Barton.

'Yes.'

'I wonder if they were the ones at Henson's place, then. We may have an eyewitness who saw them there if it helps apply pressure. Aren't they worried about being taken out?'

'I reckon they know that the brothers will take them out whether they inform or not. It's what they do. They clean up.'

'So the Peterborough operation is finished for the moment, and all the local dealers are dead,' stated Barton.

'Spot on. We've got full surveillance on the brothers. We're going to watch what they do now. They'll be nervous after their team that came here failed to report back to them. We'll give them a few days to make further mistakes, then pick them up. That will be an extremely perilous task. It's likely they will be armed to the teeth.'

Barton looked around the room while he thought.

'Do you know anything about a Jessica Craven or a skip fire?' he asked.

'No, I know this case like the back of my hand. I'd remember that name.'

'How about a Stefan Russo?'

Karen's eyes narrowed. 'Stefan rings a bell, but for a different operation. Russo is new though. Give me a minute.' Karen took her phone out and rang someone. She walked to the window and stared out over the bleak offices opposite while she spoke.

Barton glanced out of the door into the detectives' office.

Strange was there, looking agitated. She put her hand to her ear, mouthing ring me. Her face told him it was urgent. He indicated *one minute* to her. Karen finished her call.

'We busted a dealer in London recently, who had a connection to the Bates clan. We obviously end up knowing most of the people they sell to, even though we don't prosecute them if it's clearly recreational. There was an SR, who we later suspected to be a Stefan R, in East London, who was a heavy user. He was smarter than most and we never identified him.'

'Could he have been involved in the dealing?'

'No, he was paying top dollar for the best stuff. The Bates brothers referred to him as a rose, which in their code meant he was worth cultivating. There was no way this Stefan could have sold it on for a profit. He will just be one of the many rich people in London who live their lives on clean cocaine. If it's very pure, some can function reasonably normally on it despite having a considerable addiction.'

48

DI BARTON

Barton stepped out of Cox's office feeling both relieved and frustrated. It looked as if Russo had done a bunk abroad to escape any heat, but it appeared he hadn't been involved any further than being a customer. The Met wouldn't be interested in prosecuting someone like him, and he wouldn't know anyone apart from Henson anyway, or whoever the runner was when he needed his fix in London.

Barton checked his phone. There was an email from Sam Dench.

That's confirmed. Subject caught the Eurostar late last night.

Barton blew out his cheeks. He still hoped to speak to Russo about Jessica Craven. Strange was nowhere to be seen, but he found Zander at the kettle. Zander didn't ask if he wanted one, just grabbed an extra cup.

'You're back quickly,' said Barton.

'Yep, a team turned up from the Met. I told them what I knew, and they thanked me for my work. That was it. I left Mortis giving them some incredibly detailed information about lung damage in a fire.'

Barton smiled.

'I assume we've lost the van blaze?' asked Zander.

Barton updated Zander on his chat with Karen.

'Just the skip and house fires for us to solve, then,' said Zander.

'Yes, and we'll struggle with the skip fire without further intel. I'm guessing Jess got brutally dumped by Russo and ended up homeless. At rock bottom, and with no support from friends and family, she went to see Henson to ask if she could stay the night. Perhaps she was hoping to blag some drugs off him at the same time, knowing he was a dealer from being there with Russo. Henson panics when he opens the door and tells her to leave.'

'Yes, the last thing he'd want is a drugged-up Jessica anywhere near his operation, so he sends her on her way.'

'She nicks a cheap bottle of whisky from the nearest shop and climbs into the skip to get out of the wind. The fire was started deliberately by someone passing who didn't know she was there, and that's that. And now we have the blaze on Welland Road. Is Malik back yet?'

'I haven't seen him,' replied Zander. 'Strange was urgently looking for you. She's just nipped to the toilet.'

'Okay. You must have a lot of paperwork.'

Zander groaned. Barton took his phone out and rang Malik.

'Anything to report?' he asked Malik when he picked up.

'No, the only person who told me anything much lived opposite. He looked out of his bedroom window and saw a woman in the middle of the street on her own, and then he noticed that the lounge in the house behind her seemed to be on fire. There's CCTV further up the road, but it's a long shot. I'll come in and check it.'

'Okay, swing by the hospital on your way back and see if the lady who was in the house is in any state to talk to us.'

Barton finished the call and found Strange at his desk.

'About time, too,' she said. She called Zander over.

'I spoke to Sasha again this morning. She confirmed the dates from her statement and she recalled that a month or so ago, the management company wrote her a letter saying that Jess had asked for Sasha's address and could they give it to her, but she never heard any more.'

'Okay, that fits in with when Russo chucked her out.'

'Yes, I think discussing all this with me nudged some of Sasha's memories from when Jess first started dating Russo and was still partially living at Greenham. Jess told Sasha she felt guilty about him dumping his ex for her. Sasha also remembered being told by Jess that right at the start of their relationship, when Jess and Russo were in bed, this woman came around and shouted through the letter box that he was a worthless weasel and she was going to stab him.'

'Threats to kill, nice. But Russo wouldn't want any police involvement, what with his little hobby, so he probably just moved to his flat in London for a while, maybe taking Jess with him.'

'Correct. And Sasha finally remembered the ex-girlfriend had a name similar to one of the women in *Les Mis*. I don't watch stuff like that, so I asked IMDB what the names of the women were in the recent film.'

Barton was confused.

'And?'

'The girl in *Les Misérables* was named Cosette. Which probably made the girl who Russo dumped after meeting Jess on the FA Cup Final day to be Lynette, who you mentioned the other day.'

49

DI BARTON

Barton stared at Strange for a few seconds without saying anything. A feeling of horror came over him. There'd definitely been something off about Lynette when she opened the door to him and Zander that first time. He racked his brain for what Zander and he might have missed. Zander looked as surprised as he did. He was the first to speak.

'Wow. Are we saying that Lynette deliberately torched the skip after seeing Jess climb into it?'

'Well, I suppose it's a more credible explanation than saying Lynette set fire to it because she likes fires,' replied Barton.

'Before you dismiss that out of hand, it's not a completely outrageous scenario,' said Strange. 'Let's look at both sides. There have been fires around the area for ages, mostly small-scale stuff. When it comes to the skip, it could have been kids who casually threw a match in, or it could have been Lynette without knowing Jess was inside. Remember, Jess was in the vicinity to see Henson. She might well have climbed into the skip, and Lynette knew nothing about it.' Strange paused, then smiled. 'Our lives are full of coincidences that have far-reaching effects. In fact, who's to say it was Lynette, anyway? Just because she dated Russo beforehand, doesn't mean that she would want to hurt her replacement. Russo is the scallywag in all this.'

Strange looked from Zander to Barton, then shrugged.

'Okay, fair enough,' she said. 'The most likely explanation is that Lynette saw the new girlfriend climb into the skip and, in a fit of rage, set it alight.'

'Is it also plausible that she threw her in the skip, too?' asked Zander.

'Well, Lynette is curvy but slight. She couldn't have lugged a dead body up the road and lobbed it in a high-sided skip,' replied Barton.

'All the people down in those terraces were a little unusual, remember,' said Zander with a wink. 'For all we know she could have been having a relationship with a strong man.'

'Henson,' said Barton without confidence. 'I can't see that pair as an item, but let's bring her in. I have a nasty feeling she might not be an easy arrest.'

50

DI BARTON

Barton called Pigs over and brought her up to speed.

'We're going to arrest Lynette,' said Barton to the group. 'Let's discuss the dangers.'

'Pigs and I will grab our PPE and PAVA spray. I can't see her troubling the four of us,' said Strange.

'I'll arrange for a van to meet us there,' said Zander.

Barton pondered what Lynette might do. Policing had changed so much since he'd joined up. Nowadays, every time he approached a situation, he found it best to consider what would happen if there was an inquiry afterwards. It was possible, but unlikely, that Lynette would attack them with a knife or other weapon. But she could erupt, which would be dangerous if they returned her in a pool car. It was safer for her and them if she was placed in the back of what was affectionately called a 'meat wagon'.

Twenty minutes later, Zander signalled that there was a van ready to go. The four of them went down to the basement where Pigs booked out the same Volvo that Zander had taken before, and they were soon at Fig Tree Lane. As a precaution, Barton stopped a little away from the property. A minute passed, then the police van pulled up behind them. Barton turned around to his team.

'Strange, you and Pigs take point. I doubt she'd use a weapon, apart from her nails, but better safe than sorry. Let's hope her mum's kung fu isn't strong.'

Barton popped the boot, and they all climbed out of the car and Pigs and Strange grabbed their PPE. Barton wiped perspiration from his brow and looked up into the sky where the white sun relentlessly hammered down on them. Even the pavement seemed to tremble under its intense gaze. He stared across at the terraces and strode towards them.

Lynette appeared from around the side of her house, carrying a rucksack. If people were convicted based on their expressions, she would be in big trouble. She sprinted to the beaten-up red Volkswagen next to her house, yanked open the driver's door, threw her bag in the passenger seat, leapt in and started the engine.

She accelerated away at a reasonable pace, which was probably as swift as the Polo would go as the team raced back to their Volvo and got in. Lynette didn't look at them as she passed by. Pigs swung the Volvo around in a neat circle. Barton was already giving details of the 'escaping' car to Control.

The PC in the van was time served and knew what to do. He would stay put. Barton was in a predicament. The days of screeching after vehicles through built-up areas had finished even before he joined up. To pursue at speed, you needed to be fully trained, in the correct vehicle, and in uniform, unless there was a risk to life. Even then you would need to get permission from Control and they rarely gave it. The best he could hope for was Traffic coppers nearby.

Lynette, however, was surprisingly keeping within the speed limits. She wasn't following the rules on littering, though, as a variety of objects came flying out of her driver's side window.

Pigs screeched to a halt, causing Barton to put a hand on the dash. She turned to Zander.

'Out.'

Zander leapt from the vehicle and slammed the door. Pigs drove after Lynette, keeping a good distance, and Barton turned around and watched Zander fetch the items that Lynette had disposed of. As their convoy cruised down Fulbridge Road towards the parkway, Barton updated Control. There was a Traffic motorcycle a minute away. Barton could see Lynette looking in the rear-view mirror. She didn't have a chance of escaping now, especially in that tired old motor, but she could still do something reckless.

Barton was surprised then when Lynette indicated left and pulled over next to the park where the van had burned. Pigs stopped behind her and Barton and Strange got out of the car. Strange still had her stab vest on, so she walked to the driver's side door and looked in while Barton peered in the passenger-side window.

Lynette had both hands on the wheel in the ten-to-two position with her head resting on her hands. Her dark-brown hair had fallen forward and was covering her face. Strange knocked. Lynette wound down the window, but kept her forehead on the wheel. Strange put her hand into the car and turned the engine off and removed the key. Barton opened the door on his side and the smell hit him straight away. He looked in the footwell and saw a metal container. It looked like the type used for petrol. He quickly slipped a plastic glove on from his pocket, grabbed the can, and lifted it from the vehicle.

Zander had caught up by then. He jogged past them and stood in the road to stop any traffic. Pigs did the same behind them.

'Lynette, please step from the vehicle,' said Strange.

Lynette finally looked up. Tears had smudged her make-up, giving her panda eyes under huge false eyelashes. She swung her legs from the footwell while Strange gave her space to get out. Lynette wore a figure-hugging pink matching tracksuit and pink trainers.

When Lynette was fully out of the vehicle, Strange slipped a pair of cuffs onto her wrists and guided her to the kerb, where she turned her around. Barton stood next to Lynette and held her arm, because she looked as if she might fall over. She kept her gaze on the floor while Strange stood in front of her.

'Lynette Croston, I am arresting you on suspicion of arson with intent to endanger life.'

51

DI BARTON

It was the oddest arrest Barton had ever made after the strangest pursuit. Zander had recovered the discarded items, which were a large box of Cook's Matches, a green disposable lighter and a tin of Zippo lighter fuel. When they searched the vehicle, they found some barbecue cubes and a gardening coat, which stank of smoke. Lynette didn't say a word. Barton called for the meat wagon and placed Lynette in the rear when it arrived. He got in the front seat for the drive back to the nick but she was quiet throughout the journey, seemingly in a trance.

When they arrived at the station, Lynette began to come out of her shell. Barton had never seen the normally grumpy desk sergeant, Bill Donald, smile so widely when she winked at him. His smile dropped when he was booking her in and Lynette stated she had no need of representation. Barton had a chat with Donald, who put Lynette on five observations per hour. Her clothes were taken off her in a room with two female custody constables, where she was given a blue tracksuit and a pair of black trainers. They didn't have shoelaces.

A few hours later, Barton decided to conduct the interview with

Zelensky, hoping that maybe a young woman present would help Lynette open up. A detention officer brought her to interview room two where Barton and Zelensky were waiting.

'Are you okay?' asked Barton when she was seated. 'You seem very detached.'

'I'm suppose I'm in shock. You said before that whoever set the fire that killed that woman would go to prison.'

'That's likely. It's a significant offence.'

It sounded as if Lynette might confess to at least one of the fires. Barton started the tapes and conducted the preliminaries.

'Lynette, you've been arrested for arson with intent to endanger life. We're now going to question you about this subject. I must advise you that you are entitled to free legal advice at any time. Do you understand? I must also advise that you can speak to a legal representative on the telephone. Do you wish to do so?'

Barton observed Lynette, who remained silent but shook head.

'For the benefit of the tape, Lynette Croston has shaken her head indicating she does not wish to take legal advice. In light of the seriousness, and therefore the possible sentence which you may later receive, I strongly recommend that you take professional advice,' repeated Barton.

'I won't be saying much today.'

'Why not?'

Lynette shook her head again. Barton paused for a moment.

'Would you like to ring someone else for advice?' he asked. 'Your mum?'

'I'm pretty sure I don't need advice from her. In fact, I'd rather you didn't tell her. She's mad enough as it is.'

'Very well, but we'll have to search your house regardless, which means she'll know about the investigation. It's standard procedure for a case like this.'

Lynette shrugged. 'Okay. I still don't want to talk to anyone.'

'I'm now cautioning you. Lynette Croston, you do not have to say anything, but it may harm your defence if you do not mention when questioned something which you later rely on in court. Anything you do say may be given in evidence.'

'I get it.'

'You know you've been arrested. If we charge you, the next step will be for you to go to the magistrates' court, where you will probably be remanded in custody until your trial. Do you understand why you've been arrested?'

'Yes.'

'Do you understand the caution?'

'Yes. I did it, so does it really matter?'

Lynette's green eyes had a glint in them. She stared defiantly at Barton.

'If you want credit for an early plea, you can formally admit to the crime now and it will be noted,' said Zelensky. 'It won't look good if you later say you didn't do it though. Did you start the fire in the skip outside the row of shops opposite Fig Tree Lane?'

Lynette made a squeak.

'Please repeat that,' said Zelensky.

Lynette looked from one to the other with an almost vacant gaze. She tipped her head back, then returned her attention to them after a few seconds. She took a big breath, then exhaled deeply. Her eyes were clear and focused.

'Yes.'

52

DI BARTON

Barton smiled to have some resolution to the case, but the interview was a long way from over.

'Were you aware that Jessica Craven was inside the skip?' he asked.

'No, I was not,' said Lynette crisply.

'But you do know her,' stated Zelensky.

'Yes, she's the tramp who stole my man.'

Something tripped in Barton's brain.

'Wait a minute. When we first spoke to you, you asked if we'd identified who was in the skip. You said you reckoned it was just a tramp. They were your words. I think you knew she was in there. You also weren't very keen on giving a statement when we asked you for one.'

'The tramp thing was a slip of the tongue,' said Lynette, with some of her steel returning. 'I didn't want to give a statement because I already have a record. Look, maybe she didn't deserve to die, but if you do bad things, then you can only expect life to bite you on the arse.'

'We know she came to see Garth Henson down your street the night she died. I reckon you spotted her either arriving or leaving.'

Lynette's eyes flashed warning signs.

'You're fucking mad. Are you trying to say I'm a murderer now? I told you, I didn't know she was in it.'

Barton leaned back in his seat.

'There have been a variety of fires in the vicinity of your house. Are you responsible for any of them?'

'I'm not saying any more.'

'Why?' said Zelensky. 'You've admitted to the most serious one.'

Lynette fixed her with a glass-shattering stare.

'Because I don't know whether to admit to them all.'

Barton was beginning to suspect he could add the strangest interview he'd ever conducted to his oddest of cases.

'Why did you set the skip alight?' asked Barton.

'I like fire. Interview's over.'

Barton recalled what the woman from the recent house blaze had said. Although it was a stretch to consider Lynette as holy, she could be a fallen angel.

'Did you know that someone almost died in a house fire last night?'

Lynette merely scowled at him.

'I believe you started the fire thinking the home was empty, then you went back in and rescued the woman when you realised it wasn't.'

'Do I get more time off if I admit to that, too?' asked Lynette.

'This isn't a joke. A woman has died because of your actions, and other people could have perished too. The fire against the wall of the flats caused toxic smoke to pour into an asthmatic child's room. It was touch-and-go for a while.'

For the first time in the interview, Lynette looked contrite.

'I'm sorry. I wasn't aware of that.'

'But did you start the fire?'

Lynette just stared at him, then looked down and wouldn't respond to any further questions. Barton was about to end the interview when he had an idea.

'What do you think of Stefan Russo?'

Lynette's head shot up. Her eyes blazed, but then she beamed broadly, displaying beautiful teeth, which made Barton wonder if they were Russo's work. The grin turned into an ugly sneer.

'That motherfucker deserves some pain. He as good as threw Jessica in that skip. You should have him sitting in this seat. Charge him with murder.'

'Being a love rat is not currently an indictable offence.'

'Yeah, well, it should be. I could tell you some stories about him.'

'Please do,' said Barton.

Lynette frowned at him.

'Did he treat you badly?' asked Zelensky.

Lynette paused to consider her answer.

'You know what? Not all the time. I was walking through town and he came up to me. He said I was beautiful, and he reckoned I deserved a man who would treat me like a goddess.'

Zelensky cringed, and Barton almost followed suit.

'Yeah, and I fell for it. But he was nice. He paid for these.'

Lynette unzipped her top, and for a moment Barton thought she was going to take her bra off.

'I didn't want them this big, obviously, but he was paying, so I said okay.'

She zipped her top back up.

'Now I'm forever destined to walk around with men staring at my chest. I dread to imagine what effect they'll have in prison.'

'They must have cost a lot, so he was very generous,' said Zelensky.

'It depends how you look at it. These are a curse. People believe I exchanged my brain for them.' She stared hard at Barton. 'I bet you judged me the moment I opened that door to you, when you first came to my house.'

Barton had the grace to nod.

'Please, carry on,' said Barton. 'So, Stefan spent lots of money on you at the beginning. He spoilt you.'

'Very much so. All the way through our relationship, in fact. He made me chuck my job and move in with him, so I gave notice on my flat. We stayed at his place in London most of the time, which was okay, but I got bored. I didn't know anyone. He wouldn't let me have my friends down.'

'He isolated you,' said Zelensky.

'Yeah, I suppose. I never thought of it like that until after, but I was totally dependent on him. That's why it was so terrible when he dumped me.'

'Did it come out of the blue?' asked Zelensky.

Lynette gave her a sad smile.

'No, not completely. He'd started getting snippy with me about spending his money. Stefan had given me his credit card, but he took it back. He stopped giving me certain things.'

Barton suspected those things were drugs, but he didn't say anything because Lynette was on a roll now.

'We came back one weekend in May because he said he wanted to watch some football with a mate. I took a train to visit a friend of mine in Spalding on the Saturday. She had twins, poor thing. Her bloke had done a bunk, too. I came back on the Monday and found all my clothes, make-up, jewellery, fucking everything, outside in a bin bag. Even the happy-couple photo of us two that I paid to have made into a canvas. I tried my key and it wouldn't work. That was it.'

'What did you do?' asked Zelensky.

'Smashed some of his windows.'

'I meant, where did you go?'

'The only place I could. My mum's. We aren't close either. I moved out when I was sixteen and said some unpleasant shit to her. She was in her rights to tell me to do one, but she didn't.'

'And that was the last you saw of Russo?' asked Barton.

Lynette blushed a little.

'Kind of. I embarrassed myself by shouting through his letter box afterwards. It was hard. I really liked him, you know. Men have been treating me like shit all my life, just because I'm a bit scatty. I give my all, then they leave me, or worse. I thought he was the one, I actually did. We looked at rings and everything. I would have done anything for him.'

'It sounds like a serial philanderer,' said Barton, although his mind was wondering what 'anything' might mean.

'Yeah, and I did meet that Jessica. She was at the house once when I went around. He'd told me to fuck off the previous time or he'd call the police, even though he wouldn't have. Anyway, this time she came out and apologised. It was kind of sweet. Although she also told me to be careful. I don't suppose she knew he had a girlfriend when she first met him. After our chat, I stopped bothering him. I gave up and just sat inside, smoking and drinking with my mum. She eventually encouraged me to give life another crack. Then I recognised Jessica looking like shit coming out of Henson's place a while before she died. No prizes for what she was there for.'

'Was he dealing drugs to her?' asked Barton.

'I don't want to talk about that, but it was obvious Stefan had dumped her. She looked like she was homeless, dragging a little suitcase around with her. I let myself down again after I saw her like that, and I went and visited him. I allowed him to fuck me a few times, then the bastard blanked me again. I'm an idiot, and I'm back in the gutter. I might as well be in prison.'

53

DI BARTON

Lynette clammed up after that. She declined to answer questions on her methods or how long her offending had been going on so after Lynette had been returned to the cells, Barton asked Zelensky what her gut feeling was.

'I believe her. She didn't speak about Jess as though she wanted her dead.'

'No, but she was fairly heartless. I didn't hear or see any real remorse about Jess dying.'

'That's true, but she seemed genuinely sorry about the child, and we suspect she went back and saved that old lady. It sounds like she's a pyromaniac, setting these fires on impulse. She'll solicitor up eventually, and that's what they'll say before sentencing.'

Barton sucked his teeth while he thought. Zelensky had made a good point. They had a CPS solicitor in today, who would help on whatever they charged her with. Arson with intent to endanger life gave the judge an enormous range of options from a high-level community order to many years behind bars. Barton suspected Lynette didn't understand that she could be looking at a lengthy time in jail.

She would probably get away with a short prison term or maybe even a suspended sentence if they charged her with plain arson, especially as she admitted her guilt at the first opportunity and had a clean record for that type of crime. It was highly unlikely her solicitor would advise her to plead guilty to arson with intent.

However, the level of proof required to prosecute was not that she specifically wanted to kill Jess. All they had to prove was that her actions were reckless enough to endanger someone's life. If the Crown could prove that, Lynette would probably receive a life sentence.

If truth be told, Barton felt a little sorry for her. Lynette was also a victim, but which part of her story was true and which was lies? Barton found the CPS solicitor, Jane, in the canteen and sat next to her. She seemed old to Barton, but he knew she was only a few years older than him. She was an austere woman, dressed in a very sensible wool suit. Two inches of her roots were showing; a common problem with multiple lockdowns. Barton respected her. She had a strange sense of humour, but she was rarely wrong.

'John, have you decided to start annoying me on my breaks now? Perhaps I should take a recording of your voice and play it next to my bed.'

Barton froze, with no idea what to say to that.

'Relax, I've already eaten,' she said.

Barton didn't relax, but he did explain the case to her. She sipped her coffee while she thought.

'Okay,' she finally said. 'Lynette knew this Jess, and for obvious reasons didn't like her. There's your intent. She also said she was aware Jess was homeless. As for the house fire, who's to say the person who saved the old lady was Lynette? Could have been a passer-by. If it wasn't Lynette who went back in, then she really is a dangerous piece of work. Charge her with arson with intent. Let a jury decide on her guilt. Who knows what information might crawl out of the woodwork in the meantime?'

'Right,' said Barton under his breath.

Jane looked over her large tortoiseshell glasses at him.

'You believe this girl, don't you?'

'Yes. I don't think she meant to do it.'

'I knew you were a big softie at heart. Nothing to do with those giant bazookas that all the idiot men in this place are talking about?'

Barton smiled. He would get the ball rolling and charge Lynette for the more serious offence. It wasn't his job to conclude if someone was guilty or innocent. That was the court's role. The police's job was just to put the offender before the court and present the evidence. The judge and jury would decide if Lynette should spend the next twenty years in jail.

54

DI BARTON

Barton turned his computer off at ten p.m. after hours of paperwork. He'd formally charged Lynette and she had returned to her cell, speechless when he'd explained the sentencing guidelines for arson with intent. Strange and Pigs had searched her house, but found nothing unusual. Her mother seemed oblivious to what was going on. All she said was that Lynette had been a troubled child, and she'd been in court before.

Pigs was the only other detective still at their desk. Barton stopped next to her.

'Time to call it a night.'

Pigs looked up at him with a fresh face. Oh, to be young again, thought Barton, ruefully.

'Five more minutes, sir.'

'Make sure it is five minutes,' replied Barton. He was about to leave when he remembered an email he'd received from Cox earlier in the day. 'Last thing. I've been receiving a lot of good feedback about you from a variety of people, including my boss. You've really hit the ground running.'

'That's great to hear. It's a bit weird to say it, but I feel like I've ended up where I belong. Uniform was a great learning curve, but after three years it felt like I'd seen most of it before. Watching drunks get tasered, quickly gets old. I joined up to make a difference, which might sound a little cheesy, but solving major crimes really does save lives.'

'Remember to keep a good balance at home. Any goals?'

'Promotion. I'm a bit of a petrol head and I'd love to get a fast sports car.'

'Like Zander's?'

'No, something a bit more manly than that.'

Barton beamed at her. He couldn't wait to tell Zander that. He wished her goodnight and plodded down to the car park. The day's drama had made him forget that Holly was picking Gizmo up earlier. He drove home with a smile.

Strange and Zander had agreed to come in early the next morning to ensure Lynette was processed smoothly. She might be at the station for a couple of days before she went to court. Barton had worked like a Trojan recently and planned to take a few days off. He could sense he was mentally drained and ready for some much-needed home time.

Barton bumped up onto the drive and hurried into the house. He found himself tiptoeing towards the kitchen like the Pink Panther, with a huge childish grin plastered on his face. Lawrence had his head buried in the fridge.

'Hey, who ate all those caramel yoghurts?' he said by way of greeting.

Barton blushed slightly and left him to it, noting the new dog basket that had been placed in the corner of the kitchen with toys and a blanket on the top. It looked unused. Luke would usually be in bed at that time of night, so Barton headed to the lounge.

When he opened the door, Holly and Layla were watching TV. The little greyhound's head popped up from his paws where he was lying on the carpet next to the fire. Wide, big brown eyes stared at Barton. The dog rose, then trembled.

'Sit down, Dad. You're scaring him.'

Barton sat on one of the chairs and tried to call the dog over. But Gizmo lay back down again.

'Have you got any treats for him?' asked Barton.

'Loads,' said Holly. 'But he hasn't eaten anything since we collected him. They said to leave him to get used to his new environment. I saw your text. Well done on your result.'

'Thanks. It's been an up-and-down case. A lot of people's lives have been damaged, though, so I don't feel like a winner.'

Barton reclined in his seat and, with his mind still on work, he considered the London aspects to the van fire. The Met would arrest and charge the Bates brothers and he'd bet Russo would then crawl back into the country.

It did seem tough that Russo had emerged unscathed from all this. Barton would speak to the Met and ask if he was allowed to inform Russo that his name had been mentioned multiple times in connection with class A drug use. Russo could just deny it, but at least he would spend some time looking over his shoulder.

Out of the corner of his eye, he noticed Gizmo rise from his position on the floor. He pattered towards Barton. Gizmo smelled Barton's ankles for a few seconds, then lay down between his feet. Gizmo closed his eyes. Barton did the same.

55

LYNETTE

I woke up this morning after no more than a couple of hours of sweaty sleep.

Why don't I get up during the night when I can't nod off? Instead, I roll around in the twilight feeling that the morning will only bring further heartache and problems. I'm not sure I can remember what it feels like to have eight hours of uninterrupted sleep. Not without filling myself with drugs or drink first, and I don't think that really counts.

Inspector Barton had me brought back to the interview room two days ago and I was charged. He told me that I could go to prison for years, decades even. I don't understand why. How could anyone reasonably be expected to know someone is unconscious in a skip?

After the shock of the house fire, I checked the Internet before I tried to hide the materials used. For a first conviction for arson, the worst I expected to receive was a year, with only half of that behind bars. Barton told me I could speak to a court-appointed solicitor this morning before I have my initial hearing in front of the magistrates. Barton was kind enough to warn me that he doubted I'd get bail. He seems a decent man. I thought the police were there to slam you, but he came across as fair.

I spent yesterday trying to look for positives. What are my future prospects? Do I have anything good to look forward to?

They offered me a shower last night, which I refused, and brought me food, which I didn't eat. I feel so spaced out.

I took the shower they offered me at seven a.m. and ate the microwaved breakfast meal. Anything to feel more with it. I thought I was going to have to go to court in my old clothes. Just my luck to get nicked in a tits-out pink tracksuit, but they said what I was wearing would be kept for evidence.

I was surprised when they brought me some size ten black jeans and a size twenty light blue blouse with a pair of flat shoes to wear. I also got given a size twenty sports bra and a pair of knickers my mother would think were old-fashioned. They all feel new, though. I don't suppose it's fair to send me to court in the frayed tracksuit they gave me two days ago when I was first arrested. I even got a comb and a hair bobble.

They're opening my cell door when I realise this is it. I will be judged shortly, then maybe on my way to prison. The magistrates' court doesn't scare me, which perhaps should be a worry. Although they were kind throughout my previous case.

I remember that time. The lad who dumped me then was similar to Stefan. I thought he was the one too, and I was his. Turns out I was one of two and had been for a year. That was different, though. I didn't want him back, but I wanted him to suffer. Stupid, really. It took ages to pay off the compensation for all the slashed tyres. I should have just carried on turning up at his place of work.

What is tough to wrap my head around is that I could get sent straight to prison. I'll have to tell them I'm my mother's carer or something. It's all happened too fast. It's hard to keep my emotions stable in my mind. With so little sleep, everything feels surreal.

Even my vision doesn't appear to be working properly. The custody sergeant smiles at me as he signs me out to a man with a Serco shirt on.

They don't bother cuffing me, just walk me towards a big van with blacked-out windows. For the first time in what seems like ages, there are a few clouds in the sky. I shiver when I step inside the transport vehicle. Not because it's cool out of the sun, but because I hear sobbing. When they put me into the tiny compartment, shut the door and lock me in, it reminds me of being clipped in on a roller coaster. The sensation in my stomach is the same. It's a nasty ride, this one, where you might never get off.

They bring men out as well as other women and put them onto the van. A few of them argue and swear but it's half-hearted. The sun beats on the dark windows. I can feel myself beginning to cook. When the engine starts and the vehicle pulls away, everyone is quiet. For most of us, it's the road to hell.

I stare out of the tinted window at people passing by. No court for them today. No journey in this tin can. They are free, but don't know it. That was me before all of this. I was complaining about work and relationships; I should have been celebrating that I had my freedom and health.

We trundle through the security gates of the court and into the darkness of the underground car park. I'm taken off last and booked in. They offer me a solicitor, which this time I accept, then lock me in another cell. It's cold and empty, just like my heart.

There's a knock at the door, which is opened, and the solicitor comes in. He says his name is Andrew Donnelly, but I should call him Andrew. The guard leaves the door open and Andrew sits on the bed next to me. I tell him what's happened. He smiles and says to relax. What's done is done. He'll ask for bail, but with arson of this magnitude, it might be a risk the magistrates will be loath to take.

He tells me not to admit my guilt at this point. I'll have time for that further down the line. I explain that I did already but he smiles again and says that's fine. Andrew is smartly dressed and reminds me a little of a shy Tom Cruise, but I feel reassured. He says he'll come back and see me after the magistrates have listened to the charges.

'Can't they deal with it today?' I ask. 'Just sentence me to whatever. I want to get it over with.'

He slowly shakes his head.

'The magistrates' sentencing powers stop at six months.'

He's gone before that comment registers. I lie down on the thin blue plastic mat and try to think of my mother's face when the police turned up. Will she be missing me yet? It's daft, but I was hoping that I wouldn't need to explain what I've done. I expected a court case in a few months, thinking they'd release me until that date. I planned to tell my mum I was moving out to live with a mate for whatever sentence I received. She probably wouldn't realise. She rarely watches the news, and she hasn't got any close friends. In fact, she's barely aware of what goes on in the garden, never mind further afield.

She knows enough not to talk to the police if they turn up. There isn't anything incriminating in the house. I don't suppose they'll search too hard now I've admitted to setting the fires. They certainly won't look in the rockery where I buried my Zippo lighter collection.

I lost my watch ages ago, and my phone wasn't returned to me, so I'm not sure what the time is when they take me to the courtroom. I'd guess it's been an hour. Two serious, middle-aged female officers escort me along a gloomy corridor, and I come through a wooden door into a light room. There's a plastic window separating me from the rest of the court. People in suits sit at lines of desks. The door closes behind me, and I find myself alone in the dock. I'm told by a stern-looking man to remain standing. Raised up behind him are three magistrates sitting behind what I know is the bench. They look at me in the same way you would a small, unremarkable goldfish.

A grey-haired man in the middle of them asks me my name and address, which I give to him with a croaky voice. He tells me to take a seat. A slim black woman in a green pencil skirt who is seated two desks up from Andrew stands and begins talking about my case. Andrew gives me a little thumbs up. I find it hard to listen from behind the glass, but after she's spoken for ten minutes, I clearly hear the last sentence.

'We ask that bail be denied in these circumstances.'

The magistrates confer in hushed voices. They nod in unison, after barely a few seconds.

'Lynette Croston,' says the grey-haired man. 'Please stand. Due to the severity of the charges, we decline jurisdiction in this case and pass it to Crown Court.' He looks at Andrew. 'Will your client be entering a plea today?'

'No, your honour.'

'In that case, we will set a date for a plea hearing at Peterborough Crown Court. With regards to bail, do you have anything to say?'

Andrew explains about my mother and what he calls my insignificant offending history, but it seems half-hearted. The magistrates confer briefly again.

'In light of the nature of the offence, we deny bail. Ms Croston, you will have another chance to apply for bail in a month's time. In the meantime, you will be held on remand at HMP Peterborough. Probation will prepare a report to look into the matter. Do you understand?'

I nod. For a moment, I want to blurt out that it isn't fair.

'Take her down.'

I feel like I should say something, but the door opens behind me and the same two guards enter the dock and cuff my hands in front of me. Before I know it, I'm back in the cell I was in fifteen minutes ago. Andrew arrives before I've even managed to sit down.

'If you'd like me to represent you, I will.'

'I haven't got any money.'

'That's okay. The courts pay. I'll visit you in the prison next week and we'll talk through your case.'

'I don't want to go to prison,' I say to him.

'I know,' he says, but his smile fades.

I wait for him to tell me it won't be too bad, but he doesn't.

56

LYNETTE

I sit in the court cell for what must be hours. They bring me a white-bread cheese sandwich, some plain crisps and a bun that tastes like it's ninety-nine per cent sugar. It all goes straight through me and I'm forced to hover over the tin toilet. The toilet paper is cruel.

Eventually they take me out to a bigger van than the one I was in before. This is more like a bus. The smell inside is terrible, a combination of fear and unwashed humans. The sun has returned with a vengeance and getting into my compartment is like being slid into an oven. After half an hour of sweating, we trundle off towards the prison, which I've driven past many times although idling outside is the first time I've properly looked at the high walls. It's hard to imagine living behind those barred windows.

I swallow and take a deep breath, despite the aroma. I won't let this break me. The bus jolts forward and we enter a huge cavernous garage, which feels like entering a monster's mouth. We stop again. Loud machinery closes the gate behind us and plunges us into twilight. Then the huge vehicle gate opens in front of us and we turn left towards a plain, high metal gate covered in barbed wire.

Looking outside, I see male prisoners in green overalls and orange vests pushing large trolleys full of bulging black bin liners. They disappear from view behind me. A young male prison officer with ginger hair and sleeve tattoos on both arms comes out of a side gate and opens another big metal gate lined with razor wire. We are driven in. I'm the first off and escorted straight into a single-storey building.

In the bright early evening sunshine, the place doesn't seem so bad. I can tell the staff are relaxed. At a desk, there's a heavy-set male officer, who beckons me over. He is professional, but cool.

'Full name and address.'

I give him both.

'Put your finger in there.'

I push my index finger into the scanner.

'Any drugs or weapons on your person?'

I shake my head.

'Go with the officers,' he says, while staring at his watch.

I walk down a narrow corridor between two women who could still be teenagers. We enter an area with a 'searching' sign on the wall. I step into a booth, but don't turn around. Straightening my shoulders, I pull my T-shirt off. I put my hands behind my back and unclasp my bra.

'Woah!' says one of the officers. 'Just down to bra and pants.'

After a perfunctory glance over both sides of me, they tell me to get dressed. I follow them to a desk. An older woman stares at me like we're in a clothes shop.

'Anything with you?' she asks.

I shake my head.

'Here's a bag of toiletries. What are you, a ten bottom, big top?' She smiles. 'I'd keep them under cover if I were you. Shoe size?'

'Five.'

Before I know it, I've seen a nurse and been weighed, been given a prison tracksuit and pumps and I've eaten a gigantic jacket potato covered with cheddar and gooey baked beans. I was tempted to refuse it, but I'm glad I didn't because it was amazing to eat something that wasn't completely processed. Me and a short, thin girl, Smith, who looks and smells like she was dug out of a grave this morning, are then escorted to what they tell us is the induction wing. We both have little to carry.

The prison is vast and I'm disorientated, but it's quieter than I imagined. I've watched jail movies and obviously I'll get to share with Peterborough's equivalent of Myra Hindley. The escorting guard hands over our files to an Asian woman in her thirties who opens a door to a cell near the gates.

'Smith, in you go. You know the rules.'

The small room seems clean, but the sunken-faced girl on the plastic chair in there gives us a filthy look. Smith edges in and the door is slammed behind her. I try to steel myself for what's about to happen, but I feel weak and crazy. The officer takes me upstairs and stops outside cell twenty.

'First time?'

'Yes,' I whisper.

'I'm Mrs Hussein. Treat the others how you want to be treated yourself.'

She opens the door and I almost weep with relief when I see it's empty.

'Am I on my own?' I ask.

'Of course. You're an arsonist.'

57

DI BARTON

Barton had three pleasant days off in a row. There were a few calls about preparation of the case for the CPS, but he was able to catch up on some reading and go for long walks with Holly and Gizmo. The first time they let the dog off his lead in an enclosed field near their house, they expected him to race away. Instead, Gizmo walked towards Barton and stood in between his legs. Barton had to walk home as if he were about to lay an egg.

When Barton returned to the office, he was refreshed and ready to get stuck back in. He turned his computer on and discovered his inbox had two hundred emails. After a skim through them, he found two that morning from Karen at the Met. The first told him that the van fire bodies' identities had been confirmed through their DNA as being Henson and Dihoud. No surprise there. The second message asked him to give her a ring. He picked the phone up on his desk.

'Townsend.'

'Hi, Karen. John Barton here.'

'Hi, John. Thanks for ringing back. I wanted to let you know that we decided the time was right to arrest the Bates brothers. They own a large house out in the Essex countryside. Both men were armed, and they chose to fight. It'll be on the news by lunchtime.'

'Any fatalities?' asked Barton.

'Three. One of their underlings was with them and he had a gun, too. That's more or less the case over. The Bateses ran a tight ship with few others involved at any serious level. We might get a bit of heat from the press, but these men were the worst of the worst. England should sleep easier tonight.'

Barton was about to finish the call when he remembered Russo. He reminded Karen of Russo's peripheral involvement in the case and said he'd like to speak to Russo again and mention the illegal nature of his class A habit. Karen said she had no problem with it.

'Actually, there was one thing that I thought I'd mention,' she added. 'We probably won't crack those phone codes now everyone's dead, but we're guessing Russo warned Henson the police were sniffing around, and he told Dihoud,' said Karen. 'That motorbike you saw outside Henson's house will have been a contact checking it out. It might not have been Dihoud, because we think he was elsewhere that day. Whoever that was must have reported back to the Bateses after seeing you lot. It was that which probably put in motion the kill order for Henson and Dihoud.'

Barton scowled at the ruthlessness of it all. They exchanged final pleasantries and said goodbye. Barton put the phone down and tapped a finger on his chin while he thought. He had a busy few days ahead of him preparing the casework for the CPS. Lynette was behind bars and the other people involved were dead. Yet he felt unsettled all of a sudden. The motorbike was burned as well. Barton had suspected that Dihoud was driving it, but could it have been someone else? If it was, what were they up to now?

Something stank about Russo. Barton expected Russo to turn up now that anyone who could cause him damage was out of the picture and when he did, Barton would be waiting for him. Barton picked up the phone and rang Sam Dench. He wanted to know the moment Russo stepped onto British soil.

58

LYNETTE

I've spent a week in jail now and I'm already bored out of my mind. I haven't seen any of the violence I was expecting. Perhaps that's because we're locked away for twenty-two hours a day because of the pandemic. It's hard to assault anyone through a foot of concrete.

Mrs Hussein has actually been very helpful and brought me up to speed on prison life. She's the only one who's keeping me sane. Apparently, there isn't much trouble on the remand wing where I've now been moved to. After all, we still have a chance to be found innocent, although, from talking to the rest, it seems unlikely if you're in here before the trial.

The newspapers have started calling me The Fire Killer, as have many of the inmates. It's such a catchy name, I don't suppose I can blame them. Even the laundry worker who gave me fresh bedding and is a quiet soul said, 'Here's your clean sheets, Fire Killer.'

All this time with nothing to do has made me sure of one thing. I could not handle a long sentence. My mental health would disintegrate. I can see it on the faces of most of the others in here. They've given up. What is the point of living, if this is life?

Luckily, I have a plan. I wouldn't have admitted to the crimes if I knew I would get years and years. I'd at least have made them work for it. My idea is a long shot, but the consolation is, if it fails, Stefan's life will be damaged, hopefully beyond repair. He thought I was stupid, but his overconfidence will either be his downfall, or my saviour.

A few days ago, I spotted two faces that I recognised on television. Stefan, the cocky twat, had taken me to a party at one of their houses when we first dated and he was really keen on showing me off. From the news article, it seems they were very bad boys. It was the break I needed.

I need to speak to Stefan. He's my only hope, but his telephone number is still not on my PIN. I can only ring people who they've rung to ask if they'll accept calls from me. It's pot luck though whether he'd answer his mobile phone to a number he doesn't know. I've booked him for a visit next week in the hope of persuading him to help, but I need somehow to let him know. Another prisoner said that when the prison is busy, nobody processes the requests, so it can take weeks and weeks.

The softly spoken officer who looks as if he'd be more suited to working in a care home than a prison is on today. Someone told me he'd only started two weeks ago. No wonder they keep him on the female side. I tried to flirt with him this morning, but he looked as though his head was going to explode.

I manage to catch him on his own when we're brought out for lunch.

'Sir, can I have a quick word?'

'Of course, Lynette.'

I try my best to appear desperate, but I'm not sure how convincing I am.

'My visit with my boyfriend is next week, but the prison hasn't put his phone number on.'

'Okay. I'm afraid you'll have to wait until your numbers are on,' he says.

'But what if they aren't put on in time? I haven't spoken to him since I got here. You can imagine how upsetting that is.'

He avoids eye contact and scratches at a whitehead on his neck. He draws blood.

'What do you want me to do about it?'

'How about you let me use the office phone?'

'We're not allowed to.'

'I saw someone using it the other day.'

'That was for an emergency.'

'What do you think this is? Please, pretty please.'

I watch him wavering.

'Tell you what, I'll go and ask the senior officer for you. No guarantees though,' he finally says, and leaves the wing. I frown, but at least I still have a chance.

He enters the hub area, which is like a round, windowed office so the staff can look down the spokes of each wing. The bottom half of the windows are opaque. He talks to someone out of view. An older bald man's head pops up and looks my way. I wave and regret it. The head disappears and the young officer returns. He hands me an envelope.

'What's this?'

'You get a postage-paid envelope each week to send home. You've got plenty of time to post it to him.'

He smiles and I feel like punching him.

'What do I do? Just write it and give it back to you?'

'No, you place it in the box over there.'

My brain whirs. It might work, and I do have time to send it. But I'll need to be specific and convincing with what I put in the letter.

'Don't seal the envelope, though,' says the officer. 'Security read them all to make sure you aren't harassing anyone.'

59

LYNETTE

The next morning, before we're unlocked, a slip is pushed under my door informing me that I have a legal appointment this afternoon. It must be my solicitor, Andrew. I spend the morning writing and rewriting my letter to Russo. When they let me out of my cell at two p.m. for the visit, I pass it to Mrs Hussein.

'Put it in the box, please,' she says.

'It's important that it goes today, miss.'

I explain about my boyfriend's phone number not going on my PIN but Mrs Hussein wasn't born yesterday.

'May I?' she says, opening the envelope.

I nod. She reads it out loud.

'Dear Stefan,

I'm sorry I can't get hold of you, but it's been a nightmare time. If the prison rings you, make sure you pick up and say it's okay and they'll be able to add your number. I've booked you in for a visit next week on Wednesday at three in the afternoon. I'll talk to you then.

Speak to those brothers' solicitors before you come. Or I'll ring them myself and explain your connection. All I need is proof that I wasn't where they believe I was, and I will be eternally happy.

All my love,

Lynette.

'I can't see that being a problem. I'll take it to Security on my way out.'

The morning drags in my cell and I don't manage to eat any of my lunch. Just before two, Hussein escorts me across to the visits block where I'm given a thorough rub-down search, as though I'm likely to attack my solicitor. He's waiting for me in a small room with big plastic windows.

'Hi, Lynette. How are you?'

'How do you think I am?'

His smile has cooled since I first met him. He's getting irritating. They were right to search me, or I might well have stabbed him.

'I've changed my mind. I'm not pleading guilty to the skip fire.'

'Okay. Why?'

'I was confused and scared when they asked me. I'd have confessed to anything.'

'That's plausible, but not a great way to start a trial.'

'No, but I'm hoping to get an alibi. I was at my boyfriend's house.'

Andrew's eyes narrow. His half-smile drops and I have the feeling his nicey-nicey, shy persona is a show. Maybe he will be an asset after all.

'And he can provide you with an alibi? A concrete one?'

I cross my fingers under the desk.

'Yes.'

'What about for the other fires they've charged you with starting? The house fire and the one against the wall of the flats that affected the asthmatic child.'

'No, I did them. They're not as bad though, are they?'

'No, but it's not going to look good, changing your mind about the more serious incident. Especially after you admitted to it under caution.'

'My boyfriend is coming to visit me next Wednesday. Come back afterwards and I'll confirm all of it. What will they do with me for just the other two cases?'

Andrew blows out his cheeks.

'If they fall for it, which I doubt, you could end up going down for a year. If I play the mental health angle and convince them they were impulsive crimes, I might even get that suspended. Why did you admit to it if you didn't do it?'

I take a deep breath for my Oscar-worthy performance.

'I got a shock when I set fire to the house with the old woman inside. I raced in to save her, but it was close. Whatever I am, I'm not a murderer. I panicked in the police station and was ashamed of myself. I admitted to everything, thinking I was better off locked up where I couldn't hurt people.'

'And you don't think that now?'

I smile. Clever boy.

'No, I didn't realise that I could get life for a bloody skip fire. I'm not taking the fall for someone else.'

'And you can prove that you weren't there with a firm alibi from a reputable witness?'

'Of course. My boyfriend's the dentist to the stars.'

60

DI BARTON

Three days after her arrest, Lynette's file had been passed to the CPS and Barton was tackling a case of GBH with intent from an illegal poker game when his email and mobile phone pinged in unison. It was the message informing him Stefan Russo had returned to the country at eight that morning. Barton smiled. He asked Malik to drive to Russo's property and keep an eye out for him.

Barton was on his way to a meeting with Cox when Malik rang him. Russo had just turned up in a taxi so Barton told him to wait, and he'd be there in fifteen minutes. He excused himself with Cox and left the building. He was outside Russo's house within ten minutes, where he gave Malik the heads-up.

'I don't have anything concrete on Russo. The Met believe he's probably just a wealthy user, but I don't like him at all. He's bad news for women. I hope we can rattle his cage at the very least by telling him we know about his illicit drug use. I've a feeling he may do something daft, and I want him to think I'm watching him, even if I'm not.'

'Okay,' said Malik. 'Expecting any trouble?'

'Nothing me and you can't handle.'

Malik nodded and got out of the car. Barton grinned. Malik was becoming a real asset. What with Leicester, Zelensky and now Pigs, the team's future looked assured. Barton pressed the posh doorbell. No one came to answer it. Barton reckoned the video on the doorbell would be showing Russo who was at the door via his mobile phone.

Barton pushed open the letter box.

'Shall I go around the back?' he shouted through.

A few seconds later, the door opened. Russo looked tanned, but he didn't look relaxed.

'What?'

'Can we come in?'

'No.'

'Don't you want to help the police?'

'Please waste someone else's time,' said Russo, starting to close the door.

'We heard about your cocaine problem,' said Barton.

The door stopped moving and slowly glided back open.

'What is this bullshit?'

'Is it true?'

'Who said I took cocaine?' asked Russo.

Barton admired Russo's cool, but Sasha had no reason to fabricate anything about the night when she and Jessica met him. It was good for Barton to know that Russo could lie so convincingly.

'That's a secret,' said Barton.

'That lying asshole Henson?'

'No. He was burned to death before we could speak to him, along with his county lines contact.'

Barton detected a tiny movement around Russo's right eye, but he might have been mistaken.

'Or that whore Lynette?'

Barton heard real venom in the slur.

'Well, she is still alive to talk,' he said.

There was a definite twitch on Russo's face this time. What is it you're guilty of? thought Barton. Russo shrugged.

'Hardly a reliable witness seeing as she's looking at life inside for burning her competition.'

'It's nice to see you're keeping up with current events from your holiday. Although I can see you aren't much of a gentleman. You certainly don't seem upset by your ex-girlfriend's run of terrible luck. Your friend's agonising death hasn't appeared to bother you either.'

'That's not a crime.'

'It makes me wonder why it hasn't affected you.'

'Lynette is a psycho! I bet she burned Jess up deliberately. She set fire to my TV once. Maybe I had a lucky escape.'

'You're guilty of something.'

Russo blew out a long breath.

'Look, even if I dabbled from time to time, it wouldn't warrant any interest from Major Crimes. Leave me alone. That's a warning. Or I'll speak to Mr Walpole, the Police and Crime Commissioner, and have you investigated for harassment.'

Russo slammed the door in their faces but not before leaving them with food for thought. Barton couldn't remember telling Russo he worked in the Major Crimes department. And what kind of person knew who the Police Commissioner was?

Barton had a lot to think about.

61

LYNETTE

I receive another appointment slip for a visit at three p.m. and as soon as my door unlocks for breakfast, I race out to the nearest officer.

'Mrs Hussein, does this mean my visit has been confirmed?'

'We don't ring visitors to ask if they're coming. That's your job.'

'That's not fair. My numbers still aren't on, so I couldn't call him.'

'Listen, I checked with the team myself yesterday. They've tried your boyfriend's number five times. Nobody ever picks up, so they can't add the number on. They also repeatedly tried the other person you requested, and that was the same. You said you wrote a letter to your boyfriend last week, so if he wants to see you, he'll be here.'

I'm tempted to kick off, but it's not her fault. It's still bloody annoying. It's this place. My anger grows all the time. Not like a blooming flower, more like a creeping mould. This place brings out the worst in people. I think if I could get blind drunk then I'd have some kind of release. It's no wonder some walk around completely off their faces. I'm tempted to join them, although how I'd pay for anything would be a worry.

I tried to meditate last night. But forests and seas seemed a long way away from my concrete world. Instead, I'm in a pressure cooker and the gas is on. It's not just me. Most have haunted eyes here. Hope has gone, but a simmering anger remains.

As remand prisoners, we don't have to work. Innocent until proven guilty and all that, but as our court cases approach our shoulders droop further. Women scream in each other's faces over next to nothing. Some come out for meals with fresh cuts and scratches, which are mostly self-inflicted. A few take their frustrations out on the staff, assaulting them when their backs are turned. Afterwards, the troublemakers shriek loud and long, as though it's their souls not their bodies that are being hauled to the block.

The rest of us mope around like the undead, barely casting an eye at the drama around us, until it's our turn to explode.

The wing next to ours is for lifers. How do they cope knowing this is as good as it gets? Judging by the regular thunder of guards' boots towards their wing, I suspect it's with sporadic bouts of violence. Maybe it's the only way they know they are alive. I guess they have nothing to lose.

I return to my bed and lie perspiring on the sheets. My cell gets the morning sun and the dawn gives me hope, but the fiery rays are too much by lunchtime. Some of the girls frantically exercise in their cells. They are gaunt and sweaty, but at least they have found a way to survive.

My only thought is of my visitor at three p.m. Visits have been restricted with the current situation, so I'm lucky to have one at all. I'm taken from my cell at two thirty and escorted to where I had my visit with Andrew. After a bored rub-down search by a tired-looking officer called Kowalski, I'm left in a large holding cell with two others. We stare at the floor, ears straining with hope that our names will be called. The same officer who searched me returns to the cell.

'Delia?'

The shorter woman leaps to her feet.

'Sorry, your visit has rung in to say he couldn't get transport.'

Delia's face has the look of someone who's been given a terminal diagnosis. Maybe in here she has. I swore this shitty place wouldn't break me, but I don't know what I'll do if Stefan doesn't come.

Kowalski returns a long ten minutes later.

'Lynette.'

'Yes.'

'Your visitor is here.'

I leap out of my seat. Even though it's cruel, I can't resist giving the remaining prisoner a triumphant smile. What am I becoming?

The officer takes me a different route from the legal visit I had, through two locked doors, and I see Russo sitting in the centre of a big room containing over twenty tables. There is only one other visit going on, and they are in the opposite corner. Russo doesn't get up as I approach and I sit down opposite him. He looks so out of place in his sharp grey suit and big gold watch. I feel grubby in comparison.

Yet he is the reason that I'm in this hole. My fingers tighten into fists. If he hadn't exploited me, I would still be working in PR at posh events. All I had to do was turn up looking pretty. I used to moan that I was bored, but I realise now that the job gave me money and independence.

He discarded me so casually that it ruined my confidence and took away my future. People think I'm stupid because I'm voluptuous and attractive, but I'm not. I got Bs in English and maths. I made something of my life, even though I didn't go on to further education, but I was in too much of a rush to escape from home and see what was out there. That's not a crime. At the very least, he owes me, but I need to use my brain. I force myself to unclench my hands.

'Thanks for coming.'

'This had better be good, Lynette. I'm a busy man.'

'I need an alibi for the night Jess died.'

'What's that got to do with me?'

'You're going to give me one.'

He leans back in his seat, legs wide, shaking his loose, heavy watch by flicking his wrist.

'And why would I do that?'

'I was at your house.'

'You left hours before the fire.'

'Yes, because you threw me out. You got me drunk, screwed me, then told me to leave. I was too drunk to drive, and you wouldn't even pay for a taxi. I had to stagger home. Then walk back in the morning to fetch my car.'

'Keep your voice down. So what?'

'That makes you a shitbag, that's what. Will you do it?'

'No.'

'Then I'll tell the police everything I know about you.'

'You know nothing. I'm leaving.'

He stands and straightens his tie.

'I heard about your childhood. Your school.'

His eyes narrow.

'And I know about your cousins.'

He slowly sits, face twisted with rage, lips white with fury, his voice low and rasping.

'You're on ice so thin an ant could fall through. You've got one minute to tell me what you think you know, or I'm gone. Then you might as well set fire to your cell and pull the door shut.'

'Remember that party you took me to, when you wanted to

show off my new tits to all your pals. Justin and Tony Bates were very attentive to me when your back was turned. They were clearly very dodgy and also very high. Nothing loosens tongues like cocaine. Stefan's a wonderful man, they said. We owe him everything. He's our cousin, and we all grew up together with nothing, so we're a tight operation. Oh, how they bragged.'

I stare at him and it all slots into place. He is a dentist, that much is true. A great one, and he is bright and intelligent to boot. But how can I have been so naive? What kind of dentist makes enough money to drive Porsches and Jags, wears Rolex and Cartier, and lives in a million-pound house with holidays at his gîte in France? Even a dentist to the stars couldn't make so much.

Stefan was always cancelling appointments and lying around in bed with hangovers. He'd tell the clients he was stuck in Monaco, when he was stuck in me, or making furtive phone calls from his locked office.

Now I lean back and smile. He bares his teeth and quietly snarls in reply.

'You fucking bitch. You don't know who you're dealing with. Who's going to listen to a fucked-up fire-starter like you?'

'They'll all hear me in court in two weeks' time when I tell them who you are.'

His jaw is clenched so tight, he can't respond.

'I hope you can account for all the money you have, Mr Russo. Isn't there a new law around that?' I drive my advantage home. 'I also took a few pics of you when you were snorting coke off the table in nothing more than your socks and shoes. I'm sure the stars will love that.'

'You must be able to imagine the consequences for crossing me.' It's my turn to snarl.

'I don't have any choice. I'm not doing twenty years inside.'

Stefan's too angry to reply, so he looks around before blowing out a long breath. He stretches his shoulders and inhales deeply. His jaw bunches as he stands. Then he replies without looking at me.

'I'll do it. But if I ever hear from you again, they won't even find your ashes.'

He turns and ambles coolly towards the exit, nodding at the officer who has been watching us with interest.

He's right. I'm playing a dangerous game. When I get out of here, I'll have to leave the city and never come back. I saw on the news what happened to Henson and Dihoud. I should never have got involved with Russo. Now it's me who could get burned.

62

DI BARTON

Not long after Barton had handed the case over to the CPS, he found a note on his desk to ring an Andrew Donnelly. The name was familiar, but he couldn't place it. He rang the number.

'Andrew Donnelly speaking.'

'DI Barton here.'

'Inspector Barton. Thanks for ringing. There's some new evidence in the case against Lynette Croston. I'm her solicitor. In the spirit of disclosure, I thought I'd tell you before the court case next week, so my client doesn't spend any further time in jail unnecessarily.'

Barton almost dropped the phone.

'What?' was the best he could manage.

'Lynette has a concrete alibi for the night of the skip fire. She was at her boyfriend's that evening.'

'What?'

'A Mr Stefan Russo has given me a written statement. She went to his place around six p.m., then left in her car at ten the next morning.'

'But she confessed to the crime here at the police station,' said Barton, with his mind racing.

'Lynette explained that she was overwhelmed by the occasion. She's a troubled girl, but when we get her out of prison, we'll find her the help she needs.'

'What about the house fire and the bin fire?' asked Barton.

'She admits to doing them.'

'She does?'

'Yes, Lynette's been under a lot of pressure. She saw the skip fire, and I think she copied it for whatever reason. She's very sorry.'

Barton knew exactly why she wasn't admitting to setting the skip on fire. Without that, the charge would be reduced to arson without intent and was much less serious. She would probably go down for a while for almost killing the old lady. Pulling her out as an afterthought wasn't a hero's move if she started the fire herself.

Barton rubbed the sides of his head. Why the hell would Russo give Lynette an alibi? Was it possible that she didn't do it, but if she didn't, then who did do it? Perhaps it was Russo himself, although Barton couldn't imagine him taking any risks. He was getting the impression that he was a man who never got his fingers dirty. If the shit hit the fan, Russo was elsewhere.

Yet, why would Russo provide Lynette with a false alibi after dumping her so mercilessly? Barton struggled to see what was in it for Russo, unless Lynette had something on him.

'Are you still there?' asked Andrew Donnelly.

'Yes, I was just thinking that this Russo might not be such a strong alibi.'

'No? How so? Does it matter anyway? Either she was there or she wasn't.'

'Yes, but his word can be challenged.'

'I agree, which is why we have the footage of her arriving on his doorbell cam, then leaving the following day. I'll get it to you in the next few days.'

'How about you send it today?'

'I'll do my best.'

Barton shook his head at that, but he was focusing on Lynette. If she was blackmailing Russo, what had she been blackmailing him about?

It was only a week to the hearing. Barton finished the call, rose from his seat, and knocked on Cox's open door. She smiled at him.

'Sit down, John.'

Barton did as he was told and then updated her.

'Wow, that puts a spanner in the works. You've always suspected this Russo was up to no good.'

'Yes. Not only is he a rotten human being, but I wouldn't be surprised if he was up to some actual crime. I'd like to talk to the Met and ask them to search again to see if they can link him to anything in the Bates case. I'm sure they must have looked at every angle, but I'll double-check in light of what I've just been told. It also occurred to me that Russo seems very rich even for a top dentist. The Met might want to analyse his bank accounts if they haven't already, because that's where we might find some proof of wrongdoing.'

'Speak to Karen at the Met, then. The court case is next week though.'

'Yes, do we ask for more time?'

Cox took a sip of her coffee and Barton smiled at the underneath of her mug, which had arrows pointing upwards and said, *This is what an awesome manager looks like.*

'Lynette's in jail on remand. She has an alibi from someone who is reputable, at the moment. You'll struggle to persuade a judge with hearsay about Russo that a delay is necessary. The Crown

Prosecutor could try, but we should proceed with the other two cases. If the judge gives her a year for those two fires, we have time to dismantle her alibi, or the reputation of the man who provided it. Besides, we don't want to give Lynette any more opportunity to change her mind on those two pleas as well, do we?'

63

LYNETTE

It's two days before the court case. Andrew has been in and given me an update. I'm so tired, but I can't sleep. Reading is my main distraction and I've started doing press-ups in my cell and going to the gym. Anything but think about what might happen on Wednesday. Stefan was good to his word. The recording of me arriving and driving away the next day was a bonus. I wonder how he didn't show me leaving when he threw me out. I suppose with his money, he can pay for whatever he needs.

The gym is really quiet today. There are only four other women in here. Two of them are playing badminton on a court at the other end even though they don't know the rules. The other two girls are spotting each other on one of the weight benches, but they don't appear to have a clue either. The screw on duty is reading a newspaper in her office.

I can't get into my session at all. Even the lightest weights seem too heavy. The showers at the gym are minging, so I'll skip them and see if I can take one on the wing. Someone had taken a dump in them the last time I was here.

I return to the changing rooms and splash water on my face.

There are huge bags under my eyes. I grab my towel, shower gel and spare underwear, turn to leave and find the two weightlifters at the entrance. Their expressions are pinched, hands clenched at their sides. One has something in her left hand. It's a blade. My mouth goes instantly dry as I look around. My knees weaken. The only way out is through them.

I've been a fool again. If Stefan is the head of his organisation, as I suspect, then he could reach me in here. My poor neighbour was burned to death. Another lad died with him. Would Stefan risk me talking in court?

Focusing on my rage at Stefan, I try to summon its power. After a deep breath, I widen my stance while keeping the weapon in my eyeline. That small blade will be going through my throat or between my ribs if I'm not fast.

They stride forward and there's no time to cry out. The shorter one lunges forward with a clumsy uppercut but I tense my stomach and leap back, removing the sting from the blow. The fatter one drives the pointed weapon directly at my heart. I jerk to the side. Her wrist grazes my breast as her hand flies past and I grab it with one hand, and her elbow with my other. Then I bend and sink my teeth into her forearm.

I get real purchase and bite as fiercely as I've ever done in my entire life. The thinner one's fingers scratch at my forehead, searching for my eyes. The bigger one screams as I thrash shark-like from side to side and feel the flesh coming away in my mouth. She drops the spike and falls to the floor as my head jerks back leaving my mouth full of warm blood.

A razor blade in a wooden block appears over my left shoulder towards my eye. I twist my head and the blade sinks into my cheek. My attacker drags it hard down my face and blood pours freely now, hot down my chin and neck, drenching my T-shirt in seconds.

I open my mouth, spit out the skin, and scream like I've lost my mind. Then I ram my thumbs into the thin one's eye sockets. She knocks my hands away, but I'm beyond stopping now. All the resentment and anger that I've repressed over the years finds a release.

With a howl from deep within, I grab her long, greasy hair and smash her forehead into the changing room rail. Again, again, again. Then I shove her falling body over a bench where her head meets the ground with a thud. Her companion has been trying to crawl away, holding her arm. I boot her as hard as I can, right under the chin, snapping her head back.

The officer appears in the doorway. She looks at the scene, taking an involuntary step away in horror. My vision glazes over as I step in her direction. Her hand reaches for her radio. My eyes are already closed when I hit the floor.

64

DI BARTON

Barton stood outside the Crown Court building for a moment to gather his thoughts. He didn't need to be here, but he wanted to watch proceedings. The rapidly diminishing time before the plea-hearing had been intense.

Malik had checked the recordings from the doorbell cam and quickly noted that they only had them from the times when Lynette turned up and left. The sixteen hours in between weren't there. Barton had rung the solicitor, who'd said he would forward them, but Barton had needed to chase it up yesterday and hadn't been entirely surprised when Andrew Donnelly had told him that the system had been playing up and only worked intermittently. He'd sent some more videos from that night, but there were still a couple of missing periods. Any further requests had been ignored.

Barton's hackles had risen. Lynette could have visited Russo at six p.m. as the picture stated, then gone back to her own place. She could have returned earlier the following morning, then the camera would have seen her leaving again the next day. Strange suggested he check the road cameras because she would have driven along the main roads to Russo's house. This blew the theory out of the window because they could see her driving there just before six, but the next time her car appeared on any cameras was her returning home after ten the next day.

Feeling the case getting away from him, he'd asked Malik to check the CCTV in town to check if she'd somehow walked home and gone that way but they'd found nothing. There were many routes to her house, and it had been a misty, dark night with a low cloud that had spoken of bad weather, which had never come.

The Met had looked into Russo again, but if he was involved in the county lines business, his part in it was too well hidden. That case was now closed, pending further information.

Barton had spoken to the CPS about delaying all the hearings due to the shaky alibi, but the CPS didn't think the judge would agree. Why would a man who cruelly dropped his partner, then give her an alibi if it wasn't true? Even if the alibi was weak, they still had to prove that Lynette set fire to the skip knowing Jessica was in it. Unless Barton could provide further evidence, they would drop the case at this point and just proceed with the lesser charges. It was possible they might never get a conviction for the skip-fire death.

Barton had also received a call from the Prison Information Officer to say that Lynette had been assaulted in the prison gym, but she would still be attending court. Barton had no idea how today would go. All options were open to the judge for the two lesser offences. She could send her back to jail pending pre-sentencing reports, or she could easily give her two years. Barton strode up the steps and joined the queue at the scanner.

With the restrictions in place, the courts were grinding to a halt and only people directly involved were being allowed in so Barton told a guard he had late evidence to submit. The woman gave him a sceptical look, but he was permitted inside. The gallery was empty.

Lynette's case was the only case scheduled for that day and was due to start at ten a.m.

The court usher came in through the swing doors.

'All rise for the Honourable Judge Craythorne.'

Barton stood, then sat when directed. He watched the judge converse with the legal clerks, then, after a nod from the judge, Lynette was brought into the dock. Barton's mouth fell open at her appearance. She wore baggy blue trousers and a billowing white blouse, but her arms looked thin and wiry. On the side of her right cheek was a thick ten-centimetre plaster running from the corner of her eye to her chin. Without make-up, there was a grey tinge to her skin.

Lynette stared back at him as he observed her face. Her eyes were dulled like a trapped animal's.

'I understand that the prosecution has requested a delay for charge 42561, is that correct?'

The Crown prosecutor rose. He was a short, rotund man with a florid complexion.

'That's right, Your Honour. We need further time to analyse a witness's alibi. In light of the offence, we expect bail to remain declined.'

The judge, a sprightly woman who Barton would guess was somewhere around the age of sixty, looked up at the prosecutor from the bench. She gave him a tiny smile.

'Do you? Either she was there or she wasn't. If you haven't disproved the alibi, I suspect it may stick. Your thoughts are noted, of course.'

The prosecutor proceeded to read out the details of the other two arsons. Afterwards, Lynette was asked to swear an oath. She seemed upset and confused. Barton didn't think it was an act. She no longer looked beautiful. Her hair had been cut without care. The pizazz, the light in her eyes, it was all gone. If, when that plaster was removed, there was a scar of similar length, he wondered if she'd ever get it back.

The judge read out the details of the lesser charges then paused to observe Lynette before she spoke again.

'How do you plead to these two offences?' she asked.

'Guilty,' said Lynette, raising her chin.

'To both crimes?'

'Yes.'

'Anything you'd like to tell the court?'

'I'm sorry.'

The judge stared at her impassively, but Barton noted her gaze slide to the plaster.

'What say you?' she said to the defence solicitor. Andrew Donnelly stood up.

'Your Honour. These are sad cases with no winners. I heard that the lady who was saved from the house blaze will soon be living at her daughter's house after responding favourably to treatment, but hasn't been well enough to comment. The child affected by the other fire is back at home and much improved. My client has had a troubled life having been raised by a lone parent. At the time of these fires, she was still struggling with depression after an unpleasant break-up with the man who has now provided the alibi and recorded evidence to support it.

'Under considerable strain, she saw the aftermath of the skip fire and, for a reason she can't explain, threw a match in the bins near the flats. It gave her some kind of release. She later set fire to the house after seeing it was empty. She hoped the excitement would make her feel better, but it did not.

'The shock of almost hurting another person haunts her to this day. We understand you have a range of options at your disposal, but we would like you to consider a community sentence. Keeping Lynette behind bars will do nothing to tackle her health issues or manage any further risks to the community. As you see, prison has already taken its pound of flesh. She will gladly do as many rehabilitation days as you require and attend any courses you deem necessary. Lynette will work with Probation on a daily basis so she can put this sorry episode behind her.

'She pleaded guilty to these crimes at the earliest opportunity in the police station, and I ask for the credit for that to be taken into account. She has a clean record for this type of crime, having not been before the courts for any other reason for many years.'

Donnelly sat down. The Crown prosecutor stood.

'The crown accepts there are a range of factors in play here and this is the first time the defendant has been before the court for a crime of this nature. However, there is no getting away from the seriousness of these charges. It's pertinent to note at this point that she previously confessed to the skip fire, which she has since rescinded. It's fair to assume that she only changed her plea on understanding the length of any potential sentence she might receive. It is my belief that Ms Croston set three fires in close succession, making her an extremely dangerous lady.'

The judge looked around the room, deep in thought, and Barton found he was holding his breath.

'Why did your client change her plea?' she asked Donnelly.

'She was disorientated and confused at the police station. The guilt of knowing what could have happened to the lady in the house fire meant she believed she should be punished, even though she went back in and rescued her.'

'And she no longer feels like that?'

'Lynette Croston has been punished enough. Let her get the assistance she so clearly needs.'

* * *

Judge Craythorne retired to her chambers. She said she would pass sentence or defer at two p.m. For one of the few times in his life, Barton wasn't hungry. The weather was warm, but the intensity of those few weeks of the fires had faded. Barton still hadn't put his tie back on.

He spent the time walking up and down the river, staring at the swans. At times like these, he envied them the simplicity of their lives. A large part of him hoped that Lynette wasn't guilty of killing Jessica, but that didn't make it so.

At two, the judge returned to pass sentence. The case had grabbed the attention of the media, so Barton was glad the journalists weren't allowed in. Barton stared at a trembling Lynette as they brought her back to the dock. The judge told them to sit, all except Lynette. Was she The Fire Killer?

'After careful consideration and perusing the report from Probation, I will sentence you now. Lynette Croston, you have admitted your guilt to these two dangerous crimes. There was considerable damage to the house, which will cost thousands to repair. While lower in value, the bin fire could easily have cost a young child his life. With that in mind, I sentence you to two years in prison.'

Barton forced himself to breathe while the judge continued with her verdict.

'Due to your previous clean record in this regard and your willingness to seek help, I am suspending this sentence for two years. You will attend appointments with Probation until they tell you otherwise. Any further incidents of this nature will result in the activation of the two years, plus a further period for the later offence. In conclusion, if you are convicted of arson again, you will be sent to prison for a significant period of time. Do you understand?'

Lynette could only nod.

'You are free to go.'

65

LYNETTE

I stumble from the courthouse and wander down the steps but what should be a moment of triumph feels very low-key. There are some press gathered outside, but they don't recognise me. The person they are looking for has gone.

Andrew shook my hand inside and said he'd be in touch, but that was it. My clothes and a few belongings are still at the jail. They said I could return and get them immediately, but I assumed they meant in the prisoner transport bus. I can do without another ride in that, but I feel vulnerable out here on the pavement on my own.

Surely Russo wouldn't try anything in broad daylight. Just thinking of him makes me so fucking angry. He clearly provided the alibi to shut me up, then planned to have me taken out in the jail shortly after. I glance over my shoulder, moving my gaze from face to face. Perhaps I've saved myself from one prison to live in another.

I haven't any money for a taxi, having come to court with nothing. I remember the £40 my mum sent me, half of which is still sitting in my prison account. Maybe I should have gone back after all, because walking home is now my only option. I spot a familiar face in the street ahead of me. It's Inspector Barton. I haven't got the energy for a conversation, but he stands in my path. Keeping my head down, I sense his eyes on me.

'Lynette. Wait a minute.'

I take a few more steps, but then I can't help myself. Even though he was the one who arrested and charged me, I can't help thinking he wants the best for me. I ended up in prison, but only I can be responsible for that. I drag the remnants of my sass to the surface.

'Happy, Inspector?' I say with venom.

He doesn't look unhappy with the verdict. I can tell he's thinking before he replies.

'To be honest,' he says, 'I don't like how this is playing out. Something's out of kilter. The detective in me likes finished puzzles, and this one has big pieces missing.'

'Will you leave me alone now?'

'I hope we don't have to speak again, but I have a feeling it might be necessary. Stefan Russo is still on my agenda. I can protect you from him if there's something you want to tell me.'

I look into his face and maintain eye contact. He seems genuine, but I can't risk believing him.

'Protection, eh? There are too many dead bodies for you to be throwing that word around.'

'Talk to me, Lynette. Tell me what you know. Your alibi doesn't hold up to scrutiny, but at this point I don't understand why.'

For a moment, I'm tempted to tell him everything, but I need to speak to Mum first. I need to go away, I know that. All I can manage is a sad smile for Barton. I turn and wander down the street.

'Wait,' shouts Barton. He jogs up to me and hands me his business card. Strangely, his firm nod is reassuring. I put his card in my pocket and begin the walk home. Still, it's not too far. No more than an hour, and I have nothing else to do. The same could be said for today, tomorrow and seemingly forever. My hand reaches to my cheek, but I consciously pull it away. I felt high as a kite when I realised I was free again, but it lasted seconds. What's the point?

I force myself to move forward at a pace, and soon the exercise lifts my spirits a little. They said my scar would heal and be almost unnoticeable. They didn't know my line of work. The clouds part and a warm sun beats on my shoulders. I'm heading home, but is that what it is? Or am I just going to my mum's place. Apart from a shitty car and a bad credit rating, I have nothing.

It's nearly four p.m. when I arrive at our street. It looks like Clive has just had a supermarket delivery van leave and as I walk past him he glances up from his bags and grins.

'Hey, Lynette. What's up?'

'Hey, Clive.'

'I'm here for a chat if you need one.'

I smile, conscious of the plaster on my face, then rush by him, past Henson's empty house, which reminds me of Russo living free of worry, desperate to get inside. I haven't got my key, so I knock and my mother eventually comes to the door.

'You're back,' she says without emotion. 'Come in and tell me about it.'

I stroll by her and flop into an armchair. She walks to the kitchen and makes a pot of tea.

'Are you hungry?' she asks from the small hall.

I shake my head. 'Just tired, but we need to talk.'

And we do. We speak for hours and for once we're honest. It's a big shock for both of us, but more for me than her. She does care, but her childhood meant she didn't know how to be a parent. She tried, she says, but failed. Exhausted, I rise and climb the stairs. After a few steps, I stop and turn to her.

'Why didn't you answer the phone when the prison rang? I

never had a single call while I was inside. You could have visited me.'

'I sent money in for you,' she says with hope.

I can't stop myself tutting.

'It's hardly the same,' I reply.

'You could have written,' she says. 'You know I hate answering the phone.'

She's right. I suppose that's the truth of our relationship. We don't connect. There's always a barrier between us. We are the sun and the moon, always apart, destined to be alone.

'I'm sorry. I've been a terrible mother,' she says.

Tears roll down her cheeks and I can't remember the last time I saw her cry. I'm pretty sure she didn't shed any tears after Dad's horrific death, but I don't think I did, either. He wasn't worthy of them. I offer her the same smile I gave Barton earlier.

She gets up from the sofa, but I've had enough of talk. She arrives at the bottom of the stairs as I reach the top.

'Lynette!'

I pause, but don't turn.

'You can start again. You're young still. You need to get away from here. I'll help.'

I don't comment, open my bedroom door, then flop onto the bed. Free to start again? Without any money, I can't go anywhere. I'm stuck in this city. There to be shot at. Perhaps talking to DI Barton is my only option after all, even though Russo might then withdraw his alibi, but otherwise, I'm a sitting duck.

There's a knock at my bedroom door. My mother walks in and closes it behind her.

'I need to say something else. I've never been completely honest about what happened when you were young, but perhaps I was wrong to keep you in the dark. You know some things, but not everything. It's time I told you the complete truth.'

66

DI BARTON

The morning after the hearing, Barton had to attend a wash-up meeting with Zander in Huntingdon with higher management: DCI Cox and CI Brabbins. He awoke early with indigestion, so got up and wandered downstairs. Gizmo jumped out of his basket, stretched, wagged his tail and came for a stroke. He shivered, then clambered back into his warm bed and curled himself into a tight ball. Barton put his blanket back over him.

Barton made himself a coffee and put a couple of slices of bread into the toaster. After they popped up, he slathered them with butter. He grabbed a big coat from the door and shot a guilty look upstairs. Then he went out into the back garden to watch the day begin and lowered himself into a deckchair, cursing as he spilled the coffee over his slippers. There was a definite freshness to the air that had been missing of late.

The sun seemed to rise with purpose over the rooftops, tinting them red and orange. He remembered a quote he'd read that each sunrise was a new page. The fiery globe hit the multitude of wispy lines of clouds, turning them crimson. It could have been a growing fire in the distance. He had a sense of foreboding. Would this be a fresh start for Lynette? Could she pick herself up or, like a falling phoenix, would she sink into the flames?

Twenty minutes later, after returning to the kitchen once for more toast and a glass of apple juice, it was time for him to get ready for his day. Barton climbed the stairs feeling melancholic and took a long, hot shower. Zander had said he wanted to give his MR2 a decent run, so he picked Barton up with his roof down at eight a.m. It was mild, but the sky still had a carroty tinge to it. What was it they said about a red sky in the morning?

After a bracing ride on a busy A1, Barton felt as if he'd smoked five-hundred cigarettes with the fumes he'd inhaled. They arrived at Huntingdon police station just before eight thirty. Zander began cursing when the closing mechanism wouldn't pull the roof back into place. They were parked in the underground car park, so they left it open and entered the building.

Barton and Zander were surprised to find the chief super from the Met, Karen, in the meeting room. There were coffee and croissants in the corner, so they all served themselves and sat down. Barton ran through the main events of the last month or so, starting at the skip fire and finishing at Lynette's suspended sentence. Karen stayed quiet throughout. Brabbins was the first to speak.

'Is there anything we missed, or could have done better?'

'Always.' Cox smiled. 'There's also John's suspicions concerning Russo, but that's all they are at this stage.' She turned to Karen.

'That's why I'm here.' Karen smiled. 'I rang DCI Cox to talk around the case and explain that we might have had a new lead. We looked deeply into Russo's affairs, but his circle must have been so tight that he was too well protected. The Europeans, however, have had a break at their end.'

'The Europeans?' asked Barton.

'Yes, we suspected the drugs were coming from southern Europe, specifically Spain. There was chatter in the criminal community when the Bates brothers died, and they managed to link a Nathan Van Damme in with other known traffickers down there. Van Damme has been a bit of a ghost in the Netherlands. They have very little on him at the moment, but investigations are ongoing.'

Karen paused for dramatic effect. Zander broke first.

'And?'

'Van Damme studied Chemistry at King's College London. I made some calls. It's been a while, but he was a well-known student and not for all the right reasons, if you know what I mean. In his last two years there, he moved out of the halls and shared a flat in central London.'

'With Stefan Russo,' guessed Barton, recalling Russo's degree from the same place.

'Correct. They have nothing on Russo, but Van Damme regularly visits Andorra for banking purposes. With Europol involved, I suspect it's only a matter of time before Van Damme is picked up. They're suspected of smuggling Pakistani drugs from a notoriously ruthless group, so Russo may disappear if he gets spooked in any way.'

'Do you mean for a holiday or for good?' asked Zander.

'Could be either. Whether Russo makes his escape is probably dependent on his level of involvement. At this point, we just aren't sure, but he's likely to have some skin in the game.'

'What's the plan?' asked Barton.

'Russo won't be aware his name is on our radar, so I'm going to see if I can get the budget for around-the-clock surveillance on him. Whatever he does, we'll know about it.'

'Do you reckon they'll permit that with what you have so far?'

'I would say it's touch-and-go. It's reasonable to ask for an intercept seeing as this appears to be a large Class A cross-border drugs operation. But yes, it will be up to the home secretary. I'm hoping

Russo will need to raise his head above the parapet now his distributors, namely the Bates brothers, are out of the action.'

They sat in silence for a few moments, sipping their drinks as they digested the new information.

'All this makes Stefan Russo deeply involved,' said Barton. 'I've been struggling to see why he would provide an alibi for Lynette unless it was true. Obviously he could have thought what the hell, I might as well seeing as how mean I was to her, but that doesn't sound like his style so I suspect she blackmailed him somehow.'

'Go on,' said Karen.

'She would probably know about his drug use, but perhaps she met a few of these characters while she was dating him. One of the Bates brothers, for example. She's got some issues, but she's actually a smart girl. If she had her eyes open, she may well have blackmailed him into saying she was at his that night when she wasn't. The recordings could have been doctored.'

'Which means she was elsewhere and therefore probably the skip-fire killer that she initially confessed to being,' said Cox.

'Maybe she worked with Russo to get rid of Jessica, who was becoming an embarrassment. Russo put her in the skip and Lynette set fire to it,' said Zander.

'No, I don't think so,' said Barton. 'It's a bit too close to home for Russo. We were bound to look into her past, which would lead us to him. And it was very close to home for Lynette, being less than a minute's walk away.'

'Unless they thought Jess's remains wouldn't be identified,' said Zander.

'No,' said Cox. 'Russo is a dentist. He'd know a fire like that wouldn't incinerate a body and that we could identify her from her new dental work.'

'My head's spinning. Is Lynette on Russo's side or against?' asked Zander.

'I think she'll want to keep him sweet now. If he withdraws his alibi and says he was mistaken, the focus returns to her,' said Cox.

'Yeah, but Russo doesn't want any involvement with the police, so he's unlikely to do that. We could charge him with perverting the course of justice, which might be enough to get a warrant and a closer examination of his banking,' said Barton.

'It's a shame that there are all these rules to protect civilians,' said Brabbins, lightening the tone. 'Let's look into what we've discussed, search warrants, phone records, the lot. What's our biggest concern right now? Who, if anyone, is at risk?'

'Lynette,' said Barton and Karen at the same time.

Karen nodded at Barton to continue.

'If Russo is one of the bosses, then he got rid of Henson and Dihoud for much less. It only just dawned on me, too. I thought Lynette was attacked in prison randomly, but it's plausible that Russo ordered a hit on her. Can we take her into protective custody?'

'It might be an option. Will she talk to us, though? Would she want protective custody?'

'I think she trusts me. I'll drive straight there after we finish here and see if she'll come in. She might be ready to talk, especially after what happened to her face.'

'Okay, protective custody is a complicated process, but we can certainly find a safe place for her to live while we see how this pans out,' said Karen.

After another half an hour of planning, they closed the meeting. As Barton and Zander rose to leave, Barton's phone rang. It was a number he didn't recognise.

67

LYNETTE

It feels like rising from a tomb, rather than waking. My eyes wander around my room. I grew up in here. Had my first kiss here. It has the same posters on the walls from when I was a teenager, the same single bed, even the carpet is the same. Should I be touched that Mum kept it like this? Or should I just smile because I have a roof over my head? Perhaps she just did her best. I wish she could tell me how she feels and what I mean to her.

My mum sat on my bed last night and talked for hours, but she spoke about what had happened, not emotions. I barely said a thing. It was late when she left, but my mind wouldn't turn off. There was too much to process. The things she said were true; I'd chosen to forget them. I have to get some proper sleep, or at least some unconsciousness, or my mind will fold in on itself. There's a sure-fire way to achieve that.

The plaster has come off my face, probably because I rolled around having my nightmares. With my dark eyes and bootleg stitching, Frankenstein has nothing on me.

I take a quick shower, then pull on a pair of jeans and a T-shirt. Both fitted snugly before I went inside, but now threaten to slide off me. I change the jeans for the trousers I came home in from court and grab a fresh blouse from the closet. My cashcard is still on the bedside cabinet, but there's very little money in the account unless my benefits have gone in. It's quiet downstairs. My mum must have nipped out, which is unusual. In fact, I thought I heard the door close around six thirty this morning, which would be even rarer for my night-owl mother.

I make a cup of tea, eat a bowl of own-brand cornflakes that are nastier than what I ate in prison, then stare in the mirror. I refix the dressing on the side of my face, but it's tacky, not sticky. That's something I need to buy straight away. Maybe I should ring the jail because the hospital gave me clean dressings to take back with me when they needed changing.

After a deep breath, I realise I can't cope with going back there just yet. I'll go to Morrison's instead and see what they've got, even though I'm not sure I can handle that either. When it dawns on me that I can pick up a bottle of vodka at the same time, the choice has been made. I'll need to be able to cope with tougher tasks than going to the supermarket.

My mum returns as I'm pulling my trainers on and I notice she looks shifty as she comes through the back door with two bags of shopping.

'I don't suppose there's a first-aid kit or any alcohol in those bags?' I ask.

'No, I got some tasty things, though.'

'Yeah, like what?'

'Stuff for breakfast. Sausages and bacon. You know, the posh bangers you like.'

I'm tempted to tell her I'm off out, but didn't I just think I wanted affection?

'Okay, Mum. Be quick. I've got a date with oblivion.'

'Good for you. I thought we could have a nice meal together before, well, whatever...'

She smiles and almost runs into the kitchen. I've never seen her be so dramatic. This version of normality, after what she said last night, is almost as hard to get my head around as what she told me. I stare out of the window with a blank mind. Thirty minutes later, we eat in silence. It's nice. She's gone all out on the sausages. I finally grin at Mum with pure pleasure, which makes her cry.

'I'm so sorry,' she says, blinking back tears. 'Look at your beautiful face.'

I'm not sure what to say to that, so I keep quiet. Many people are to blame for my predicament, but it's good to see her finally own up to her part in my downfall. She has been a terrible, selfish mother. Perhaps she is the most to blame.

'Can I borrow your car?' I ask. 'The cops still have mine.'

'Of course. How long will you be?'

'I don't know. Maybe an hour. Could you lend us fifty quid in case my card doesn't work? I'll get a pack of mince and some spaghetti for tea.'

She reaches over and ever so gently places her fingers over mine.

'I'll always love you,' she says, which makes me cry.

I finish my breakfast and nip upstairs to the toilet. All I can focus on is the release vodka will give me. After reapplying my mascara, I tell my mum I'm off. At the door, she hands me fifty pounds and an A5 exercise book.

'This is something I've written which will explain everything. It'll be good for you to have a record.'

I take it from her. I'm about to open it when she puts her hand on it to keep the cover shut.

'Read it later.'

'Okay. Is it something we should discuss together?'

'We should have discussed it long ago. Do some shopping. It'll do you some good. I'll be here when you get back.'

I shrug, put the pad under my arm, and leave the house with her keys. I head off in her car. It's only got twelve thousand miles on the clock and she's had it for years. I give it a bit of a razz on the parkways, but my heart's not in it. My exhaustion also makes me more cautious than normal. I wander around Morrison's supermarket in a haze, thinking about my mother being here when they opened, choosing the nicest sausages. Perhaps it's both of us who need to change. I'm certainly no angel, although that's not surprising.

I suspect I've been carrying my past around with me like an untreated wound. As the years have passed, it's festered and poisoned. No wonder my life hasn't worked out. I've spent my life running from the truth. Even I know that's a race I was never going to win.

My day perks up when I reach the alcohol aisle and I spot Nemiroff vodka is on offer. I decide to treat myself.

I'm idly looking around after joining a queue when I see him. Russo is at the bottom aisle, paying for his shopping. I break out in an instant sweat and crouch down behind the conveyor belt. The checkout lady, who appears to be on the wrong side of eighty, gives me a worried smile. My mind scatters. He will be walking past the end of my checkout at any moment.

I can't help looking up when he does, but in an instant I realise it's not him, just someone who looks like him, and I collapse to my knees. The middle-aged kindly looking woman in front of me glances down, then lowers herself to my level.

'Are you okay, love?'

Without answering I put a hand on the side of the conveyor belt and haul myself upwards, sobbing. I wipe my eyes with my fingers, smearing my make-up for a second time today. Somehow, I pay for my things and get back to the car. I struggle to calm my breathing before I drive home, but I can't manage it. Reaching into the footwell, I pull the bottle of vodka from my bag, unscrew the cap, and take a huge gulp. It burns like hell on the way down, makes my eyes water and my teeth bite down, but it does the trick.

After a few minutes, my breathing gradually slows, and I try to think rationally. I can't live like this. My mum told me the truth. Should I tell Barton the same? Mum said it was best to get things out in the open. She's ready to pay for what she did. Am I?

Remembering the business card Barton gave me, I put my hand in my pocket. It's still there. The police still have my mobile phone, but I know there's a public phone just inside the entrance to the shop. Dragging myself out of the vehicle, I realise I've had enough. My sanity is leaving the station with my future onboard. I will face the truth, and I won't be the only one.

At the phone booths, I speak to Barton, then return to the car with a face damp from tears. The exercise book sits on the passenger seat. I pick it up, open the first page, and begin to read.

68

DI BARTON

Barton pressed answer and put the phone to his ear.

'Detective Inspector John Barton.'

'Mr Barton, it's me, Lynette. I'm ready to talk. I'll tell you everything.'

'Where are you?'

'I'm at Morrison's in Paston.'

'Okay, stay there. I can be with you in half an hour.'

'Aren't you at the police station?'

'I'm in Huntingdon. Or you can head to Thorpe Wood station, I'll be back before you know it.'

'Look, I'm going to go home. It's probably better if I explain there.'

Barton could detect a strange drawl in Lynette's voice, as if she was tired or out of breath.

'Okay, I'll meet you at the house.'

'Bye.'

'Wait!' said Barton. 'Don't do anything rash.'

The line was dead.

'Shit,' said Barton. He closed his eyes for a moment, then rang DS Strange's number; she picked up after five long rings.

'Kelly, where are you?'

'Erm. Me and Pigs are definitely not at Krispy Kreme. No, sir. Miles away from there.'

'Grab your doughnut and get in the car. I need you to go straight to Lynette's house. She's just rung and said she wants to tell me everything, but she was sniffing and might even have been crying. We'll be about twenty minutes as long as Zander's car starts.'

'Okay, we're on it. We're on the other side of town, but we'll be there in around ten minutes. What's the worry?'

'I'm really concerned about her doing something stupid. She sounded like she was at the end of her tether.'

69

DI BARTON

DI John Barton watched all four passengers in the Range Rover they were overtaking do a double take as DS Shawn Zander accelerated past them. He supposed it wasn't every day you saw two large men, both well over six feet, one black and one white, zip past you on the four-lane A1 motorway in an MR2 sports car with the top down doing over a hundred miles an hour. At least the vehicle was light blue. If it had been red and yellow, there would have been Noddy jokes every time Zander gave him a lift.

Despite the speed, the air that raced over both their bald heads was bearable. In fact, Barton found it pleasantly bracing. The extreme weather had begun to exert its toll over the last month and it seemed as though there'd never be an end to the heatwave. It was only in the last few days Barton had worn a tie again, without it feeling like a noose.

The roof of Zander's MR2 had still refused to lift back into place when they had returned to the car park after their meeting in Huntingdon, and now they were returning to Peterborough the wind howled across the bonnet into their faces. The air smelled different. By that measure alone, a storm was coming. The men looked at each other, but it wasn't the time for smiles. No words were necessary after working together for over twenty years.

Barton observed the weather front massing on the horizon, but they didn't have far to go now. The dark clouds gathering above cast moody shadows, but there were still breaks where sunlight flooded through.

Barton shifted down in his seat so he could answer his ringing phone. It was Strange.

'Barton speaking.'

'John, we've reached the address. There's a very big problem with the house.'

'Now what?'

'It's on fire.'

Barton's phone whistled with the air turbulence, and whatever Strange said next was stolen by the wind.

'Say that again. What do you mean by on fire?'

Again, the reply was lost.

'Slow down,' shouted Barton to Zander.

They were pulling off the motorway for Peterborough, anyway.

'Please repeat, Kelly.'

This time, her voice was loud and clear.

'We can see flames licking at the back wall of the upstairs bedroom, lots of them. The blaze is building in there, but the rest of the house seems untouched.'

'Ring the brigade.'

'Pigs is on the phone to them now.'

'What about the residents?'

'That's why I'm ringing. The Fire Killer is sitting in a car outside the house, watching.'

'Pardon?'

'Yes. Hang on! There's someone at the upstairs window.'

'Don't enter the building!' he bellowed down the phone. 'Wait for the fire crew.'

'The person at the window has their hands pressed against the glass. Hang on.'

Barton listened as Kelly asked Pigs how long until the first engine arrived. Strange came back on the line.

'John. ETA for the closest appliance is at least six minutes.'

'Stand down until they get there. Arrest The Fire Killer. We'll be there in five.'

There was a gap with only static. Barton felt like crushing the phone in his huge hand. The line buzzed, then cleared.

'John, we have to try. Otherwise, anyone in there will burn to death. It doesn't look too bad right now, so we're going to check it out.'

Barton thumped the dashboard in frustration. After a small pause, where Barton listened to footsteps hitting the pavement, Strange spoke again.

'Are you with Zander?'

'Yes.'

'Tell him, tell him...'

Strange stopped talking. There were a few quiet seconds, then Barton heard a creaking sound.

'The front door is unlocked,' said Strange. 'We're going in.'

Barton shouted Kelly's name into his phone. But the line was dead.

'Drive, Zander. As fast as you can.'

Zander didn't need asking twice. He'd made out enough of the conversation, and he knew where Strange had gone. Barton looked across at his friend and colleague. He still hadn't put the weight back on since his son had become ill even though it had been years now.

Zander had enjoyed a few dates with Pigs, but there were words that remained unsaid between him and Strange. Unsurprisingly, Zander's face was stone, eyes wide. His knuckles white on the steering wheel.

Barton was pressed into his seat as Zander tore through the next roundabout, stamping the brakes to career through the bend. Zander accelerated hard again, and they roared up the slip road and down the parkway, pulling off three minutes later onto Fulbridge Road. Barton moistened his lips. He removed his tie. They were almost there.

They flew past lads playing football on the field to their right, where the van fire had been, and children screaming with delight at the play area on his left. All blissfully unaware of what had occurred or what might be about to.

They were less than a minute away now. The first heavy drops of rain fell onto them, but any concerns about getting soaked were irrelevant. They rapidly approached a badly parked white Transit van, which blocked their view of the way ahead. To the sound of screeching tyres, Barton was jerked back by his seat belt. A little girl wandered into the middle of the road and stood staring at them as Zander's car juddered to a halt, mere metres away from her. Before Barton could get out, a woman sprinted into the street, scooped the child up, and ran to the pavement and Zander was on his way again within a second.

They soon turned right onto Fig Tree Lane. A fire engine's siren wailed in the distance. Barton swallowed as he spotted a string of black fumes rising above the houses. The clouds beyond had darkened considerably and seemed to boil as the storm approached. Destruction was in the air as the wind picked up the smell of smoke and blew it towards them. Zander slammed on the brakes outside the property and Barton clocked The Fire Killer sitting in a car next to the kerb, but he had more pressing concerns.

He and Zander jumped out of the MR2 and frantically assessed the scene. Barton stared up at the bedroom window where he saw someone, looking to their left. Grey smoke swirled and amassed behind the glass, temporarily concealing the occupants. Barton noticed a hazy arm and hand appear. The window opened, but only a few inches. Two seconds later, to the accompaniment of a crack of thunder, what looked like a small bedside table bounced off the inside of the glass.

Barton knew modern glazing would withstand a brick, or even an iron bar. The smoke cleared a little. Through the teeming rain, he watched someone in a white blouse approach the bedroom window. They put a hand to their mouth and bent double. Then Barton saw a stool or a chair hit the glass. A crack appeared this time, but nothing more. With the increasing smoke, Barton couldn't tell if it was Strange or Pigs who was trying to break the glass.

He felt a blast of sound and air, combined with a throaty growl as the fire engine braked behind them but Barton kept his eyes on the house. Darkness seemed to descend as the black clouds raced overhead. The front door was ajar. The creeping smoke was now pouring around the sides of it. Barton stepped a few paces forward as another deep rumble of thunder echoed above them. He fought the urge to race in, but sensed Zander edging past him towards the door, which suddenly spewed black smoke out like a desperate, dying gasp. Barton managed to catch Zander's sleeve, and with all his strength, hauled him back.

'No, no!' screamed Zander.

Barton didn't reply. He tried to put his arms around Zander's waist to stop him moving, straining every sinew to hold him still. Sheet lightning lit the house up for a second. Zander's suit jacket ripped as he struggled out of it.

Then an ear-splitting, booming bang filled the air and Zander froze. They both looked up. The window vibrated, and then another louder explosion shattered the glass outwards, blasting shards like bullets in every direction. Barton covered his face with his hands and bent double. After a few seconds, he straightened up and frantically waved his hands to clear the smoke in front of him. When he could finally make out the window again, all that was visible were large roaring flames, which reached out of the blackened hole like the fiery claws of an escaping demon.

70

DI BARTON

Zander stood spluttering next to a half-deafened Barton. It seemed to take Zander a moment to come to his senses and realise what had happened. He staggered backwards. Barton returned his gaze to the house, and to his amazement, he saw the front door open. A gush of smoke emerged and through that smoke staggered a diminutive figure in grey and dirty clothes. Barton's view was suddenly blocked by a towering man. Barton went to move around him, but he was stopped by a big arm.

'We'll deal with it, sir,' said the firefighter.

'You don't want to go in there, John,' said another voice next to him.

Barton looked beside him and saw Vic, the fire commander. Another firefighter raced past him towards the woman emerging from the fire. The firefighter scooped her up, turned, and sprinted back, carrying her like a child. Zander stumbled forward. The woman wriggled free of the fireman's grasp and he put her down.

As she ran to meet Zander, Barton recognised Kelly Strange's soot-covered face. She and Zander clung to each other. For Barton, the world decelerated. He watched a female firefighter, face set with concentration, open her hose and a thick stream of water arced towards and into the upstairs bedroom. Another firefighter knelt next to her and repeated the action.

Barton's head slowly spun to the front door. He felt his features crack into an ugly, silent cry. His sluggish brain prayed for another figure to rush through the door, but it wasn't a person that came out. Instead, it was hungry flames. A jet of water hit the door and pushed it fully open, beating the flames back. The big man who had been in front of him moved towards the house with breathing apparatus on, wielding an enormous axe. The sounds around Barton blared and buzzed, as though he'd entered a confusing nightmare.

Barton gritted his teeth and searched for his experience and his calm. He turned away from the fire and looked into the face of Vic.

'Vic,' he shouted. 'The fire's not been going long. I suspect there are two people in there. A female detective called Nicola and an elderly woman called Eileen. One or both were in that upstairs bedroom. The stairs are at the back of the house where there's a rear entrance.'

'Got it. Move back, please, John, and I'll pass on the orders.'

Barton staggered away, feeling the heat lessen on his skin. He looked over his shoulder and realised that was also because the flames were losing the battle. Turning to his left, he saw two fire-fighters in breathing apparatus moving along the side of the house to the rear. At the front, the door was off its hinges and had been thrown onto the grass.

Barton glanced behind him and spotted Zelensky and Leicester arguing with a male firefighter who had set up a cordon. Barton felt his legs shake and put his hand on the car next to him. The metal was warm. Inside, sitting back against the driver's seat, clutching an A5 notebook, was Lynette. Barton saw a bottle of some kind of clear liquid between her knees. Zander was walking towards them with a look of pure thunder on his face. Strange was pointlessly tugging on his arm.

Barton pushed his fury to the side, opened the car door, and lifted Lynette out with one arm. The half-empty bottle rolled out with her. He recognised the label. It was vodka. She was still holding the notebook. He half carried, half dragged her to Zelensky.

'Arrest her for double murder,' he said to Zelensky. 'And get her out of here while she's still in one piece.'

Lynette struggled and the small booklet slipped from her hands as Zelensky and Malik quickly cuffed her and led her to their car. Barton picked up what she'd dropped.

'What's this?' he said.

Lynette, wobbling and barely able to focus or stand, could only lisp a reply over her shoulder.

'It's a confession.'

71

DI BARTON

Barton stood outside the smouldering house in the rain for the following hour. He didn't feel a drop. Zander told him he was driving Strange to the hospital for a quick check-up, but Barton barely heard him. Soaked, he stayed until they brought the two bodies out. He felt it was the least he could do.

Afterwards, he organised uniform to guard the scene, and he left the fire crew to do their jobs. Leicester arrived to drive him back. As he was climbing into Leicester's car, he realised the danger to Ernie's house next door, where the flames had licked across and blackened the roof. It looked relatively unscathed, but he couldn't recall the firefighters getting Ernie and Rob out.

Then he saw them outside Clive McBride's door at the end of the terrace. McBride was looking at him. He gave Barton a peace sign and ushered the old man and his grandson back into his house. Barton had put Lynette's notepad in his pocket to keep it dry. He opened it as they drove back to the police station, Leicester grim-faced beside him. There were four pages of notes, then about the same again of a rambling pen-written scrawl.

Barton flicked back to the first page and the first entry that had the number 'one', the words, 'house fire', and a date. The second entry was numbered 'two' and titled, 'bin fire', then a date. Barton frowned at the years. They were from before Lynette was born.

72

DI BARTON

It was nine p.m. when Lynette had sobered up and the on-call doctor deemed her fit to be interviewed. Barton had spent most of the time in between reading the notepad and checking the dates against the PNC. His eyes stung from tiredness and the acrid smoke from earlier, but mostly from rubbing them with incredulity.

Strange had left the hospital and returned home with Zander. Leicester and Malik had taken the events of the day badly. They'd struggled on with the necessary work, but Barton had told them to go for a coffee together, then go home. Zelensky, who was no stranger to heartache, had stated steadfastly that she would stay. It was Zelensky who came with him to interview Lynette.

Lynette had accepted the offer of a solicitor this time and she stared only at Barton when he and Zelensky entered the interview room. After the preliminaries were over, he returned her gaze.

'Your mother,' he said, 'was the arsonist.'

'Yes,' said Lynette clearly.

'I'm holding up evidence bag 8752B, which contains a notepad allegedly written and kept by Eileen Croston. Is this your mother's, Lynette?'

'Yes.'

'Have you set any fires?'

'No, I have not. Although I once left some night lights on Stefan's TV, which melted the top, shorted it, and almost caught fire, but that was an accident.'

Lynette giggled for a moment, possibly still a bit drunk, then stopped herself.

'This isn't a laughing matter,' growled Zelensky.

Lynette glanced at her for the first time, eyes blazing. She snarled her reply.

'You're telling me.'

'Yet you confessed to the fires and served a short spell in prison.'

Lynette turned her gaze to Barton and nodded.

'It was no wonder you had an alibi if you weren't there,' he said quietly.

Lynette smiled again; a big toothy grin with a total absence of warmth, but she didn't say anything. Barton changed tack, hoping to unsettle her.

'Did you help your mother to light the fire at your house this afternoon?'

'Look at the last entry.'

Barton didn't need to. He knew it said number fifty-seven, house fire, and today's date.

'Your mum committed suicide by setting fire to the house while you were out at the supermarket. That's your story.'

'No, it's her story.'

The solicitor next to Lynette whispered in her ear, but she kept her eyes on Barton. Lynette smiled the same cool smile.

'I can't incriminate myself by talking. I have nothing to hide. If you want to listen to everything that happened, I can explain now.' Her smile fell as she glanced from Barton to Zelensky and back again. 'For the benefit of the tape.'

'Go on,' said Zelensky with a scowl. 'Let's hear it all.'

'My maternal grandfather was an abusive alcoholic. My mother felt powerless, and the violence traumatised her. When she was around fourteen, she accidentally set fire to their house. She woke up and realised what she'd done, fetched her mother, and they escaped. Their home burned to the ground. They did not wake her father. Sadly, her mother's health was ruined by smoke damage and she never fully recovered. She died on the day my mother finished school.'

Lynette wiped a solitary tear from her cheek with annoyance, cocked her jaw, then continued. Barton dragged his eye away from the livid scar on her face, which was no longer covered.

'My mother never really recovered, either. She lived a lonely life, working dead-end jobs, until she met my father and had me. She repeated the mistakes her mother made, as I guess we are destined to do. Eventually she found him virtually unconscious in his car, having crashed into the garage at the rear of their house. She said to me yesterday that something snapped inside her. She went to the back of the garage, grabbed the lawnmower petrol and poured it over him.'

'Jesus,' said Zelensky involuntarily.

'Yes, but trust me, he deserved it.'

'Surely nobody deserves that.'

'He was a bully, and worse. My mother didn't realise for a long time what he was doing, because while he was focused on me, she was free from his fists.'

Barton paused as the implications sank in.

'So she torched his car with him asleep in it,' said Barton.

'I hope he was alive when he burned.'

'That's murder,' said Zelensky.

'That's justice.'

'That's not for the public to dispense,' said Barton.

Lynette leaned forward with a sneer.

'What? Leave it to you lot? She'd already spoken to you guys in hospital after he broke her arm. The nurses reported it after seeing the network of bruises over her body, but you did fuck all. My mother did what you were incapable of. She did a good thing.'

Lynette put her head in her hands, as though she wasn't sure if she believed that or not. Barton exchanged a glance with Zelensky, then cleared his throat.

'Carry on, please, Lynette,' he said.

Lynette took a few deep breaths, lifted her head, stared into the distance and continued.

'After she had her revenge, she was briefly sectioned and I got taken into care. After a year, she reclaimed her child and raised me. I was young and, over the years, I learned not to think about the past. It doesn't hurt if you push those thoughts away.

'But as I found out recently, my mother never forgot the thrill of the fire. The buzz from doing something naughty. Being in control. The men and women of the fire service. The big fire engine. Although she never wanted to hurt anyone again. I can't remember much about my father or the old her, but the new her was distant and quiet. She wasn't a great mum, and the other kids knew she was weird. School became hard. I had no idea she was setting a couple of fires every year. I had enough of my own problems.'

'You had no inkling whatsoever?' asked Barton.

'No, nothing. She said the anticipation was exciting, but I reckon it was a release from the suppressed guilt from the first fire. Not only had she murdered her father, but the blaze ruined her mother's lungs and therefore she killed her as well. She told me that setting fires became her reason for living which, as her only child wasn't great to hear, but explained a lot.

'After I moved out, I rarely saw her. There was the odd birthday card or phone call but that was it.'

'But when you split up with Russo, your only option was moving back in with her.'

'Yes. That motherfucker isolated me, then discarded me. He destroyed my life. Mum took me in, even after all the horrible things I said.'

'What about the skip fire?' asked Barton.

'You were right. I did see Jessica the night she died. I'd just walked home from Stefan's after he'd kindly shagged me again, then told me to leave straight afterwards as though I'd provided a service. I saw her outside the shop with a whisky bottle.'

Barton's brain spun at the revelations. Russo's alibi was dodgy. Lynette must have blackmailed Russo.

'It was your mum who set fire to the skip.'

'Yep. I saw her leave the house not long after I got home, but never imagined it could have been her. She wouldn't have lit it up if she'd known the girl was inside. It will have eaten my mum up, killing someone innocent again. Stefan as good as put Jessica in that skip. My mum set fire to the bin in desperation. When she heard about the young boy, she decided enough was enough. Time to stop, one way or another.'

'But she set the fire at the old lady's house?' asked Barton.

'I think she planned to die in it, or maybe it was a final treat to herself. She was out of control, so who knows? But she realised there was still someone inside.'

Barton thought back. The woman said an angel saved her. He thought of Eileen's grey bouffant that might have looked like a halo with the fire as a backdrop. Lynette continued.

'She didn't care if she got caught and was happy to spend the rest of her life in jail to put a stop to it all. You finally seemed to be closing in. I must admit, I didn't share her confidence in your abilities.'

'Why did you confess to the fire, then, if she was okay with taking responsibility for them?' asked Zelensky.

'I didn't tell her I was going to confess. I didn't know back then exactly who she was, or what she'd been doing, but I wanted to protect her. I thought I'd get a little bit of prison time at most. It already felt like my life was over, anyway, and that was before today's events. My mum wouldn't have been able to cope with being locked up. I only realised it was her who was setting the fires when I caught her coming home all out of sorts and reeking of smoke. When I saw the news of the house fire the next day, I guessed she was responsible. It doesn't take a detective to work out the rest of the fires were her. When I thought back, I could remember a lot of small to medium fires in our neighbourhood over the years. Although, I didn't know about the people she'd killed until last night.'

'When you admitted to the skip fire, you didn't realise that you could get life for Jessica's death,' said Zelensky.

'Correct. I thought I'd do Mum a favour, but coping with a few months in jail is different from decades, so the plan had to change. I blackmailed Stefan by saying I would tell the police he was involved with drugs.'

'Do you have any proof of that?' asked Zelensky.

'He gave me the alibi, didn't he?'

Barton frowned. He was hoping for more.

'And this morning,' he said. 'What's your version of events?'

'I woke up. Mum was acting slightly odd. We had a good chat the previous night where she told me everything she'd done wrong over the years. She gave me this notepad when I left to go shopping and then I read it in the car park for a bit after I spoke to you. It contained what she said it would, all ending with a confession, but then the date of the last fire registered. It was today. I raced home and turned up about thirty seconds before your people did.'

Barton considered her words. They rang true, but if they were, then Lynette was a monster.

'Why didn't you ring 999? Why not try to save her?'

Lynette replied in a monotone voice.

'I didn't have a phone anyway, but why would I? It was what she wanted. And maybe it was for the best.'

'Your neighbours could have died?' said Barton, holding his temper.

Lynette dropped her gaze.

'You can't think you're an innocent in all this,' said Barton. 'Why didn't you stop the police from going in?'

Lynette's head snapped up. Her voice rose in intensity as she spoke, finishing in a yell.

'All I'm guilty of is loving a terrible person. Only a fool would have gone into that house with a fire raging upstairs. That was their mistake, not mine. I. Am. Innocent!'

Barton just about managed to stop himself from shouting in reply, but he jabbed his finger at Lynette.

'That's wrong! You're guilty of plenty. You're guilty of perjury. You lied under oath and now *we* are suffering the consequences. If you'd told the truth, your mother would be safely behind bars, and our colleague would still be alive.'

73

LYNETTE

The blonde detective puts her hand on Barton's arm.

'Interview terminated at 21:36,' she says and presses a button on the recording equipment. 'Good time for a break.'

'I would agree,' replies my solicitor, whose name I can't remember. 'We would appreciate a few moments to talk.'

I watch as the woman detective encourages the big inspector up and they leave the room.

'I'd think carefully about what you're saying,' says my solicitor when they've gone.

Without turning my head to look at her, I bark my response.

'I don't care any more. It's all coming out. The history of my mum, the reason why I confessed, the facts about Stefan Russo.'

I lean back in my chair and wipe the spittle from my chin.

74

DI BARTON

Barton returned to the interview room twenty minutes later, after splashing his face with water and getting some fresh air with a quick walk outside. He was spent, but he wanted the truth about Russo.

'Interview reconvened at 21:58,' he said. 'Tell us about Stefan Russo.'

'About our relationship?' said Lynette.

'Specifically, his line of work, his friends, and I'm interested in how you got him to provide you with a false alibi.'

For the first time, Lynette's smile was genuine.

'He is definitely up to his ears in dodgy businesses. There's an office in his house next to the toilet where he takes his phone calls. He keeps it locked, not just with a key, but also a digital bolt controlled by a fob. He took me to what I can only describe as a gangsters' ball. They treated him like a god. I saw those Bates brothers a couple of times when we stayed in hotels in London. I think he used me and the hotels as cover because they never came to his flat.'

'Anything else?' asked Zelensky.

'He snorted cocaine all day long, but he only drank with it on Fridays and Saturdays. It didn't appear to affect him during the week, although Mondays could be rough. He was always happy and affectionate, but he'd have the odd doldrums day when I'd keep away from him.'

'Why did you stay with him if he was high most of the time?'

'To be honest, if I hadn't seen him doing it, I wouldn't have noticed. He made me feel good. I bet Jessica said the same thing.'

'How do you feel about him now?' asked Barton.

'I want him to go down. Look at what he's done. He must be involved in all this.'

'We believe you might be in danger if he realises you've informed on him,' said Zelensky.

'So what? Let him come. I've got nothing to lose now. Nothing at all.'

'Is there anywhere you can stay that's safe? You clearly can't go back to your mum's,' said Barton.

Lynette seemed to deflate in front of him. Her face fell, dropping on one side. Half sorrow, half scowl.

'That had occurred to me, but I've lost my job and my dignity. My scar is permanent so no one will book me now, and today, I lost my mum and our home.'

'We might need you to testify against him. Your evidence could be crucial. Didn't you mention you had a friend in Spalding with twins?'

'Yes, I suppose she'll let me stay. She's exhausted so I guess I could crash there for a while and give her a hand, but it feels like my life is over. What am I going to do now?'

Barton struggled to answer that, but he wanted to say something.

'Start again,' he finally said. 'People do it all over the world, every day.'

Lynette was back staring into the distance. Her mind elsewhere. Her mouth turned down.

75

DI BARTON

Barton came in the next morning on autopilot with an avalanche of work to plough through. Lynette was still in the custody suite. He checked with Reception that Jane, the CPS solicitor, was in. After firing off multiple emails and making some phone calls, he went to Jane's office mid-morning and updated her on Lynette's case. She blinked for a few moments at the end of the story, but she surprised him with her response.

'Poor girl,' she said.

'One of ours has been burned alive,' said Barton.

'Yes, and that is a tragedy too, but I'm not sure it's reasonable to place that at Lynette's door. It's been a long time since I came across anything like this.'

'I know. I can't afford to think about what Lynette's been through until I've got everything processed, but we all have some hard days ahead of us. Pigs...' Barton stopped himself, then continued, 'Nicola Pignatiello was a popular and well-liked member of the team with a great future. DCI Cox went with the family liaison officer yesterday to break the news to her relatives. I'll be going to see them tonight. In the meantime, what do we do with Lynette? Should we charge her with perjury?'

'Do you believe her story, her version of events, and do the facts back it up?'

'It seems so. CSI is ordering the DNA tests for the items we caught Lynette trying to dispose of to protect her mother. I suspect her mother's fingerprints and DNA will be all over them. We have a written confession from her mother, which we'll be able to match to her handwriting, even if it's just to the writing on her driving licence application.'

'Is the house that damaged?'

'Leigh Beddows, the fire investigator, was at the scene first thing. The upstairs of the house is completely burned out, but he doesn't think the damage is structural. He thinks Lynette's mother had been planning this for at least a few days. Maybe even years.'

Jane raised her eyebrows but didn't comment.

'The fire crew found a lot of unburnt material in the bedroom. The loft is full of stored boxes from when they bought new TVs and microwaves. We're lucky the house isn't still burning. The explosions probably put some of the fire out. It looks like she used lighter fuel as the main accelerant on old newspapers, piled up cardboard, that sort of thing, but there are tins of what seems to be paint thinners and bottles of kerosene. It will have been those that blew up.'

'Were the victims overcome with smoke?'

'At a guess, Beddows said that the deceased were probably suffocated by the fumes, but they may have been killed by shrapnel from an exploding tin. Fuel of some kind was poured over the stair carpet. Beddows assumes she did that to stop anyone getting upstairs for a rescue, so it must have burnt out before Nicola got up there. Some of the carpet itself might have ignited after Nicola went up the stairs. It's clear Eileen planned to die, but I don't think she wanted to take anyone else with her. Nicola was just too brave for her own good.'

Jane reached over and patted his hand. No words were necessary.

'The coroner's inquest should determine what Eileen was responsible for, but what of Lynette?' asked Barton.

'This will go above my head due to the media exposure the case has received. There are so many complicated elements to the case that it's hard to say what the decision will be. But I don't expect they'll prosecute Lynette again.'

'What about the cost of her perjury, which includes the loss of a young constable?'

'Lynette has been punished already for something she didn't do. She clearly has some mental health issues and any solicitor would use that to say she wasn't of a sound mind. She's lost her mum, her home, and she's been left disfigured. She has had to pay for her mistakes. I can't see it being in the public interest to punish her any more.'

Barton understood her point of view.

'Thanks for your help,' he said, turning to leave.

'What about this Russo character? Is he the big boss you suspect he might be?' asked Jane.

'I'm beginning to believe so, but he's been very clever. I wanted to know if we were going to charge Lynette with anything before I rang Karen at the Met to discuss Russo.'

'Right. Keep me posted. Where will Lynette go?'

'Once we've finished all the statements, I'll have someone drive her to a friend's place in Lincolnshire. If we don't charge her, she's more likely to cooperate if we prosecute Russo. Putting him away might be the big win for us.'

'The only win,' said Jane without humour.

Barton thought of Russo's casual attitude to all of this. He found his eyes were narrowed.

76

DI BARTON

Barton returned to his desk with a lot on his mind. He recalled something Sasha told them. She'd said Russo had given her his business card which had 'call me' written on it. They'd assumed he was trying to sleep with her. Perhaps he was merely looking for another customer for his illegal business.

He found Zander sitting with his head resting on the desk next to his own. Zander's eyes were closed, and there was a touch of drool coming out of the side of his mouth. Barton was about to make a joke, then thought better of it. There was a Post-it note on Barton's computer to ring Beth Doran but he didn't think he knew a Beth Doran.

He picked up his desk phone, accidentally unsettling a large pile of paperwork, which slid onto the floor. The noise woke Zander, who leaped to his feet. He stared at Barton for a few seconds as though Barton were pointing a gun at him. Barton got a whiff of body odour. Unshaven and unkempt, Zander looked like a man on the back of a two-day bender. Barton half expected to see a small bottle of whisky in his crumpled suit pocket.

'Everything okay? Kelly all right?' asked Barton.

'Sorry, yes. I stayed with her last night. She's fine. You know how she is. Not happy about losing her fringe, but apart from that.'

Barton felt bad asking questions, but it was important he knew as much as possible as soon as possible.

'Did she say what happened?'

'Yes.' Zander blew out a big breath. 'They both went into the house knowing that seconds counted. They hoped that Lynette's mother might have made it down to the lounge, but when they got there, it was empty. Kelly said that most of the stairs' carpet was smouldering, although there weren't any flames. The landing above was clear. They tried the rear door to see if Eileen had escaped that way, but it was locked.'

He looked at Barton with moist eyes as he recalled the conversation. Zander steeled himself.

'Okay. This is what Kelly said. Pigs told her to check the kitchen. Then Pigs just ran up the stairs and barged into the room at the top. Kelly nipped back to the kitchen. There was nobody in there. She went back to the bottom of the stairs, but there were flames billowing out of the bedroom door, and the stairs had caught fire. Kelly said she shouted to get out, but there was a bang. Apparently a lid or something metal shot out of the room like a missile. She ducked down under the stairs as a massive plume of black smoke billowed from the bedroom. Then there was a second explosion.'

'That's when she ran out?'

'She couldn't see anything. She just crawled to the front door and staggered out.'

Barton stood up and put a big paw on Zander's shoulder and sat him down. He squeezed hard.

'There was nothing you could have done.'

Zander nodded, but his head drooped.

'Does Kelly know what happened to Pigs?' asked Barton.

'Yes, Leicester rang me in the hospital, but it was pretty obvious.

I hear we were wrong about Lynette setting the fires. It was the mother.'

'Yes. We'd have got there soon enough. We were just a little too late. It can't be helped if Lynette gave us a false confession. The investigation was bound to be derailed. We caught her trying to dispose of a car full of fire-setting equipment, after all.'

'I suppose.'

'Look, get home. Have a shower. We don't need you back for a few days. Take care of Kelly. I'll tie everything up here.'

Zander sniffed, then rose and began walking out before he stopped and turned.

'Just a thought, but who's to say that they didn't concoct all of this to save Lynette's ass?'

'What do you mean?'

'Maybe they were both fire starters, or fire killers. A mother and daughter combo.'

Barton couldn't help smiling. Even in his current state, Zander was still a detective.

'It's possible.'

'Or perhaps it was only Lynette? The mother had terminal cancer or something, so she had nothing to lose. They invented this confession to get Lynette off the hook when it was her all along. A final gift from a dying mum.'

'That's not a bad angle,' said Barton. 'I'll look into it.'

Zander walked slowly out of the office, leaving Barton pondering his comments. Barton dialled the number for Beth Doran. The name Doran suddenly rang a bell, but not the Beth part.

'Hi, is that Beth Doran? Detective Inspector Barton here, you rang.'

'Yes, I'm Mavis Doran's daughter.'

'Ah, yes. The lady whose house caught fire.'

'Yes, the hospital is letting me take her home today. She's still a bit confused, but she keeps going on about the person who saved her.'

'The angel,' said Barton with a rueful expression.

Barton could almost hear the woman smile down the phone.

'Yes, she meant she was like an angel, but she's been able to describe her now. It was an older woman. I think I met her outside the house because I spoke to a neighbour who knew Mum. She had kind of big, frizzy hair. I told her that the house wasn't secure and she said she'd keep an eye out for thieves until I came back. I was supposed to be taking Mum home with me that day, but she kicked up a right stink about watching her programmes, so I said I'd come back the next morning.'

'That was unfortunate,' said Barton, unsure as to what to say.

'Well, I reckon it was lucky. Maybe if I hadn't spoken to that lady, then she would never have had the chance to become an angel and save Mum.'

Barton found a small grin appearing on his face.

'That's a nice way to look at it,' he said. 'If I find out who saved your mum for sure, I'll get back to you. We're not certain exactly what's gone on at this point.'

Barton took her email address and thanked her for ringing. It was likely he would need to ring Mrs Doran later and explain that the angel was really the devil who started the blaze, but at least Eileen had gone back to save the woman.

Barton rang Karen at the Met next. He updated her with the latest information, saying he would keep her in the loop as the case progressed.

'Actually, John, I wanted to tell you we had a lead. There's a man in HMP Brixton who we picked up for involvement in gangland stuff a while ago. Someone grassed him up, which has put him in line for a very long sentence. He's after a deal and guess who he fingered.'

'Russo.'

'Correct. We've spoken to the guy at length and, even though we have nothing watertight yet, we've built an even better picture on Russo. It's time to bring him in before he flits.'

'I wouldn't stick your grass back in general circulation.'

'I agree, he's being moved somewhere safe.'

'When's it going down?'

'We've got a warrant for both of Russo's addresses. We're nabbing him today. He's at work this morning, so we'll follow him when he leaves. His car's been immobilised, so he won't escape.'

'I wish I could be there.'

'If I have the chance, I'll put the boot in for you.'

Barton finished the call with a chuckle. It looked as though justice would be done, and Russo was going to get what he deserved after all.

77

DI BARTON

A week later, life was starting to return to normal, even though they still had Nicola's funeral to face. With numbers allowed at funerals still restricted, they had decided to line the route in uniform instead. Even with that, it seemed too little for someone so young and with such promise, who'd shown such bravery.

Barton's first task was to ring the manager of the shop.

'Rafiq speaking.'

'Morning, Mr Majid. I just thought I'd ring and let you know how everything panned out. We think the investigation is over.'

Barton gave him all the details, then listened to a quiet line for a few seconds.

'That's very sad. I remember that lady coming in the shop. She was always polite. In fact, most people were decent. In a way, I miss working there. My friend and his family have accepted their new reality and are selling the shop. They're all moving to the seaside for what they call a new adventure.'

'You're never too old for a fresh challenge.'

'I agree, and I think I need to apologise for my attitude that morning. I was having a bad day.'

'I understand completely, sir. Bad days are when we're needed.'

Barton finished the call and was checking his emails from the previous night, when he came across one from Karen at the Met.

John, I tried to ring, but it was probably too late for a part-timer like yourself. Heads up on the Russo case. We've had to let him go. He lawyered up as you'd expect. The brief really knew what he was doing. He was so well prepared it was as if he'd been waiting for just this eventuality. It was like Whac-A-Mole when we were questioning him, but we were the mole. His ass was covered more times than a pass-the-parcel. His bank records are dodgy, too straight and impersonal, but we can't connect him to the Bates brothers yet. Both his houses proved clean as a whistle. That locked office Lynette mentioned contained a desk and a chair, nothing else. We're concerned he was tipped off by an insider. We'll keep him under the microscope, but we didn't have a hope of bail being refused.

Barton emailed her back.

What about the guy in prison who pointed the finger at him?

A reply pinged through ten seconds later.

Retracted his statement. Off the record, all he would say was that he had family.

'Great,' growled Barton. He just managed to prevent himself from shouting something worse across the office.

He knew he had to call Lynette and tell her, but really didn't fancy it. Spalding was only twenty minutes away, but he had no time for a wasted journey if she wasn't there. He looked up her number and gave it a ring.

'What do you want?' answered Lynette.

'I was wondering how you were.'

'Right. Like you care.'

'Are you still at your friend's in Spalding?'

'No, I couldn't stand it. I'm never going to have children.'

'Where are you now?'

'Does it matter?'

'I wanted a quick word in person.'

'Are you coming to arrest me?'

'No, it's nothing like that.'

'Is Russo in prison yet?'

'It's about that. Where are you?'

'I'm at Clive McBride's house.'

Barton paused.

'The relaxed neighbour with the illegal gardening habit?' he asked.

'Yeah.'

'Okay, I'll come over in fifteen minutes.'

'Make it thirty. We need to clean up. We don't want you busting us for slovenliness.'

It was nearly lunchtime, so Barton took his jacket off the back of his chair and strolled downstairs to book out a car. He'd walked in for the last two days. All the events of the previous month had almost overloaded his system, so he'd been trying to take things easy for a while. Gizmo had become his ally at home, and much to the rest of the family's chagrin, he followed Barton around the house the moment he stepped through the door.

Barton said that was because he was the nicest out of the lot of them, and that dogs were brilliant judges of character. Holly reckoned that as the weather was a bit cooler now, the dog was merely attracted to the largest heat source. Luke decided it was because his dad was always eating and dropping food.

Barton had found the walks soothed his soul after witnessing so many tragic deaths. It had made him appreciate his family even more, and he loved the general banter around who the dog liked most and whose turn it was to walk him. Getting one had been a good choice. Life had a habit of teaching you to seize the day. Everyone had a clock that was ticking.

78

DI BARTON

Barton got caught by the desk sergeant on the way out. Donald was back to his grumpy self, but he was master of his kingdom, and Barton helped him with the missing paperwork he was looking for. Barton booked out a lacklustre silver Ford Focus and drove around to McBride's house.

Barton could smell marijuana when he knocked on the door.

McBride opened it with a huge smile, teeth shining.

'Mr B, what's up? Lynette said you were coming. I'm just getting Ernie home. His arthritis has been very bad, but now he is super cool.'

Ernie from number two came out of the lounge and lurched up behind McBride. He had a suit and tie on, which seemed out of place next to McBride's beachwear. Lynette stuck a pair of yellow-star sunglasses on Ernie's face. He wobbled as if he were dancing with a laughing McBride as he helped him over the step and down the path.

'Pain is in the mind,' said Ernie with a goofy grin as he left.

Lynette had taken the bandage off her cheek and the scar still looked livid. There was an empty hardness to her eyes that made

Barton feel uneasy. She had loose black jeans on and a baggy, faded T-shirt. Her face was make-up-free except for some eyeliner.

'You better come in,' she said.

He followed her to the lounge and sat on the sofa. Lynette didn't take a seat, instead she stood in front of him, so he had to look up at her.

'Well?' she asked.

'We arrested Russo, but we didn't have enough to keep him in prison while we continued our investigation.'

Lynette was incredulous.

'You what? He's got away with it?'

'No, he was released on bail. Our inquiries are ongoing.'

'Useless. You're all fucking useless. He gets to wander into the sunset, while I'm homeless and scarred, and Jess is dead and buried. This world sucks.'

Barton kind of agreed with her.

'Are you staying here now?' he asked.

Lynette slumped into an armchair and ran her hands through her lank hair.

'No, I can't. He'd probably let me if I begged, but he needs his own space. He has work deadlines. In a few weeks, he's going to America for a road trip with his friend Ceri anyway. She's already over there. He's not sure if he's coming back. It's a shame, he's a good guy. I did try.' Lynette looked away and cringed. 'It was horrible, but who would want me looking like this?'

'Come on, Lynette. You're still a beautiful woman. You've got your whole life ahead of you.'

Lynette pushed herself up on the chair's arms and leaned into Barton.

'I've got fuck all. I went to the council this morning and told them I was homeless but they said they can't help me because of the arson convictions. I'm a risk to the other women if they put me in a shared house because I might burn it down.' Lynette sneered and spoke in a cartoon-like high-pitched voice. 'We have a responsibility to the other service users who also have complex needs and are very vulnerable.'

'There is help out there for people with offences like yours. We can look to have the convictions quashed going forward, but it's not an easy or straightforward process.'

Lynette's face set like concrete.

'Ah. Corporate lingo. That's exactly what they said. There are places, but it's not straightforward. I have to be risk-assessed. They need to check the insurance. Support needs to be put in place. Meanwhile, I can go and live with some rapists in a barn somewhere.'

Barton frowned. She was right. She would be hard to house.

'There are no rules on who can stay at the Travelodge. Why don't you sleep there for a few days? It's only thirty quid a night at the moment because no one's travelling anywhere.'

'I've barely got thirty pence.'

'And there are no other friends?'

Lynette slowly shook her head, looking exhausted all of a sudden.

'I've had enough. I can't see a way forward.'

'Don't talk like that,' insisted Barton. He took sixty pounds out of his back pocket. 'I'll drive you there now. Let me look into it for you tomorrow. We have funds for this sort of thing to keep you safe. There's someone at the council I work with. We'll get you a place to stay.'

'What the fuck am I going to do in a Travelodge with no money and no friends? Eat the soap?'

'I'll get something sorted. Give me a chance. I'll ring you this evening and update you, okay?'

Lynette reached over and took the money. He saw an

unpleasant expression flicker across her face, but when she showed him to the door, she only seemed exhausted.

'Thanks, John. You might be hopeless, but your heart's in the right place. Don't worry about me. I'll be fine. I always find the strength from somewhere.'

79

Barton spent the rest of the afternoon trying to plead Lynette's cause. The problem was there was so little money to go around to deal with all the people that had problems. And if you ran a hostel, would you really want someone in it with a conviction for setting house and bin fires? Barton was on shaky ground if he said she'd been wrongfully convicted when it hadn't been overturned in court. Zander was also correct. There was still a slim possibility that she had been more involved than she had let on.

Eventually, with the help of Peterborough council, he managed to get her into a hostel on the far north of the city with twenty-four-hour wardens. It was one of the few places where the insurance didn't specifically exclude arsonists.

It was seven p.m. when he rang Lynette to give her the good news, but her line went straight to voicemail. Barton decided that was enough for one day. He left the office and stepped outside. The sun had finally fought its way out again, and he took off his jacket. He was about to walk home when an unpleasant thought occurred to him. He stood still and wondered. Donald was also leaving.

Barton watched as he waited for the lifting barrier to let the desk sergeant out of the car park. Barton waved him down.

'Can you give me a lift?' he asked.

'Do I look like a taxi?'

'It's only up Thorpe Road.'

'Go on, then, but you'll owe me a pint.'

'You're very kind,' said Barton as he opened the door of the vehicle. 'And extortionate.'

Three minutes later, Barton got out fifty metres from the turn into Marchmont Square. He walked towards the turning and looked down the street that led to Russo's house. Lynette's mum's car was parked on the drive. The white front door to the house was ajar and Barton could see there was a reddish splatter up it. Barton approached warily, taking a glove from his pocket. He pushed the door fully open. There was a smear about four inches wide where something bleeding had been dragged along the carpet and across the cream tiled floor in the kitchen. A strong smell of petrol filled the air. Puddles of a clear liquid showed up on the tiles.

He followed the smear, which stopped near the kitchen door to the rear. Bloody handprints were everywhere, as though the injured person had struggled to get to their feet. The blinds had been broken, but Barton still couldn't see into the garden. He opened the door and looked out.

The hot tub was in the middle of the lawn and Russo was slumped inside it, with rivers of blood running down his face. He'd been secured with metres and metres of packing tape. His neck had been taped to the side of the tub, so his head was facing Barton. His mouth had been gagged and the single eye that wasn't taped over was wide and blinking. Lynette was pouring a transparent liquid from a canister into the hot tub. She wore a lilac tracksuit and her ponytail shook from side to side. She noticed Barton out of the corner of her eye and looked across at him. Her face was garishly made up.

'Too late, John,' she said loudly, then threw the canister over the grass at him. It landed short.

Barton was lost for words for a moment. It was obvious what she was going to do.

'Don't, Lynette,' said Barton, slowly stepping through the kitchen door.

Lynette turned back to him. 'That's close enough.'

Barton noted four other canisters in varying parts of the garden. Closer now, Barton could see Russo's expensive suit was soaking. Lynette reached into her jacket pocket and removed a Zippo lighter. She tapped the top open while staring back at Russo, who pointlessly attempted to wriggle free.

'Stay where you are, Inspector,' she ordered in a loud, but monotone voice as she faced Barton again.

'These lighters should have been a clue. My mother bought me one for my eighteenth and most years after, even after I stopped smoking. Who knew they'd come in so handy?'

'Don't throw your future away,' said Barton, softly.

'I have no future.'

'I've found you a place to stay. Somewhere safe. You can begin again.'

'It's too late. I want revenge!' she roared, stamping back to Russo and slapping him around his head where the hair was matted with blood. 'For me!' she bellowed. 'For Jess! For everyone he's already hurt, and for everyone he will destroy.'

Barton edged forward. He spoke just a touch louder than a whisper.

'Lynette, we haven't been able to prove he's responsible. It's possible he's innocent.'

Lynette gasped a laugh of disbelief. She took a stride towards Barton, index finger jabbing with her left hand.

'I don't believe that. You don't either. It's time for him to pay. He's ruined so many lives.'

Lynette tensed her fists, and her eyes scrunched in furious rage.

'Lynette, breaking people's hearts isn't a crime, whatever that person might do afterwards.'

Lynette's eyes, when they slowly reopened and met his, were scowling and angry, ugly in their purpose.

'Yeah, well, it should be.'

'Don't do it, Lynette. You're going to prison. What you do right now will affect whether it's for a few years or forever.'

'I don't care any more. Do you know what he said before I taped him up?'

'No.'

Barton slid a little closer as Lynette's eyes glazed over.

'He said he would fix me up and get my modelling career back on track. All as though none of this ever happened. He said I can trust him. What do you think of that?'

Barton wouldn't trust this guy to water his plants while he was on holiday, but he merely gave a little shrug. Lynette's shoulders shook. She turned her back on Barton to stare at Russo again.

Barton had a moment where he thought of the cheeky, sassy, young lady he'd first met when he knocked on her door. She was long gone. Only a mean-faced woman with nothing to lose remained. Lynette marched stiffly towards the side of the hot tub. Using her wrist, she closed the lighter with her thumb so the chamber would refill with fumes. Barton shuffled further forward, but realised he was still too far away. He looked around for a hosepipe or even a water barrel. There was neither. He probably had one last roll of the dice.

'Yes,' he said. 'Russo's guilty of many things and he deserves to pay, but not with his life.'

Lynette glanced back over her shoulder at Barton, blank-faced but maybe on the edge of a smile. Despite the warm evening sun, which was shining directly on him, goosebumps instantly covered Barton's body.

'Yeah, well, I disagree,' she said.

Lynette stepped into the hot tub, sat down next to Russo and put her arm around him. His neck muscles strained as he tried to break free from his bindings. While glaring intently at Russo's terrified face, Lynette raised the lighter into the air with her other hand, flicked it open, and rolled the flint wheel with her thumb. Small sparks flew, and, with an enormous roaring whoomph, the hot tub went up like a volcano.

80

DI BARTON

Barton was stunned for a few moments, then rushed forward, but the intense roaring heat beat him back. To his amazement, both occupants of the hot tub remained silent and still. Only the billowing, raging flames made any noise. Barton sprinted into the house to look for a fire extinguisher. He yanked open cupboards and drawers before finding one under the sink. He raced outside where the blaze had died down, but he was too late.

Two charred bodies, like the petrified remains from Pompeii, were burning together in a final embrace. Barton slumped to his knees and bowed his head.

81

DI BARTON

A month later, after the furore and fallout had faded, Barton was finishing his last shift before a weekend seaside break that he'd booked on the Norfolk coast. Nothing flashy, just a three-bed caravan at Heacham with the kids. Barton always slept on an airbed in the caravan lounge, having broken one of the smaller beds on a similar vacation many years ago.

Lawrence, who had been saying he was too cool for shit English holidays, had folded rapidly. He'd got into university and knew that it might be his last family getaway, and the dog was going. They all wanted to see Gizmo at the beach.

Layla had been addicted to the penny-pushers since she was three and could barely hide her excitement after being told about the break. Two days before they left, Luke had stuffed his eight favourite teddies into his Trunki suitcase, stating if he liked it at the seaside, he and Trunki might not come home.

After a final check of his emails, Barton turned his computer off late afternoon to head home and pack the last of his things. Only Zander was still in the office.

'Enjoy your holiday, John. Bring me back some rock.'

'Aren't you a bit old for heroin?'

'Oh, very good.'

'Anything planned for the weekend?'

'I'm taking Kelly out for a meal.'

'Ah ha! Did you have the chat?'

'Might have done. Kelly said not to tell anyone. Especially any interfering gits at work.'

Barton grinned. If *he* couldn't get the goss out of Zander, Holly would be able to get it out of Kelly.

Zander frowned at his friend.

'And don't encourage Holly to ask her, either. We want to spend some time together with no pressure. All of us need some space to deal with what happened to Pigs.'

'What happened to them all!' said Barton, with a sad shrug.

Zander nodded, but made no more comment.

Barton drove home as fast as he could within the limits. He stepped through the front door, pleased to find Gizmo waiting for him. Luke was there too, but he had his arms crossed.

'My friend at school says government forces shoot people before asking questions.'

'Is that Colin again?'

'Yes, he was watching *Judge Dredd*. How many people have you shot today?'

Barton wondered whether he should have a word with Colin's parents about appropriate viewing.

'None, but if this cheek carries on, there's still time.'

Luke's scowl deepened. 'Did you really not shoot anyone?'

'Okay, I did. It was six teenagers, just this afternoon.'

Luke's face dropped. Barton grinned.

'That was the number of people in front of me when I was queuing for doughnuts. Cop's gotta eat.'

Luke's expression split into a grin. He shot off a few imaginary rounds.

'Love you, Daddy.' Luke crossed his arms again. 'Now, pack your stuff. I want to be on the way shortly.'

Barton chuckled and went upstairs. Gizmo followed him up. Holly was laughing at the top. He gave her a kiss and strolled to his wardrobe. As he packed, he couldn't help thinking of all the victims of the fires. Those people would never have this kind of simple pleasure again. It was the finality of death that was so terrible. Lives cut short for no worthwhile reason at all. The lost opportunities, the lost possibilities, the blighted lives of those left behind. No chance of redemption. Futures stopped dead.

Barton decided he was going to try not to be as grumpy this weekend. It was easy to moan about things, but doing so stopped you from living in the moment. Barton would savour all the expensive ice creams and fish and chips he was planning to buy. He'd slip the kids extra money to win cheap teddies in the amusement arcades with a wink, and, finally, he hoped he could even raise a smile when he was robbed in broad daylight at the fairground.

He thought of Lynette. She must have felt as if her life had never begun. Children, through nature and nurture, often repeated the mistakes of their parents. Perhaps, as Lynette hinted herself, it was always her destiny to be a fire killer.

AUTHOR'S NOTE

Thank you for continuing with the series. I'll look forward to reading your reviews!

There will be one more in the series, which you can pre-order now. I wanted to do a book for the Christmas market. As I was writing it, I felt like I was coming to a natural end of the series. Strong distinct characters like the people in this series almost write themselves after a while. So, in *The Santa Killer*, decisions are taken, loose ends are tied up, and crimes are solved. But it's the nature of the beast that mistakes are made.

It might just be the last Barton. Read the blurb now.

MORE FROM ROSS GREENWOOD

We hope you enjoyed reading *The Fire Killer*. If you did, please leave a review.

If you'd like to gift a copy, this book is also available as an ebook, digital audio download and audiobook CD.

Explore the DI Barton series.

ABOUT THE AUTHOR

Ross Greenwood is the bestselling author of over ten crime thrillers. Before becoming a full-time writer he was most recently a prison officer and so worked everyday with murderers, rapists and thieves for four years. He lives in Peterborough.

Follow Ross on social media:

twitter.com/greenwoodross

facebook.com/RossGreenwoodAuthor

bookbub.com/authors/ross-greenwood

instagram.com/rossg555

Boldwood

Boldwood Books is an award-winning fiction publishing company seeking out the best stories from around the world.

Find out more at www.boldwoodbooks.com

Join our reader community for brilliant books, competitions and offers!

Follow us
@BoldwoodBooks
@BookandTonic

Sign up to our weekly deals newsletter

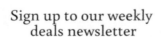
https://bit.ly/BoldwoodBNewsletter

Printed in Great Britain
by Amazon

42381301R00198